MIDNIGHT CROSSING

ALSO BY TRICIA FIELDS

The Territory

Scratchgravel Road

Wrecked

Firebreak

MIDNIGHT CROSSING

TRICIA FIELDS

MINOTAUR BOOKS

A Thomas Dunne Book
New York

This is a work of fiction. All of the characters, organizations, and events portrayed in this novel are either products of the author's imagination or are used fictitiously.

A THOMAS DUNNE BOOK FOR MINOTAUR BOOKS.
An imprint of St. Martin's Publishing Group.

MIDNIGHT CROSSING. Copyright © 2016 by Tricia Fields. All rights reserved. Printed in the United States of America. For information, address St. Martin's Press, 175 Fifth Avenue, New York, N.Y. 10010.

www.thomasdunnebooks.com
www.minotaurbooks.com

The Library of Congress Cataloging-in-Publication Data is available upon request.

ISBN 978-1-250-07628-1 (hardcover)
ISBN 978-1-4668-8768-8 (e-book)

Our books may be purchased in bulk for promotional, educational, or business use. Please contact your local bookseller or the Macmillan Corporate and Premium Sales Department at 1-800-221-7945, extension 5442, or by e-mail at MacmillanSpecialMarkets@macmillan.com.

First Edition: July 2016

10 9 8 7 6 5 4 3 2 1

To my friend and mentor, Sandra Scofield

ACKNOWLEDGMENTS

Thank you, Linnet, Mella, and Merry, for your friendship and writing support through the years. Thank you to firearms editor Frank Disbrow, for your expertise. And thank you to my agent, Dominick Able, and to Peter Joseph and Melanie Fried, at Minotaur/Thomas Dunne Books, for five great years.

MIDNIGHT CROSSING

ONE

Josie opened her eyes, her body instantly alert, muscles taut. Night-time had never scared her. Lying awake, alone in bed at two o'clock in the morning, could lead to miserable thoughts, but not fear. At the same time, she also didn't believe in coincidence. For the second night in a row, she awoke to the distant sound of a car driving down the gravel road toward her home.

Schenck Road wound through the foothills of the Chinati Mountains for five miles, and then reconnected with River Road. Two houses were located on Schenck: her own house and Dell Seapus's, a quarter mile behind hers. The only reason to drive down Schenck was to visit Josie or Dell, and her seventy-something-year-old neighbor did not have visitors at two in the morning.

She lay flat on her back with her hands folded over her abdomen as she listened to the low drone of the engine, growing louder as it neared her house and then slowing like a roller-coaster car approaching the top of a rise. With the late October temperatures in the sixties at night, she'd been keeping her windows open. She slipped out of bed and walked down the wood floor in the hallway without a sound, not wanting to rouse the dog sleeping at the foot of her bed.

Standing to the side of the living room window, she slowly slid a finger behind the fabric and pulled it back an inch from the window. The oncoming vehicle rounded the bend in the road, and as it reached the straight stretch that ran past the front of her home, the headlights disappeared and the car vanished from sight. As she heard it roll by her house, the light from the moon wasn't enough to determine the size or make.

A half mile past her house, the lights reappeared, but too far away for her to catch any details. The driver knew the road, knew her house, and knew she'd be watching.

Long after the car lights had disappeared, Josie stayed at the window, feeling the rhythm of her pulse slow to normal. She heard Chester rise from the bedroom and his paws clicking down the hardwood floor in the hallway. He nuzzled up beside her, more curious than worried. She couldn't have picked a less aggressive dog than a bloodhound.

Lying on her back in bed again, but now holding her cell phone in her hands, she stared at the time: 2:17 a.m., obviously too late to call Nick and rouse him out of a deep sleep. He was somewhere in Juárez, Mexico, living with a young woman and her three small children, negotiating the release of the woman's husband. Josie had thought her position as chief of police wasn't conducive to starting a family, and then she'd begun dating Nick Santos, a kidnapping negotiator, and all thought of a normal family life, whatever that meant, had ended.

She tried to imagine him, curled up on his side on a lumpy foldaway mattress in the temporary bedroom constructed for him on the family's back porch. Or maybe he was crouched down behind a garage in a dark alley, waiting for movement, for the quiet approach of someone who might lead him to the terrified victim. Josie pondered how strange their life was, avoiding the criminals while all the same seeking them out.

When her cell phone alarm rang later that morning, Josie turned it off and fell back asleep instantly. Ten minutes later the alarm across the room on her bureau buzzed, forcing her up and out of bed, swearing as she tripped over Chester, who insisted on sleeping in the direct path to the alarm clock.

By 6:45 a.m., Josie had locked up the house and sent Chester down the lane to spend the day at Dell's ranch. Dell was a bachelor with little patience for people, but infinite tolerance for animals. Josie figured as far as a dog's life went, Chester was living the dream.

As she unlocked the driver's door on her retired Army jeep, her department-issued vehicle, she noticed something lying just behind her back tire. She bent down and picked up what appeared to be a plastic sandwich bag with bread crumbs in the bottom of it—what the Border Patrol would refer to as a sign, usually the remnants of someone crossing the border and leaving behind their trash as they made the long trek.

The problem was, the odds of the bag finding its way to her driveway were incredibly slim. Artemis had many more miles of unpaved roads than paved. Most people lived miles apart. The closest businesses to her home were located downtown, a ten-minute drive down remote roads that sometimes saw no other cars for hours at a time.

Driving to work did little to diminish the unease she felt from the night before.

She wondered if the baggie might be connected to the car driving by her house. A few months ago, she and Nick had found signs of crossing and two kayaks on the Mexican side of the Rio Grande, just a few miles from her house. Crossing the Rio from Mexico into West Texas made no sense at that particular location. Josie lived in the middle of the Chihuahuan Desert, with the Chinati Mountains located just beyond her home. If someone from Mexico wanted to illegally make the trek into the States, they would cross five miles beyond her house, where the land was wide open and mountains wouldn't add dangerous and unnecessary travel to the journey. And any coyote working out of Piedra Labrada, the Mexican sister city to Artemis, knew where along the Rio the cops lived. They wouldn't choose to cross by her home, unless crossing by her home was their specific intent. In that case, the crossing probably had little to do with illegals, and more to do with the Medrano Cartel.

Josie tried to clear these thoughts from her mind as she approached her one-stoplight town of Artemis, preparing herself for the day ahead. As a female chief of police in a speck of a town on the border with a country whose criminals had more resources than the federal army, every day was a new drama.

She pulled her jeep in front of the Artemis PD. The words ARTEMIS POLICE DEPARTMENT were painted in gold across a large plate-glass window to the left of the main door, and their motto, TO SERVE AND PROTECT, was painted across the window on the other side of the door. It looked like Mayberry: old-fashioned, small-town paradise. But the issues brought on by the drugs and guns that fueled the cartels had long overtaken paradise.

Josie parked next to Officer Otto Podowski, who stood on the sidewalk, holding a plate covered with plastic wrap. Josie slammed her car door and smiled. "Delores baking again?"

"The woman is amazing. She stayed up late last night to make us apple dumplings for breakfast. And, of course, she made a plate for you and Lou."

"Lou won't eat those. She's boycotting sugar again."

Otto winked and grinned. "I know that."

"Ah. Which means you get Lou's share. On top of the ones you already ate for breakfast. You're a sneaky one."

"Josie. A man has to have a vice in his life. It keeps me young. Gives me something to look forward to."

At sixty-something, Otto was a good fifty pounds over the department weight limit, which was set thirty years ago and had since been ignored. He and his wife, Delores, had left Poland when they graduated from high school so that Otto could attend medical school in the U.S. and then move back home to take care of the village. School had proved too much in an unfamiliar country at such a young age, and so he and Delores had stayed on and made a new life for themselves. Josie knew the hint of melancholy that lay just behind his smile was linked to his faraway homeland and parents who had passed away.

The silver bell clanged against the door to the police department, announcing their entrance. Lou scooted her chair back from her computer to see who had come in.

"Good morning, Lou. You're looking lovely today," Otto said.

"Please," she said.

Lou didn't get friendly until after nine o'clock, and even then it was a stretch some days.

"Delores made apple dumplings, if I can interest you."

"You know I don't eat that stuff."

"Just checking," he said. He turned and grinned at Josie.

Josie said hello to Lou and picked up a stack of paperwork and sticky notes, and then they headed upstairs to the office.

Josie and Otto shared an office with the third officer in the department, Marta Cruz. She typically worked the night shift, and Josie and Otto split day and night shifts with the sheriff's department so that Arroyo County had at least one patrol car, preferably two, on the road at all times. In charge of running the Arroyo County Jail, the sheriff was often shorthanded due to a jail overrun with problems caused by an international border and not enough staff to patrol it. That left the city police to take calls well outside of city limits.

Josie unlocked the office door and the rows of fluorescent lights hummed on. Otto filled the coffeepot with water at the back of the room and they both settled into the comfortable early-morning routine they had developed in their ten-plus years of working together.

Josie sat down at her computer and started through the several dozen emails that had come through since the evening before and began making return phone calls regarding a vandalized water tank behind the gas station and a burglary at an apartment downtown. A young couple had reported a thousand dollars was stolen from their apartment, but Josie had talked to the sheriff that morning and he said they'd also supposedly lost fifty thousand dollars' worth of heroin and cocaine earlier in the week. If true, the domino effect would travel along the drug trail that started in Mexico and chugged up north into the U.S. from dealer to dealer, until the drugs were recovered, or someone paid the price. The police carried out an investigation while the criminals conducted their own, which often resulted in a faster, more violent conclusion.

At two o'clock Marta called from home.

"What's up?" Josie asked.

"I got a follow-up for you. I'm off duty tonight and just wanted to make sure to get this on record. I had a busy night and didn't have time to leave you a note."

"No problem. What do you need?"

"It's Slick Fish. He's back at it again. I thought we ran him off, but he just changed locations."

"Somebody saw him?"

"Agnes Delaney, of all people."

Josie grinned. "Was he naked?"

"Oh, yeah. He's coming up out of the water just south of Agnes's house," Marta said.

"Okay. I'll check it out." She hung up the phone and turned to Otto. "Slick Fish resurfaced. Out by Cotton Canyon. Want to go take a look?"

"You bet," he said. "You got your bathing suit?"

Josie shuddered. "Slick and I will not be swimming together."

———•———

Josie drove with the windows down, enjoying the cooler mid-eighties temperature while Otto cranked up the air-conditioning and pointed all the vents toward his face.

"Four decades I've spent in this desert, and I still haven't adapted to the heat," he said.

"I'm over a decade into it here, and I wouldn't go back to Indiana winters for anything."

Josie slowed her jeep to take a long curve in the road that hugged a bend in the Rio, and then pulled up in front of Agnes's double-wide trailer. The trailer sat about fifty feet off the road and was the only house for several miles. Boxes and old bedsprings and tires and every kind of worthless junk Josie could imagine were piled around the base of the trailer

"I think it's gotten worse," Otto said. "I hope we don't have to go inside. My stomach can't take the smell today."

"That's what you get. Too many dumplings."

They exited the jeep and a woman in her fifties with fuzzy gray hair walked outside, leaning on a cane.

"Morning, Agnes," Josie called.

"Hello, hello," she said. "Give me a minute."

Agnes hobbled down the lopsided concrete-block steps and

Josie cringed, afraid her cane would get caught in a crack and send the woman tumbling down.

"I hear you had some excitement out here yesterday," Josie said.

"That man is taunting me. He makes me feel dirty in my own backyard."

"Why don't you tell us what happened?" Josie said.

"As you probably know, I'm a birder. I can show you the photographs in my house. I've spotted black phoebes, kingfishers, the great kiskadee. And my prize, the Colima warbler."

"Were you looking for birds when you saw the man crossing the river?" Otto said.

"I wasn't *looking* for birds," she said, scowling at Otto. "There's a difference between looking out your kitchen window at the birds in your backyard, and actually birding. I have journals filled with notes of my trips, and—"

"My apologies," he said. Otto raised a hand in the air and spoke slowly. "Were you *birding* outside when you saw the man in the river?"

"Yes. I was. I'd walked out into the backyard and had traveled maybe a few hundred feet down toward the river. It's a hard walk for me through the thicket with my cane, so I'm slow and quiet. I had my eye on a painted bunting. A real beauty. Blue and red and green. A little bird that looks like it's straight out of the tropics."

Josie heard Otto sigh and she glanced over at his slack face. She had noticed Otto had begun to lose patience when people being questioned about a topic relevant to the investigation rambled on about something unrelated. A significant number of people in far West Texas lived in remote solitude, so when unexpected visits happened, they occasionally got chatty. It mostly led to wasted time, but every now and then a golden nugget surfaced between the details.

"That's when I saw a pale blob in my binoculars. I put them down and saw this man dragging a big rubber inner tube by a rope, up and out of the water and onto the riverbank. There was a woman who climbed off the inner tube and stood there onshore with a big black backpack over her shoulders. I almost screamed at them to get off my land, but then I worried they might have a gun. Well, obviously he didn't have a gun, because he was stark-naked. But she could have. So I just stood there in the tall grass and watched."

"He only brought one person over?" Josie asked.

"There was a man standing onshore, already waiting there. I hadn't noticed him until the woman came ashore. Then the naked man jumped back in the river and swam over for another man. He put the rope over his arm, like a woman's purse, and swam the man over in the inner tube like a fish. He has a heck of a strong stroke. I'll give him that. I bet I stood there maybe ten minutes and it was over."

"Was anyone else on the bank waiting for them? A coyote picking them up?" Josie asked.

"As soon as the last man got to the shore another fella in jeans and a shirt and cowboy boots appeared out of nowhere, and the three people followed him out toward the road. I stayed right where I was until I heard a car take off. I couldn't see them on the road. I was down below the bank."

"What time was this?" Otto asked.

"About five. It was about dinnertime."

"Have you seen him here before?" he asked.

"No, sir. But I've heard about the naked Mexican. He charges people for that!"

"About a thousand dollars a person," Josie said.

Agnes's jaw dropped. "Well, I'll swim them across for that kind of money!"

Otto smirked. "Don't try it. It's a bit easier to arrest you, on U.S. soil, than it is to catch a guy who just has to jump back over the river to avoid arrest," Otto said.

"We call him Slick Fish," Josie said. "He's been doing this for years. He has runners up and down the river that he pays to watch for police and Border Patrol. When the area's clear, they radio

Slick and he strips down, gets his people on the inner tube, and swims them across. No engine noise, no commotion."

"Why on earth would he come here where he has to swim across?" she asked. "There's places in the river upstream where you can practically walk across."

Josie looked downriver to where Agnes was pointing. "He's got a perfect spot here. The river splits this long low hill." She pointed to where the river dipped down a fifteen-foot bank and disappeared from view. "The cottonwood trees and the salt cedar give him cover. His scouts look up and down the road here to ensure there aren't any cops. And he has easy access to a road. When you cross in the open desert, you can cross the border easy enough, but you're an open target on the run. Here, it only takes fifteen minutes and he's got three people across the border, loaded into a pickup truck, and headed north to freedom."

"And three thousand bucks for his trouble," Otto said.

Agnes looked horrified. "Well, you can't just let this naked man ferry people onto my property!"

"We'll get someone out here." Josie handed her a business card. "You call me if you see anything else. By the time we get here the transport will probably be over, but we'll track what times he comes and goes. We'll get him eventually.

"And, whatever you do, don't get involved. No yelling at him to get off your land, or firing shots, or you're likely to get shot yourself. Understood?"

Agnes nodded, her expression grim, and slipped the card into her shirt pocket.

They got back in the jeep and Otto buckled his seat belt, clearly agitated. "Explain how a multimillion-dollar border fence is going to stop a guy like Slick Fish."

"No clue," Josie said. She'd heard the same rant from Otto for years.

"We spend a small fortune building a fence that they'll go under, or over, or cut a hole in and drive straight through. Makes no sense."

"It's a deterrent. It slows them down," she said, which was the same response she always gave.

"It's like shoving your thumb into a hole in a dam and expecting to stop the water. The water always wins. It doesn't work."

Josie changed the topic. "I'll work with Marta to set up an observation post to track Slick's movements. It'll be tough to find her time to get over there in the evening, but we'll give it a shot."

"We'll never catch the bastard. He's naked and he's slick. Unless you're right down there on the water and plan on jumping into the river and wrestling him back onto U.S. soil, he's home free. What's the point?"

"What are you so grumpy for?" she finally asked.

He ignored her question as she parked in front of the PD. They entered the building and found Lou behind the entryway counter, leaning against it with her hands folded in front of her, grinning as if she had a mouthful of gossip ready to spill.

"Okay. Let's hear it," Otto said to her.

Lou grinned wider. "Can't. It's a surprise. And, boy howdy, is it ever."

Josie refrained from rolling her eyes and walked through the swinging door at the end of the counter and back toward the stairs that led to their office. Pointless gossip annoyed her almost as much as meaningless small talk.

She reached the top of the stairs and was surprised to see the office light on. Marta had another half hour before her shift began, and she wasn't one to come in early. Then Josie smelled cigarette smoke. She knew it wasn't from Lou sneaking one in the bathroom because she'd given up the habit several months ago and turned into an anti-smoking zealot.

Josie pushed the office door open and the "surprise" stood and smiled, blowing smoke out in a stream and dropping her cigarette into a Coke can sitting on the conference table.

Josie pushed past her shock and said, "Mom! It's great to see you."

"You bet it is!" She gave Josie a quick hug and turned to Otto, who had been right behind her. She walked up to him and poked a finger into his chest. "And I remember you. Officer O. Right?"

"Otto," Josie said. "His name is Otto."

"It's good to see you, Beverly," Otto said, reaching his hand out but accepting her enthusiastic hug instead.

"Of course I know this is Otto! That was my nickname for him!"

Josie didn't remember that at all. Her mom had made the trip from Indiana to Texas once a few years back, and it had been a disaster.

"This is a big surprise," Josie said. "What brings you here?"

Her mom planted her hands on her hips and looked offended. "Seriously? You have to ask? I came to see you!"

"Beverly, it's a pleasure to see you again. I'm sorry to leave so soon, but I've got a meeting I need to get to." Otto laid his notebook on the conference table and headed toward the door. He turned to Josie when he reached it, his eyebrows bunching up as he offered what she assumed was a sympathetic look. "I'll see you tomorrow?"

She nodded. He didn't have a meeting. Their shift was almost over and he had just mentioned going home to feed his goats. "See you in the morning." Josie didn't blame him. She didn't want the drama either.

"I figured, you won't call me, so I'll just come visit in person!" Beverly said. Her voice was loud and overly cheerful in the otherwise quiet room.

"The phone lines run both ways," Josie said.

"You going to take me out to dinner tonight? Introduce me to your friends?" her mom asked.

"A friend of mine is coming over for dinner tonight. His name is Nick. Why don't you come by about six, and I'll have dinner for us."

Beverly's face fell and her shoulders slumped. "I thought I'd be staying with you. I drove all the way out here. Gas cost a fortune. And buying all my meals along the way. I just figured you'd put me up."

Josie felt blood rush to her face and she struggled to contain a smart remark about the visit that she'd had no time to prepare for. "I have a small place. I think it—"

"You have two bedrooms!"

"—would be better for us if we got you a room at Manny's. You stayed there last time you were here. I'm sure he'll have a nice room for you. And his rooms are very reasonable."

Beverly huffed and Josie motioned to the conference table, where they both sat down. Her mom was wearing a short denim skirt and a T-shirt that fit her like a second skin. Josie acknowledged in her mind that it had been several years since she'd seen her mom, but she was fairly certain that her mom's chest was a size or two larger now than she remembered.

"Surprised?" her mom said. "I could tell I got you when you walked in the room."

Josie smiled, trying to warm up, to be gracious and show some appreciation for her mom. As happened with almost every visit, she felt nauseating guilt for the irritation she felt over her mom's presence.

"You surprised me. That's for sure," she said. "How's everyone back in Indiana?"

"Did I tell you Aunt Sugar got married?" Beverly asked.

Josie shook her head. She hadn't talked to her mom in almost a year. Her mom knew that she'd not told Josie about her aunt. She'd never understood her mom's insistence on pretending they had a close relationship when it so obviously was not the case.

"She got married a month ago and moved to Oklahoma last week. She's my last family. Everybody else either died or deserted me. I figure, maybe it's time to move west. Be closer to Sugar. Closer to you and my grandkids."

Josie raised her eyebrows. She was an only child, mid-thirties, never married, no kids.

"You're old enough. I figured I'd show up and find out you were married, with a kid on the way. You and the accountant. What's his name? Drake?"

"His name was Dillon. And he no longer lives here. He moved back to St. Louis about a year ago. And no. I have no plans for marriage or kids in the near future."

The intercom buzzed on Josie's desk phone. Josie took a deep breath and walked over to her desk and pressed the button, telling Lou, "I'll be with you in a minute."

As she sat back down at the table, trying to avoid the feeling that her mom was baiting her, she heard the steady clomp of cowboy boots, the precursor to a visit from Mayor Moss. She briefly closed her eyes and wondered if her day could get much worse.

Thirty seconds later the mayor walked into the office, glanced from Josie to her mom, and stopped as if he'd suddenly forgotten why he was here. He played like he'd just walked into the middle of a pleasant surprise.

"Afternoon, Mayor. What can I do for you?" Josie asked.

He looked from Josie to her mom and back again. "Sisters? I definitely see a resemblance here."

"Mayor Moss, this is my mom. Beverly Gray."

He gave Beverly a big skeptical grin as if he couldn't believe it. "Mother? No way. You have to be sisters."

Beverly stood and walked around the table, stretching her hand out to shake his. Josie was relieved she didn't go straight for the hug, or, worse yet, the kiss on both cheeks.

"I am so glad to finally meet you!" Her voice was a flirty sing-song. "You happen to be the first mayor I have ever actually talked to in person. It is a *real* honor."

Moss lit up like a Christmas tree.

"Josie told me all about you. I know she feels very lucky to work with you."

Josie stared at her mom like she had lost her mind, and then felt the mayor's eyes on her. She turned to the back of the room. "Anyone want coffee?"

"No, I'm fine, honey," her mother called.

Honey? And why on earth had her mom told the mayor that Josie had talked about him? Her mom had no idea who she talked to or about, or the fact that Josie and the mayor had a contentious working relationship.

After another five minutes of interminable flirting between the two, Josie repeated, "What can I do for you, Mayor?"

He glanced back at Josie and cleared his throat. "I have intelligence that we need to discuss."

Josie gritted her teeth. Her tolerance had evaporated.

"I got an anonymous phone call. There's some bad customers taking up in town."

Josie turned to her mom and said, "I'll have to connect with you later."

Beverly seemed shocked, like she couldn't believe she was being dismissed. "So, I should just take my bags to your house? Is that what we decided?"

Josie glanced at the mayor and said, "I'll be right back. Let me walk her out."

The mayor extended his hand again and said what a pleasure it had been to meet such an outstanding woman. He turned to Josie. "You make sure and show your mama a good time while she's here in Artemis. Bring her by my office one afternoon, and I'll give her the big tour around town. You hear?"

"I sure will," Josie said.

———

Moments later, standing in front of the police station, Josie pointed down the block. "You remember Manny's Motel? Just remind him that you're my mom. I'm sure he'll give you a good rate. Do you need directions to my house for dinner?"

"Nope. I got you in my GPS."

"Okay. I'll see you at six, then." Josie reached out and they hugged awkwardly. "It's good to see you again."

———

Back in the office, Moss had regained the stoic expression he usually wore when talking with her, one of a stern, disapproving superior. Josie wondered if he'd been so friendly with her mother just to irritate her, and she realized if that had been his intention it had worked.

Moss sat at the conference table texting on his cell phone. When Josie sat down he laid the phone on the table.

"I got an anonymous tip that something's going down in Artemis."

"What kind of tip? A phone call?"

"Somebody left it on the office voicemail. Helen heard it this morning when she got to work."

"What exactly did it say?"

"There's the problem. Helen isn't too techno-literate. She erased the message. But she says a male, not too old, not too young, said there's some bad business taking place in town and the police had better get a grip before it gets out of hand."

"That's all she remembers?"

"You want more?"

Josie laughed, incredulous. "More would be helpful. An anonymous man leaves a vague message about trouble in town. That's not much to go on."

"It's not like we get anonymous tips left on the office answering machine on a daily basis. Obviously something's up. Be vigilant. Inform the officers that there's possible trouble. Do I need to do your job for you?"

"No, sir."

They both stood and she watched him pick up his phone and slip it into his back pants pocket. Josie was five-foot-seven, and Moss was slightly shorter than her, although he made up for it in cowboy boots with a custom high heel. His body was shaped like an inverted triangle, with large muscular shoulders and biceps and a narrow waist. His build, coupled with a significant underbite, had gained him the nickname Bulldog with the local law enforcement.

Before he left, the mayor admonished her once again to be vigilant. Josie texted Otto, *Look out. Bulldog's got a bone.*

TWO

Josie arrived home in time to change clothes and make it back into the kitchen before Nick pulled up in the driveway. She'd told her mom six because Nick was arriving at five-thirty, and she wanted time to warn him about their dinner guest before she arrived. Dinner was already made—vegetable soup in the Crock-Pot that she'd turned on when she woke up that morning. It was about as home-made as Josie could muster: frozen vegetables, chunked up potatoes and carrots, beef broth, and roast beef from a can. Nick claimed it was his favorite soup, either because he was a nice guy or because he had simple tastes. Either way, Josie was fine with it.

Josie met him at the front door, where he carried a loaf of French bread and a six-pack of Killian's Red. She smiled at the sight of him. It had been two weeks since he'd been able to visit, and she'd missed him more than she had realized. He wore a pale yellow summer-weight button-down shirt and jeans with well-worn cowboy boots. His hair was black, military-cut, and he carried himself with the same confidence and purpose as a street cop. When he noticed her standing at the door he smiled back at her, and the floor tilted beneath her. She'd never felt such an intense physical attraction to anyone else, not even Dillon, whom she'd dated for so many years.

She pushed the door open and he walked inside, laid the bread and beer on the floor, and wrapped both arms around her in a tight hug. He put his mouth beside her ear and whispered her name. "I lay in bed every night for two weeks and imagined you lying beside me. I thought about you on stakeouts. I thought about you instead of my job." He pulled his head back and looked into her eyes. "You are one dangerous lady."

She grinned, feeling her body temperature spike as blood rushed to her cheeks. "I missed you too."

He laughed at her simple response and kissed her hard. He ran his hands up under her shirt and pulled her tight against his body. She finally pulled away slightly and said, "I have something to tell you."

He closed his eyes and rested his forehead on her hers. "That phrase never brings me good news."

"It's not necessarily good," she said, "but it could be a lot worse."

"Does this mean we're not skipping supper and heading to bed?"

"You're very intuitive."

He dropped his arms and grabbed the beer and bread off the floor, heading into the kitchen. "Give it to me straight."

"My mom's here. In Artemis."

He dropped the items on the kitchen counter and turned back to her, appearing as shocked at the news as she imagined she had.

"Is she here? In your house?"

"Not yet."

He looked like he wasn't sure what to think. "That's good, right? You haven't seen her in a long time."

She smiled and turned on the oven to heat the bread. "It's been a long time. Yes."

"Did you know she was coming?"

"I got back from a call this afternoon and found her in the office at the PD, smoking a cigarette."

He laughed and Josie finally smiled at the absurdity of it.

"Are you going to see her tonight?"

Josie glimpsed the clock on the stove. "She'll be here in about twenty minutes."

At that moment they heard a car pull into the driveway and someone honked several times. Nick grinned. "That's her, huh?"

"No doubt."

"Do you want me to go so you can spend some time with her?"

"No. Stay. I need all the support I can get."

Josie walked outside to greet her mom. She had on a different outfit but it was the same combo she'd worn earlier—a short skirt and tight T-shirt. She had pulled her hair up into a messy bun behind her head. She looked a decade younger than she was until you saw the wrinkles and dark age spots on her hands and face. Josie tried to imagine her own self in twenty years, and wondered if she might be facing the same upheaval as her mom. She mentally vowed to be patient and kind.

"It's good to see you," Josie said.

"You too, darlin'!" she cried. She held up a bottle of wine in each hand, and then noticed Nick walk outside. "And who's this handsome man behind you?"

"This is Nick Santos. A good friend of mine," Josie said.

"Well, Nick. If you're a friend of Josie's, you're a friend of mine," she said.

———

Nick put his beer in the fridge and poured them each a glass of Beverly's wine while Josie served the soup and bread. Nick was not a wine drinker and Josie found the gesture sweet. As they sipped their wine Beverly sat at the table telling Nick about her solo drive cross-country, and about the various truck stops she'd slept in along the way.

"I came across every sort of trucker and lot lizard you can imagine," she said. "Some fella even said he'd marry me if I'd keep him company on his haul up north to Canada. Told me when we were done I could divorce him and have half of everything he owns."

"Were you tempted?" Nick asked.

"Not even. He was nice enough to look at, but I figured half a nothing won't get me too far."

By the time they finished dinner and moved onto the back porch to take in the sunset, it was clear Beverly had won Nick over. This wasn't the same mother Josie had grown up with, nor the one she fought with during every visit and phone call she'd had since leaving home. Had she changed, or was she the same manipulative woman Josie had expected? And more importantly, would Josie have time to tell the difference before her mom won over her friends and staked her claim in the midst of Josie's life?

It was after one in the morning before Beverly left. Josie closed the front door after her mom drove off and sat down on the couch next to Nick, worn out from the night.

Nick said, "I have to tell you. I don't get your irritation toward your mom. She seems like a sweet lady. She's just looking for family and friendship."

Josie groaned. "Seriously, Nick. You spent one evening with her. She's a manipulator. She shows you what she wants you to see."

"I get that. She's no angel. My dad was a son of a bitch while I was growing up. But he's my dad, you know? Sometimes you forgive, just because it's family, not because it's right."

Josie felt her face flush. She would have liked to have said, *Shut the hell up. You don't know what you're talking about.* Instead, she said, "At least he was a son of a bitch. My mother was nothing. When my dad died, that was it. I was eight years old and she shut down on me."

"She couldn't cope. I see it all the time. Some people don't have that coping mechanism."

She raised a hand to stop him. "I'm done, Nick. She's here. I'll deal with her. But I don't want to talk about her parenting skills right now."

They sat for a moment without talking. Josie wished the TV was on, but it wasn't, and if she turned it on it would feel like she was silencing him. This was the part of relationships that she disliked. Always second-guessing herself, tensing up over her inability to do the right thing, or even knowing what the right thing was.

"Look. We're no good at this. Right?" Nick asked.

She turned to look at him. "At what?"

"At this. At talking about"—he shrugged—"whatever this is."

She sighed. "I think you're right. We should probably quit talking before we say something that gets us into a fight."

He grinned. "Exactly. We're no good at whatever this is. So let's skip it."

"Skip it," she repeated.

"That's what I said. You're getting mad. I don't know what the hell I'm talking about. So we skip it and go to bed. You give me a back rub. I'll give you a foot rub. And then we go to bed happy instead of mad."

"You could be a marriage counselor."

"Call me Dr. Nick."

———·——

Once they finally made it to bed they skipped the back and foot rubs. Nick curled around Josie's body and they both settled into an almost instant sleep. Until Josie awoke with the same jolt she'd experienced the previous two nights. She'd intended to tell Nick, but had forgotten with her mom's visit.

As she lay in a tangled mess of sheets, trapped under Nick's leg, Josie's skin prickled and her body was suddenly covered in a thin sheen of sweat. She pulled her leg from under Nick's and rolled over on her back to focus on the sound. Across the room the clock on the bureau read 2:13 a.m. She was certain it was the same person coming down the gravel road.

She laid her hand on Nick's arm, which was stretched out beside her. "Nick," she whispered.

She felt the instant flex of muscle in his forearm, an automatic response from too many years of working in law enforcement. "What's the matter?" His voice was hoarse with sleep but already worried.

"Do you hear the car coming down the road?"

He propped himself up on an elbow, and they both lay completely still, listening through the open bedroom windows to the faraway engine.

"I hear it," he said. "What's the problem?"

"People don't come down this road at two in the morning. It's just Dell and me. This is the third night in a row I've heard it."

Nick rolled out of bed, stepped into his jeans, and grabbed his pistol off the nightstand in one smooth motion. Josie slipped a T-shirt and shorts on, grabbed her Beretta, and shoved her bare feet into a pair of work boots beside the door. She quietly shut the bedroom door so that Chester wouldn't follow them, and walked behind Nick down the hallway. In the living room she placed her hand on his back.

"Let's go out the back door," she whispered.

Nick put on his boots while she disengaged the alarm system and they stepped outside.

The night spread before her in black and gray shapes, making depth perception difficult. From where she was standing ten feet from Nick, his form was clear, but the features of his face were not. Without a word she took off walking around one side of the house and Nick took the other. She held her Beretta at the ready position, her right hand gripping the gun, her trigger finger extended along the side, and her left hand held underneath to support.

She hugged the side of her house, controlling her breathing as she saw the headlights appear around the curve of Schenck Road. The headlights went off.

Josie and Nick both reached the front of the house at the same time and crouched behind his black SUV, an armored vehicle necessary for his job. She wanted to run to the side of the road to catch the make and model of the car, but the driver was driving slow enough to signify he was looking for something or someone and might have night vision gear.

"We need to stay behind the SUV. There's nothing for cover out in the front yard," she whispered. "The best we can hope for is to see where they slow down. Maybe we'll narrow down what they're searching for."

"If shots are fired, you get back inside and arm the security system. I have my car."

She didn't argue. Like it or not, since serving as her negotiator in a kidnapping case the year before, Nick automatically assumed the lead role when it came to any safety issue. Eventually she would confront him about this, but now wasn't the time or place to take it on.

About five hundred feet from Josie's house the car slowed to a crawl. As it rolled by she heard the gravel crunch under the wheels. She could only make out the shape of the car as a mid-sized vehicle. The front passenger window was open. She could see moonlight reflected off the back passenger windows, and the front windows appeared completely black, which meant someone had turned off the dashboard lights. She was too far away to see shapes in the car.

Then the car passed by her house, and as it reached the pasture containing Dell's cattle, it stopped. For almost a full minute they watched the car sit idling. It finally pulled away, heading in the same direction, and rolled along for a quarter mile, then the lights were turned back on and the car picked up speed.

"You heard the car last night too?" Nick asked, his voice remaining low.

"This is the third night. Last night I got up and watched it roll by about the same time, and do the exact same thing—slowing down and killing the lights."

"Why didn't you call me last night?" he asked.

"There wasn't anything to call about."

He didn't respond and Josie switched topics.

"It's odd the car didn't stop in front of the house. It continued on toward the pasture. It didn't last night either. It makes me think they aren't after me. Maybe the kayaks you saw down by the river really are coyotes crossing. They're just too stupid to realize a cop lives here. Maybe they lost someone crossing through the pasture."

"A coyote's not going to spend three nights in a row looking for a lost traveler. They already got their money. They couldn't care less if someone gets lost."

"I forgot to mention, I found a baggie with crumbs in it under my tire this morning. Looked like someone's sandwich bag."

She could see him shrug, like it didn't make sense to him.

"Maybe a load got lost," Josie said.

"They wouldn't be cruising by a pasture if they thought dope was lying out there. They'd have boots on the ground." He pointed at the place along the road where the car stopped and they both started walking toward it.

Josie heard a sound coming from behind her on the front porch and put out her hand to stop Nick. "You hear that?" she whispered.

He shook his head. They were standing near the end of the driveway. She switched on her flashlight and shone it back at the house and around her jeep and Nick's SUV.

They crept between the vehicles and up to the front of the house. The front porch was the length of the house, about ten feet deep and thirty-five feet long, with just one low step that ran the length of it. Josie shone her light along the porch, from left to right, to the far right corner where there was a chair, and froze.

She held her light steady on what appeared to be a person, hunched up into a ball and hiding behind the chair. Nick made a move forward and Josie grabbed his hand. "Stop," she said, keeping her voice low. "I'm the cop. This is my jurisdiction here. You need to back off."

He hesitated but pulled back without a word.

Josie took a step forward and called out, "This is Police Chief Josie Gray. I'm coming up to talk to you. Can you tell me your name?"

There was no response.

Josie stayed off the porch, walking through the sandy front yard, carefully avoiding the cactus plantings and landscape boulders. When she reached the end of the house she could see the person was female, with her legs pulled up to her chest and her arms wrapped around them. Long black hair fell over her shoulders and on both sides of her legs. She was wearing ankle boots, shorts, and a T-shirt.

"I'd like for you to nod your head if you can hear me," she said.

Josie took a few steps closer. Her gun was still drawn, but held down to her side so she wouldn't alarm the woman if she suddenly looked up.

"Are you hurt?"

Josie stepped onto the porch and the woman flinched, pressing her balled-up body farther into the corner.

Josie pulled her cell phone out of her shorts pocket and called Brian Moore, the night dispatcher for the PD. "Brian, it's Josie. Is Marta available?"

"Yes, ma'am. She's sitting at the intake desk doing paperwork. You need her?"

"I do. I also want you to call the sheriff's department. Send backup to my address."

"Emergency?"

"Yes."

"Injuries?"

"No. But I need backup as a precaution."

"Yes, ma'am. Hold the line."

"Hang on. Who's on duty at the sheriff's department?"

"Dave Phillips."

"Tell him we have a possible immigration issue. Let me talk to Marta."

Seconds later Marta came on the line.

"I'm on my front porch. There's a female, most likely in her teens or twenties by the way she's dressed, curled up in the corner. She hasn't spoken yet."

Marta broke in. "I'm walking out the PD now. Headed that way."

"Okay. Brian said he'd send Dave Phillips too." Josie went on to describe the car that had driven by her house and stopped. "Obviously someone's looking for this person. I'm guessing it's an immigration issue or a domestic. Just keep an eye out for any other cars on your way out here. If you see a mid-sized car as you approach Schenck Road, follow it and call me immediately. There shouldn't be anyone out here this time of night. Got it?"

"Will do. Be there in ten."

Josie slipped her phone back in her pocket and shone the flashlight on the porch floor so she wouldn't spotlight the girl. She crouched down and lowered her voice.

"Don't be afraid. I'm going to scoot the chair out of the way so we can talk. Okay?"

When the woman didn't answer, Josie reached out and slowly dragged the chair from her. As the wood scraped across the wooden decking she cringed again, burrowing her head down farther like a child attempting to hide.

Josie turned back to Nick, who was standing just behind her watching. "Would you get a bottle of water out of the refrigerator?" she asked.

He left and Josie stood again, taking small steps until she was directly in front of the woman. "My name's Josie. Can you tell me your name?"

Josie continued to ask questions and converse quietly, trying to establish herself as someone friendly who wanted to help. When Nick came back and handed her the water, she opened the lid and held it toward the woman. "Water?" She repeated the word in Spanish.

Josie touched the water bottle to the woman's arm. She flinched but raised her head enough to peer at Josie. Her eyes were wide and unfocused. Josie heard Nick make a sound behind her. She knew that he'd seen the look too many times through years of negotiations, but seeing a person in that kind of pain never got easier to take.

"She's in shock," he said.

When the woman heard his voice she cried out as if slapped and buried her head again, dropping the water bottle onto the porch. Josie set the water upright and turned to Nick. "I hate to think what's happened to her. Can you wait out by the car, and I'll try and get her inside?"

Josie continued speaking in a soothing voice, and eventually knelt beside the woman and placed a hand on her back, rubbing slowly, trying to calm her. The woman finally raised her head again at the mention of water. As she closed her eyes and drank half the bottle, water dripping down her face, Josie was able to study her for signs of abuse.

Josie figured she was in her late teens to early twenties, with dark brown eyes, black hair, and full lips. Her clothes were not typical of someone crossing the desert. Noticing her reaction to

Nick's voice, she wondered if she was looking at a horrible domestic situation. Maybe the woman had come to Josie's house knowing that a female police officer lived here.

Josie put a hand out and tried to get the woman to stand but she seemed too terrified to move. Josie pointed to the living room window.

"Let's go inside. You're safe now. I promise." Josie reached down and slid her arm underneath the girl's and slowly pulled her up. "No one is going to hurt you here. We just want to help you."

Josie helped the girl inside the house and sat her at the end of the couch, where she once again pulled her legs up and hugged her arms around them. Josie took a blanket that lay over the top of a chair and wrapped it around the woman's shoulders.

She sat next to her on the couch and said, "The car that drove in front of the house. Was it looking for you?"

She began crying and Josie was hopeful that she spoke at least some English.

"Are there other people with you?"

She whimpered like a child and finally looked out the front door and in the general direction of where the car had stopped on the road.

"Is there someone outside?"

She closed her eyes as if she wasn't able to stand the image.

"Are the people who hurt you back there?"

Nothing.

"Is someone else back there? In the pasture?"

The woman sobbed at the question and Josie pulled her cell phone out of her pocket and called the night dispatcher. "Brian, this is Josie. Call Border Patrol. Call Otto too and tell him I need him out here. I don't know what's going on, but I want to be prepared."

Brian told her Marta was on her way and should be there within five minutes. Phillips, from the sheriff's department, was on a call but would be there within twenty minutes. "I talked to Sheriff Martinez. He's on his way as well."

Several minutes later Marta Cruz pulled up. Josie introduced her to the girl, who remained curled up on the couch and under the blanket. Marta sat beside the woman and placed an arm on her back, trying to reassure her while Josie briefed her on the situation and gave her instructions. "I'd like you to stay with her while I arrange a group of officers to search the pasture beside the house."

Outside, Josie found Nick pulling a flak jacket from the back of his vehicle. "Let's have a look around the house," he said.

"Not until we have help. I just asked for support from Border Patrol but don't have an ETA. Otto's on his way. So are Deputy Dave Phillips and Sheriff Roy Martinez. We'll partner up and head out when they arrive. We'll each have an officer. I'll leave one man posted at the house."

Nick nodded. "How long?"

"We should have everyone here in twenty minutes."

Josie called Dell to fill him in. It was three o'clock in the morning. He answered after the first ring.

"What's the matter?"

"I need to make you aware of a situation. Nick is here. We heard a car drive by at about two this morning. This is the third night I've heard it. Nick and I went outside to check things out and watched it stop in front of your pasture."

"They get out of the car?" he asked.

"No, it just sat idling along the road. After it pulled away we found a young woman hiding on my front porch. Physically she's okay, but she's terrified. She can't speak. I'd guess whoever was in the car was hunting her."

"I'll be right down."

"No. Don't leave your house. Stay indoors with the lights out and gun ready until you hear otherwise. I don't know who might be out here right now."

"You have backup with you?"

"I do. We'll fan out in groups. I'll call you back as soon as I know something more." She paused and he didn't say anything. "Everything okay?"

"I ought to be out there helping you. At least checking my pasture."

Josie sighed. "Dell, please. Promise me you'll stay put. We can't be worrying about running into you while we're outside. You could accidentally get shot."

"All right, then," he said. Not one to sit idle, he was clearly frustrated. "You let me know what you find."

Sheriff Roy Martinez was a burly retired Marine Corps sergeant. Roy spent most of his time running the jail and dealing with the dramas that come with supervising staff and criminals, but Josie trusted him as a solid officer.

Josie reintroduced Nick to Otto, Roy, and Phillips, who knew him as the kidnapping negotiator who had helped recover Josie's ex-boyfriend. They also knew Nick by reputation as one of the best negotiators in northern Mexico. He had brought home an Arizona state senator after a nationally publicized kidnapping two years before.

Josie quickly briefed the group on the situation. "Let's get our cars facing the road with lights on. We'll travel in the dark, but I want whoever was stalking my house to think twice about driving up here while we're out on foot. Marta will remain at the house with the victim. I'd like to leave Phillips positioned by the house to watch for anyone approaching the area. I'll take Nick with me. Roy, you and Otto work together?"

"You bet," Roy said.

"We'll fan out in a line, about a hundred feet between each of us. At the back of the property Nick and I will head to the base of the mountain. You two check Dell's barn and around his house."

Each of the officers walked into the night, aware that something horrific had happened to the woman sitting in Josie's house, and that someone, possibly multiple people, had come back to finish the job. Flashlights were necessary to check the pasture for evidence or clues to the woman's terror, but the light also broadcast their presence to anyone who might be out there, waiting to strike.

THREE

Marta carried a cup of hot tea and a bowl of canned pineapple chunks into the living room. She'd dug around in Josie's refrigerator and cabinets and marveled at the lack of food. *No wonder she stays so thin*, she thought.

Marta placed the food on the coffee table and sat back down beside the woman on the couch to study her. She was hardly a woman, probably just beyond her teenage years. She no longer sat in a rigid ball, but had collapsed into a puddle at the end of the couch, her head lying on the armrest as her eyes stared at the opposite wall.

The woman had warmed up to Marta, and no longer seemed afraid. She sat up and hungrily ate the fruit and sipped at the warm tea flavored with milk and sugar. Marta tried to get her to carry on a conversation, to simply answer a question with a yes or no, but she wouldn't speak or even shake her head. Her face was void of any expression, as if she had lost her ability to experience anything beyond fulfilling her basic needs.

When whimpering and scratching noises came from somewhere

at the back of the house, the girl looked at Marta in alarm. Marta smiled and patted her leg as she walked past her and to the hallway where the sound was coming from. "It's Chester," she said, keeping her voice cheerful. "He's a good dog. No worries."

Marta stopped at the closed door at the end of the hallway and opened it a few inches. Chester poked his nose out. He was a gentle giant, and Marta thought he might be a good distraction for the woman. She reached her hand around the door and held tight to his collar as she let him out. He walked into the hallway, his tail wagging and his hind end shaking back and forth.

When they reached the couch the woman sat up and smiled at the dog, which was trying to lick her face and nuzzle his nose against her arm. She petted his head and stroked his back. A few minutes later he was lying down on the rug directly underneath her curled-up body on the couch. She rested her hand on his belly, watching it rise and fall as she cried quietly. The sight made Marta want to cry with her.

Marta's own daughter was a freshman at Texas A&M in Corpus Christi. When she'd helped Teresa unpack her belongings in her dorm room just a few months ago, it had seemed like she'd moved her daughter to a different country, not just across the state. Nine hours separated her from Teresa, who was now living on the Gulf Coast. Her daughter's dream was to study marine biology, a funny choice for a kid who'd spent her life in the desert, but Teresa had always wanted what seemed out of reach: a sober father, money to spare, a mother who wasn't overprotective.

Since childhood Teresa had been Marta's supreme joy and greatest anxiety, causing her countless nights of hand-wringing and praying. Now Marta looked at this young woman lying on Josie's couch and wondered if there were similarities between the two. Maybe this young woman shared Teresa's impulsive need to strike out on her own and declare her independence. And maybe it had even caused her to land here, in a strange person's home, devastated over something Marta dreaded to uncover. She wondered what the young woman's mother was thinking at that moment. Did she know her daughter was gone? Did she care?

Josie's house sat back approximately two hundred feet from Schenck Road. Dell's driveway, located to the left of her house, was a half-mile-long lane that led straight back through pasture to his barn and home. To the left of Dell's lane were several thousand acres of wide-open pasture, small groves of piñon pine, and a small mountain range that ran through the middle of Dell's ranch. Josie planned to search the area between the road and Dell's house where the car had stopped earlier that night.

The four officers lined up in a row parallel with the road, with Nick on the far left, farthest from Josie's house, then Josie, then Otto, and finally Roy, who walked alongside Dell's driveway. With their flashlights, they swept the land in front of them, looking for any tracks or sign of crossing.

Just a few hundred feet from the road Josie held her flashlight steady and quietly called Nick's name. He jogged over to where her beam of light was trained.

"Jesus," Nick muttered under his breath.

Josie's heart clenched in her chest at the sight of a young woman lying flat on her stomach, her arms thrown out to the side, a bullet hole in her back.

Worried that someone else might be hiding in the distance, she called Otto on her cell phone rather than holler for him. "You find something?" he asked.

"There's a body," she said. "A female, probably the same age as the woman inside the house. Let Roy know. Then you'd better keep going. Check the barn and outside Dell's house. I'll call Cowan and start processing the scene."

"You'll let Dell know we're checking his barn? Make sure he stays inside?"

"I'll call him now."

Josie called Dell and told him they were surrounding his house, and he agreed to remain indoors until further notice. She wouldn't tell him about the body until she knew more details. He was probably already worried enough. At seventy-plus years, Dell was in good physical condition, and a self-proclaimed hard-ass, but he'd suffered a heart attack a few years back during a nightmare ride in her police car that involved a chase through the desert with the Medrano Cartel. She would do everything in her power to protect him now. She couldn't imagine losing Dell.

Nick had served as a police officer for years. Now, as a kidnapping negotiator, he was forced to investigate crime scenes as horrific as anything a cop would see. Josie trusted he knew the protocol and the necessity of looking carefully for evidence while not disturbing the crime scene. While she started scouting the area directly around the body, he walked to her jeep and brought her evidence kit back with him to the pasture. He established a thirty-square-foot perimeter around the body with the crime scene tape and small tent stakes while Josie updated Border Patrol. Next, she called the coroner, Mitchell Cowan.

Cowan was in his late forties, never married, with a solemn demeanor and awkward social manners. He didn't get cop humor, rarely smiled, and had a difficult time participating in conversations that didn't involve dead bodies. He considered himself a physician for the dead. He had confided to Josie that he'd tried his hand at private practice, but the social aspect of practicing medicine for the living made him miserable. He'd said he was better equipped to work for dead people. She respected his self-awareness and had wondered if she was that aware of her own shortcomings.

Many of the police officers, especially Otto, found Cowan to be overbearing and unfriendly, but Josie had always liked him. He was a man who cared deeply about the job he performed, and she appreciated that.

Cowan answered his phone, but just barely. The line was connected, but it was several seconds before he spoke, and his hoarse voice sounded confused. If she hadn't already known Cowan didn't believe in what he called "imbibing," she'd have guessed he'd gone to bed drunk.

"Yeah, yes," he said. "Who is this?"

"Cowan, this is Josie. I'm sorry to wake you like this. We've got a dead body."

He cleared his throat, and after another moment he finally said, "What's happened?"

Josie gave him a brief summary and asked how long it would take him to arrive on scene.

"Give me thirty minutes."

Training the lights from her jeep between the road and where the body was found, Josie and Nick slowly walked a twenty-foot section of pasture from the body to the road, searching for evidence, including tracks or footprints, but found nothing.

Next, Josie took photos of the area surrounding the girl and again noted there were no footprints. Nick walked concentric circles, searching with his flashlight for anything the killers may have dropped. Josie began photographing the scene from various angles. This was all part of the initial walk-through. The body wouldn't be touched until the scene had been documented with video and photographs.

Next, she knelt beside the body and examined her clothing for signs that it had been torn in a scuffle, or even removed and the girl later re-dressed, as might be the case with a rape victim. She studied all sides of the body and found nothing to dispute what appeared to be the obvious cause of death: a gunshot between her shoulder blades.

Josie used a ballpoint pen to lift the girl's long black hair away from her face and grimaced at the swollen discolored sight. She took close-up shots of her face and neck before she stood, turning her back on the body and taking a deep breath.

After Josie had graduated from the police academy, she worked for the Indianapolis Police Department for three years before moving to Texas. Initially, her intent had been to work CSI, but her roommate had been a crime scene specialist for the PD, and she'd come to understand the stress the techs endure. Josie had watched her roommate go from a well-adjusted new recruit to a woman suffering from nightmares and relying on prescription sleep aids and vodka shots to erase the visions from her head long enough to sleep a few hours each night. After the horrors of what her roommate had experienced—the smell of blood and death, touching the flesh of a dead body, being at the scene with the dead victim long after everyone else had left—Josie had changed her mind. Now, in a small-town department without the funds to pay a crime scene tech, the job fell to her anyway. The TV shows were far from reality. There was nothing exhilarating about lifting a dead girl's hair to view her bloated face. Only sorrow.

Josie's thoughts returned to her roommate and she wondered if she still worked in law enforcement. Josie contemplated when she would hit a wall and no longer be able to face the nightmarish scenes that occasionally accompanied her job.

"Josie," Nick called.

She turned and saw Nick on his hands and knees, staring down at the ground. "I found a casing."

Josie counted her steps off. The spent case lay on the ground approximately twenty-three feet from the body. "Maybe she was gaining ground on them. They gave up the chase and shot her."

Nick stood and brushed off his hands on his pants. He looked tired at the sight of one more statistic to log in his memory. "The sad thing is, she's probably better off now than if she'd been caught."

Josie took a photo of the casing and its relationship to the body. She then took measurements and drew them on a crime scene template that she would later log into her computer using a drawing program. As she was getting the location of the body oriented to the position of the road behind her, she saw a car traveling down Schenck Road toward her house. She and Nick both turned off their flashlights as a precaution. Otto and Roy were in the barn where they couldn't be seen. She radioed Phillips. "That's probably Cowan. Tell him to leave the hearse on the side of the road. The tires will get hung up in this sand."

"Will do."

While Cowan made his way over to the body, Josie called the mayor to fill him in. In the past he'd made it clear that he should be called in the event of any major crime that could affect public safety. She wasn't sure this crime fit that description, but better safe than sorry. He didn't answer his cell phone, so she left a message and said she'd call later with an update. She'd begun to wonder if the anonymous call left on the mayor's answering machine could have something to do with the body.

Cowan joined Nick and Josie. "Good morning," he said, sounding surprisingly energetic for four in the morning.

He wore a white short-sleeved button-down shirt tucked into polyester pants held up with a wide black belt. A large canvas bag was slung over one shoulder and a camera bag over the other. The walk had clearly winded him and he dropped his bags onto the ground with a huff. He had a wide midsection that made his bald head and narrow shoulders seem out of proportion.

Cowan unzipped his duffel, pulled out a blue tarp, and laid it on the ground. He then moved his bags onto the tarp and began pulling out the various pieces of equipment he would need for the exam. When he stood again, he turned to Josie. "You've gotten the photos and measurements you need?"

She nodded. "I'm done with her until we can roll her over. I'm anxious to determine the time of death. I'd be shocked to discover it happened at night. I'd have heard the gunshot."

"Wouldn't Dell have heard the shot during the day?" Nick asked.

Josie tilted her head to concede the point.

Nick stood beside her. "Hard to imagine the girl running in the daytime, getting fatally shot, and then the killers coming back at night to search for her."

"More likely the killers were coming back for the girl who was hiding on my front porch."

"That's what I'm thinking," Nick said. "Which means they'll be back again."

"It's a shame we couldn't keep this quiet for a day or two," she said. "We could watch the area and hope the car returned."

"Why can't you?" Nick asked.

"I called it in to dispatch. Border Patrol has been notified, plus the coroner call. I'm sure some of the local cop junkies already picked it up on the scanner. Rumors will be running like water through the Hot Tamale by breakfast."

"If the car's from Mexico, the driver may not be aware the

body's been found. As a precaution, I'd like to put a man outside your house for twenty-four hours," Nick said.

Josie gave him a skeptical look. "When you say 'put a man,' you mean one of your men? Because I can't afford to lose an officer out here for a full day."

He gave her a half smile. "I got you covered. At least through tomorrow morning."

"That would be great," she said. "I'll take all the help I can get."

———

Otto and Roy both arrived back on the scene with nothing to show for their walk. They stood outside the area cordoned off with crime scene tape, and Josie and Nick walked over to fill them in. Several minutes later Cowan finally joined the conversation.

"Given the color in her skin, the passage of rigor mortis, and so on, I'd estimate she's been lying here for a full two days. The bullet entry point is consistent with the casing Nick found. I'll take the body back for an autopsy, but I don't expect any major surprises."

"That ought to be on every cop's headstone," Roy said. "He didn't expect any major surprises."

"I'm ready to transport," Cowan said, ignoring Roy. "I've got a new body bag, better for decomposing bodies with fluid. But we'll need to get her out to the hearse. Josie, can we load her into the back of your jeep?"

Josie winced.

"I got the department SUV. It's bigger. We can put the seats down and drive it over here." Roy looked at Cowan. "You sure that bag won't bust?"

"It's designed not to."

Roy sighed and headed back to the road where his vehicle was parked. As they watched him walk away, they saw a vehicle flying down Schenck Road. Lit up by the other headlights, they recognized it to be Mayor Steve Moss's black pickup truck as it pulled off onto the side of the road. Otto groaned beside Josie.

Moss walked quickly toward Josie and Otto. He glanced over at the body and then turned to Josie. "You find anything yet? Local newsies already got wind. They want a story."

She pointed toward the body. "Just what I told you in my message. We're ready to transport the body. Cowan will start on the autopsy today."

"What did I tell you? You don't take me serious, and what happens? A dead body in your backyard is what happens. What the hell is going on here, Josie?"

"That's what we're trying to find out, Mayor."

He swore loudly. "Your phone message said two women? What the hell does that mean?"

"We found a second woman hiding on my front porch. She's the reason we went looking in the pasture and found the body. She's fine physically, but she's not talking."

"What are two women doing out here in the middle of nowhere? Hiding at your house?"

"The other woman hasn't talked. I called the trauma center and they're going to take her in, see if they can stabilize her so we can talk with her."

He squinted at her. "Any ID on either one of them?"

"Nothing. We're estimating they're in their late teens or early twenties, and of Latin American origin." She paused as he continued squinting at her. "Have you heard any other gossip about something going on in town?"

He scowled, looking at Josie as if he didn't like what he saw. "This have something to do with your involvement with the Medrano Cartel?" he said, ignoring her question.

She looked at him dumbfounded. "I'm not involved with the Medranos. That's a ridiculous thing to say."

"Well, hell, yes, you are! Your boyfriend sure was!"

"Look. They committed a crime against Dillon that took place over a year ago. That doesn't make me involved. Please don't use that expression. And, no, I don't think the two crimes are related. At this point, it's safe to speculate that this could be an illegal immigration issue. Beyond that, when you talk to the media, tell them this is an ongoing investigation and the police aren't ready to comment further."

"You'd better be ready to answer some tough questions come tomorrow. The media's going to be all over this. And they're going to wonder how you're involved with a dead girl beside your home and another hiding at your house."

"I'll call you later today with an update," she said, turning from him. She crossed the crime scene tape, aware that she'd rather stand next to a corpse than her boss.

She heard Otto and the mayor talking for a few minutes and after the mayor left Otto approached her. "I don't know what's wrong with him. I've never understood his beef with you, other than you're a female."

"You think that's true, that the media will want to know how I'm involved, since the murder took place next to my house?"

"I think it is if he plants that seed," Otto said. "You think he hates you enough that he'd tarnish an investigation just to put you in a bad place?"

Josie thought about Otto's question. It was hard to imagine the mayor would purposely mislead an investigation, but if he could turn the public against her, or cast doubt about her ability to lead the department, she had no doubt he'd do it.

With the body finally loaded into the hearse, Josie and Otto called Marta out to the front porch to discuss what they'd found.

"That poor girl. I suppose she's been hiding out here for days, knowing her friend was lying alone in the pasture," Marta said. "Makes you wonder what could have happened to make her so afraid to ask someone for help."

Josie described the plastic bag she'd found the previous morning, but explained she'd not seen any other signs of someone hiding around her home.

"Has she spoken at all?" Otto asked.

"Not a word," Marta said.

"Vie said they have a room ready for her," Josie said. "Vie said her shift ends at eight this morning, so she'll get her checked in."

"Any ideas on what happens now?" Otto said. "She's not a criminal. We can't hold her."

"I don't know where she'd go. If she knew someone, she'd have found a way out of this mess days ago," said Josie. "I'll have a translator meet me at the trauma center as soon as Vie clears it. For now . . . Marta, I'd like you to get her settled into a bed there. Surely we can keep her for observation for a day or two."

"I'll start running missing persons reports," Otto said.

"That's good. I'll finish up here and meet you at the office."

FOUR

The trauma center in Artemis was equipped with a one-room sur-
gical unit not typically seen in small towns along the border. The
center was located in a building shared with the county health department. Emergency room doctors served the trauma center on
rotation, and a federal grant had at least ensured that the facility
could handle some of the increased violence the area had experienced over the past decade.

Marta pulled into the rear parking lot. It had been a quiet drive
from Josie's house into town. Marta had talked about her daughter's
first few weeks living away at college, trying to engage the woman
in conversation, but she had remained quiet.

Marta opened the jeep door and walked around to the backseat
to lead the young woman into the center. The woman was staring
at Marta as if she had no idea what was happening to her.

Marta spoke to her in Spanish, explaining that the doctor
needed to check her to make sure she was okay. The young woman's
eyes were wide and her mouth downturned into an exaggerated

frown. Her arms were drawn up and crossed at her chest, as if she thought Marta was going to drag her out of the vehicle. Marta still had no idea if the woman spoke English or Spanish, so she alternated between the languages.

After several minutes the woman timidly put a foot onto the pavement and stepped out of the jeep. They walked slowly into the reception area, where a young female receptionist picked up the phone and waved a finger in the air for Marta to give her a minute.

A moment later, Vie Blessings, the trauma center head nurse, came bustling out from the nurse's station in bright purple scrubs and neon green glasses. Her hair was short and spiked. Marta would have thought Vie's vibrant personality would have frightened the young woman into retreating, but Vie came across as so incredibly competent that people just gave in to her. Marta had seen it before with great ER nurses; they could take control of anyone, from babies to crack addicts, all of them in crisis and needing help.

Vie wrapped her arm under the woman's and took her in to the patient wing. She motioned with her head for Marta to follow.

"I've got a bed ready for her," Vie said. "No sense processing paperwork if she can't talk with us yet. Let's just get her stable and feeling safe."

———⋅———

Forty-five minutes later Vie was able to sit down with Marta.

"Obviously I'm not a psychiatrist," said Vie, "but I'm quite sure she's suffering from psychological trauma. I think she'll need to be treated for acute stress disorder."

"How is she physically?"

"Her vital signs are good. She's dehydrated, but not severely. I'll call Dr. Brazen, a psychiatrist out of Odessa, and see if he'll pay us a visit later today to evaluate her. He has a good reputation for working with military personnel with PTSD."

Marta looked at her watch. It was almost seven-thirty a.m.

Vie continued, "We'll be lucky if we get him today. He's a busy man."

"The other problem is a possible language barrier," Marta said.

Vie sighed. "For now, we have her stabilized. I'll give her a sedative to help her sleep this morning. We may be surprised what a meal and hydration and a bed might do for her by late afternoon."

"I'll post outside her room. Until we have a better handle on the investigation we'll work with the sheriff's department to have someone here with you."

Vie patted Marta's arm. "I'd appreciate that. Let's get you set up in the hallway."

As they walked down the hallway Marta said, "I keep thinking about Teresa. She's not that much younger than that poor woman in there. I can't help thinking our lives are just one bad decision away from tragedy. I just wish I could get Teresa to think that way."

Vie smiled. "Come on, Marta. You were young once too. If we all second-guessed every decision we made in our youth we'd never leave home and experience the world."

Marta pointed back toward the patient room. "Leaving home isn't always a good thing."

———•———

At nine o'clock that morning Josie walked into the office at the police department and found Otto typing something into his computer, his phone pressed between his ear and shoulder. Josie's desk was full of paperwork and pink "While you were out" messages. She wondered how many were checked "Urgent," and felt a weariness settle into her bones. In her mid-thirties now, she'd noticed working a twenty-four-hour shift affected her differently than it had ten years ago. The adrenaline surge didn't last as long as it used to.

Josie filled her coffee cup from the pot at the back of the office and sat down at her desk. She found a package of cheese crackers in a drawer and opened them for breakfast.

Otto hung up and scowled as he turned to face her.

"Nothing. No leads on two young women missing over the past week. At least not in the surrounding areas. Cowan called and said he's already entered information into the NamUs system from the Department of Justice."

"That's the unidentified persons database?"

"Yep. No hits. I checked Texas missing persons and a few other databases."

"You checked Piedra Labrada?"

"Nothing connects with anything that's happened in the past week. I'll expand the search parameters." He took his glasses off and rubbed his eyes. "How's the other woman doing?"

"Marta just called with an update. The woman's still not said a word. Vie said she'll call a psychiatrist from Odessa to come talk with her later today, after she's had some sleep. And on my way over here I called Ms. Beacon to see if she'd meet me at the trauma center later today to translate."

The phone on Josie's desk buzzed and Lou said, "Mayor's on his way up."

Josie leaned her head back and looked at the ceiling. "Otto. I do not have the patience for him right now."

"Pick up your phone. I'll deal with him."

"You're a saint."

It was pathetic, but she blamed it on sleep deprivation and picked up her phone. She pressed the handset to her ear and turned from the door to face her computer monitor, eavesdropping on the conversation taking place behind her.

"Morning, Mayor," Otto said.

"How the hell are you?" the mayor said.

Josie pressed her lips together in irritation. The mayor had never once in her career addressed her in such a casual, friendly manner. Generally, he greeted her with a disapproving nod of his head. She imagined he viewed their relationship as drill sergeant to lowly private. And it ticked her off.

She opened the drawing program on her computer and began entering measurements from her crime scene diagram. With the measurements in place, she'd be able to print a drawing to scale. Josie occasionally muttered yes or no into the phone, hoping the mayor would get a quick update on the investigation and leave.

"You keep me updated, you hear?" she heard him tell Otto.

"Yes, sir," Otto said.

"Who's she talking to?"

Josie heard Otto hesitate. "I'm not sure, Mayor. Can I give her a message for you?"

"Tell her Caroline's sponsoring a tea for the women of Artemis to support her mission project. I expect Josie will want to attend. Tomorrow at six in the basement of the Methodist church."

"Yes, sir. I'll do that."

"Tell her to invite her mom. I'm sure she'd enjoy the event. You take care, now."

Josie listened to his boots clip-clop down the stairs and replaced the handset. "So now I'm required to support his wife's charity work? That bastard infuriates me."

"It's not like he's asking you to do something immoral. It's a charity event."

Josie's eyes widened and Otto threw his hands in the air. "All right, all right. Just tell him you're busy."

"I have a murder to solve. I'm not worried about his wife's latest do-good cause."

"So send your mom. It'll keep her occupied for the evening."

Josie clocked off at ten a.m. to get a quick shower before returning for an eleven to seven-thirty shift. In order to get their shifts straightened out again, she would be back at work at eight the next morning. The swing shift was the worst. It would take her a day or so to get acclimated to the new sleeping schedule, and she had her mom visiting from Indiana, hoping to be entertained on Josie's off hours.

Josie called her mom on the drive home to fill her in on the situation.

"What am I supposed to do tonight while you're working?" she asked.

"Just hang out at the motel for tonight and get caught up on your sleep. Tomorrow, the mayor invited us to his wife's charity event." Josie winced as she said the words. She couldn't believe she was using his summons to buy off her mother.

"At least that's something." She paused. "He's married?"

Josie sighed. "Yes. Her name is Caroline. She's a senator's daughter with money. Her goal appears to be getting the mayor elected into the state senate, but so far, no luck."

"That's hard to believe. Seems like he'd be a great politician."

Josie stifled a sarcastic comment and promised to stop by the motel later that evening on her break to check in.

Otto drove home to his ranch on the outskirts of town and found Delores standing on the front porch when he pulled into the driveway. She appeared to be placing something on the ground. Then he saw the gray cat weaving in and out between her feet, and he realized she was setting down a bowl.

Otto opened the jeep door, hollering to Delores before his feet even hit the driveway. "No, no, no. We've had this discussion. No more strays. Especially cats. They're evil animals. They leave prints on my patrol car."

"Oh, Otto," she said. Her tone was irritated, and she waved her arm at him dismissively. "You can't call that old jeep a patrol car. And with all this dust on the roads, who'd notice a paw print anyway?"

"Cats multiply like rabbits. We have enough animals to feed. We don't need another one, that will eventually turn into twenty, milling around my feet every time I walk in the barn."

"We'll get him fixed. You have your goat herd to take care of. I just want one cat. And he showed up looking for love. Look at him. He loves you already."

The cat was greedily lapping up the bowl of milk Delores had given him.

"My goats serve a purpose. Cats are pointless rodents."

"They aren't rodents." Delores opened the screen door and ushered Otto into the living room.

He stopped just inside the door and took a long deep breath through his nose. He closed his eyes and stood perfectly still. "Do I smell corned beef?"

"And?"

"Sauerkraut?"

"You have a nose like a chef."

He opened his eyes and turned to face her, feeling a mix of betrayal and excitement. "Sauerkraut balls for breakfast?"

"It's almost ten-thirty. Brunch," she said.

"Bribing me with food. You want this cat bad, don't you?"

"I do."

Otto sighed, knowing he'd already lost the battle.

He followed his wife into the kitchen, where she pulled a platter of deep-fried sauerkraut balls out of the oven.

He snatched one as she carried them over to the kitchen table, and popped it into his mouth. "A perfect, mouth-sized piece of Polish goodness."

"Since we're having the rest of the apple dumplings for dessert, I thought we'd best just eat the kraut balls and nothing else. Josie will cut you from the department if you gain any more weight."

"She's got bigger problems than my midsection."

Delores poured them both tea and sat down across from him at the table. "Fill me in."

Otto had called Delores after they'd found the women to let her know he'd be working at least a double shift. He'd given her the basics but no details.

"Josie and Marta took the woman they found hiding on the front porch to the trauma center."

"Was she hurt?"

"Josie said physically she's fine, but she's not said a word. She acts as if she doesn't understand any English or Spanish."

"Maybe she's from Latin America. They speak other languages besides Spanish."

"We can't even get a yes or no out of her, not even a shake of the head."

"She didn't carry a purse or any ID?" she asked.

"Nothing. The woman who was shot in the pasture didn't have an ID either. She was running away from the road and was shot in the back. I imagine the women were traveling together, and after her friend was shot, she hid at Josie's."

"I'm surprised Josie's dog didn't sniff out those women," Delores said.

Otto spread horseradish sauce on another sauerkraut ball and looked at Delores like she'd said something ridiculous.

"What?" she asked, looking slightly offended. "He's a bloodhound. Surely he knew the woman was hiding there."

"He's the laziest dog I've ever seen. He probably kept her company during the day while Josie was gone."

"What's going to happen to her now?"

"She's been admitted to the trauma center for now. They'll treat her for PTSD, I guess. We don't have any kind of victims' assistance here in Artemis, so we'll have to work with one of the bigger cities to see if she can get help. See if we can find her a place to stay so we can keep tabs on her." Otto suddenly felt irritable and realized his lack of sleep was catching up with him. "I don't know. It's not a good situation."

"Let her stay here. We've got a spare bedroom," she said.

He sighed and stifled a yawn. "However unlikely, she's still a suspect in a murder investigation."

"That's awfully coldhearted to say, after what she's been through."

"Delores, you've been married to a cop for too many years to make comments like that. You know very well we can't take this woman into our home right now."

"Fine, then. If you won't let me help this woman, then I'll be helping out that poor starving cat."

Otto scooted his chair back and stood. He kissed Delores on the head, thanked her for breakfast—or brunch—and headed down the hallway to drop into bed for a few hours' sleep. People thought he was married to the sweetest lady in Arroyo County, but she was awfully bossy for someone so sweet.

FIVE

Later that afternoon, after several hours of slogging through paperwork, Josie told Lou she was headed to Marfa to meet with Jimmy Dixon, a Border Patrol Agent with the Big Bend Sector. Agents in the Big Bend Sector were responsible for the entire state of Oklahoma, as well as seventy-seven Texas counties, which included over four hundred miles of the Rio Grande border. While making the thirty minute drive to Marfa, Josie scanned the vast desert that spread out in all directions and thought about the hundreds of miles of unsecured border. Considering the incredible cartel violence in Juárez, Mexico, located just a few hours from Artemis, she marveled that the crime had primarily remained across the border. But she also wondered, as remote as the area was, how much drug smuggling and gunrunning went on completely undetected.

Dixon was standing under the shade of a massive live oak tree on the courthouse lawn talking on his cell phone. He was in his mid-forties, wearing the standard olive-green BP uniform. Jimmy was trim and well turned out: brass polished, uniform starched, and boots shiny. She liked Jimmy, and respected him as a competent officer. He'd asked her out to dinner a few times through the years, but she'd been in a relationship with Dillon Reese. With Dillon out of her life, she hoped Jimmy wouldn't pursue it. He was attractive and a good guy, but his manic intensity wore her out. She couldn't handle his energy more than a few hours at a time.

He saw Josie get out of her jeep and waved.

She reached him as he was slipping his phone in the holder on his belt. She held her hand out and they shook. "How's it going, Josie?" he asked. "It's good to see you again."

"You too, Jimmy. How's life in Marfa?"

He motioned toward the park bench under the tree and they both sat down. She listened to his story about a two-hundred-pound load of marijuana they'd confiscated a week ago, and the ensuing chase through the river that brought down the smugglers. Josie laughed at his retelling, full of drama and mishaps.

He finally asked what she'd learned about the body that had shown up in Artemis.

"Did you hear we found the body in the pasture beside my house?" she asked.

He looked shocked. "No kidding?"

Jimmy had been part of the investigating team when the Medrano Cartel had shot up Josie's bedroom several years ago over a cartel homicide that took place in Artemis.

"What about the other woman that survived?" he asked.

"I found her cowering on my front porch. I suspect she'd been there a day or two."

He raised his eyebrows.

She lifted her hands. "I know. It sounds absurd. I searched outside this morning when I got home. She'd been staying in the toolshed on the side of my house. I haven't been in there in a week or so. I don't know what she was going to do when I finally opened the door and found her."

"You think she ended up at your house by coincidence?"

"I don't know. I was hoping you could tell me," she said.

Jimmy settled back against the bench and then turned slightly to face Josie without addressing her comment. "You have any leads yet?"

"Nothing. The woman who survived hasn't spoken a word and neither woman had any identification. Marta is trying to track down the clothing brands to see if we can narrow down a country of origin, but beyond that I'm at a loss. Prints didn't show up anywhere, and the missing persons databases haven't matched with two females traveling together."

"They could have been crossing the border with a larger group too. Gotten separated," he said.

"I keep going back to the illegal immigrant idea and it just doesn't fit." Josie described the vehicle that had been driving by her house the two nights before they discovered the women.

Jimmy nodded as she finished describing the turn of events. "You're thinking a coyote transporting these women across the border isn't going to come back for them."

Josie shrugged. "Why would they? They collect their money up front. If the women wanted to split from the group, it's less hassle for the coyotes. Two less people to deliver."

"Unless the women took something from them," Jimmy said.

"They didn't have anything on them. No money or ID, nothing."

"Sounds more like a human trafficking case."

Josie nodded. "Traffickers would have a lot more at stake if two girls escaped."

"You bet. They get money from the girls to transport them into the U.S. Then they get a second payment when they deliver the girls to whoever is paying for the service," Jimmy said. "And it fits that the girls had no money or passports. The transporters take everything from them, knowing they're less likely to leave if they don't have any ID or way to get back home."

Josie frowned and watched a young woman with two small kids enter the PD across the street. "What kind of person takes someone's desperation and turns it into profit?"

"It's a pretty sound moneymaker," he said. "The girls get dropped off to a pimp or a labor broker in Houston or San Antonio. They don't speak English. They have no money, no ID, no passport, and they're here illegally. They work sixteen-hour days for enough money for only food and board in a crappy motel room they share with half a dozen other people. Then the room and board is deducted from their paycheck, and they get nothing."

"Indentured servants," she said.

"That's it. They'll work for years in those conditions. And the labor broker moves the maids or factory workers around so they can't form friendships or figure out ways to partner up and break free."

"Have you heard of traffickers working in this area?" she asked.

"No, but we're so overwhelmed with illegal entry—so that's not a current target for this area," he said. "I'll get back to the office and pull together the intelligence we have. I know there was a ring running out of Guatemala last year that got busted. They were coming through Juárez and into El Paso. Sex-trade workers."

"When these girls leave home do they know that's where they're headed?"

Jimmy scowled. "Hell, no. They're fed stories about how rich they'll be in the U.S. Their families scrape together thousands to send them here. They count on the girls getting high-paying jobs and mailing home the cash. Then the girls just disappear."

Josie didn't respond for a while. She watched the woman come back out of the police station, smiling, holding both her kids' hands. Josie turned to look at Jimmy. "You ever wonder when you'll hit the wall? When you'll get up one morning and think, *I just can't do this job anymore. I can't deal with one more piece of scum today.*"

"Some days, by the time I get home, I can almost feel the dirt on my skin. You know? I worry all that bad we're surrounded by is rubbing off on me." Jimmy paused and pointed to the lady strapping her kids into car seats in the back of a minivan. "And then I think, some people can't do this job. But I can. And if people like you and me give up, then what?"

Josie caught up with Otto in the office and described her conversation with Jimmy about human trafficking.

Otto gave her a half grin. "A few months ago Delores came home from the beauty shop complaining about a new hair-cutting place downtown. The one that offers massages?"

Josie nodded in recognition. "Selena's Cuts. She called herself a massage therapist and sent the Holy Water Church into spasms."

"That's the one. The women at Delores's old lady's beauty shop claimed she went beyond the basic massage."

"I talked to Selena and Marta looked into it, but nothing ever materialized," Josie said. "I think it was a young woman wearing short skirts giving back rubs to men that had the old . . ." Josie paused, realizing she was about to refer to Otto's wife.

He smiled at her discomfort. "That had the old women in a frenzy?"

She tilted her head. "Something like that."

"Still might be worth a look. She came here from somewhere in South America, and there were rumors about how she came into the country," Otto said. "Want me to talk to her?"

"Why don't you let me talk to her, and you check in with Cowan on the autopsy. See if he found any matches on the woman's fingerprints." Josie turned to her desk to find Marta's notes from her shift. She typically left Josie a brief summary and listed anything that needed follow-up the next day. Josie read through Marta's notes, repeating key pieces for Otto. "Regarding the clothing the women were wearing, she says the brands were all too global to narrow down, except for the dead woman's cowboy boots, which were tooled in Petrolina, Brazil."

Otto jotted down a note and considered Josie for a second. "Delores and I talked about languages in South America this morning. Portuguese is the main language in Brazil. Maybe that's the language barrier."

"Except I think Brazilian Portuguese is fairly close to Spanish. I think the woman would recognize the basic questions we've been asking in Spanish."

"All right. I'll check missing persons in Brazil," he said, "but a pair of boots is hardly a lead."

"It's all we have right now. Can you call one of the nurses at the trauma center? See if they'll check with the translator about the Portuguese/Spanish language issue."

"Will do."

⬦

Josie sent Jimmy Dixon a quick email and asked him to look specifically into human trafficking intelligence from Brazil with a connection to West Texas. She worked through a pile of return calls and emails and set out for Selena's Cuts at 4:58, knowing Selena closed her shop at five on weekdays.

Selena Rocha was a tall woman with long legs, deep blue eyes, and satiny black hair. When Josie pushed open the door to the salon Selena was bent over at the waist, pulling a brush through her hair. The black mass was so long that the tips grazed the floor. When Selena heard the door open she stood and flipped her hair up and back to let it fall around her face.

Selena gave Josie the once-over and seemed to quickly deduce that Josie hadn't come into her salon in a police uniform to have her hair styled. She pursed her lips into a thoughtful pouty expression.

Josie knew Selena from the trouble she'd experienced earlier that year when the salon opened. Several anonymous complaints were filed against her. One woman left a message on the department hotline about *lewd and lascivious* conduct taking place at the salon. Josie had talked with Selena and felt confident nothing illegal was happening. No doubt there were men who left their barbers for the new woman with the long legs, but it wasn't a crime.

Josie held her hand out and Selena shook it, still pouting.

"How are you, Selena?"

"I'm well, and you?"

"I'm doing okay. I have a few questions, if you have just a minute."

Two middle-aged women who appeared to work at the salon poked their heads out from a curtain at the back of the salon that hid a stockroom. One of the women said, "We're leaving now. Okay?"

Selena waved. "See you tomorrow. Lock the door behind you." Her speech was heavily accented and her voice low-pitched—the kind of voice that commanded authority. She pointed to the plastic chairs in the waiting area and they took seats next to each other.

"Do I remember right that you moved here from South America?" Josie asked.

Selena raised her eyebrows in response and Josie noticed their perfect arch.

"Yes. I came from Venezuela. I've been in Texas almost two years now and came to Artemis just a year ago," she said.

Josie nodded. "That's what I thought. I'm hoping you can give me your perspective on a current investigation we're working on. A young woman was found shot to death early this morning. Another woman was found hiding nearby. She's in shock and hasn't said a word."

"You think they're from Venezuela?"

"We're not sure. We're investigating a possible human trafficking connection. They aren't from the area, and we've not been able to match them to a missing persons database for the surrounding areas."

Selena looked confused. "You want me to translate?"

"We have a Spanish translator, but we can't get the survivor to talk. Honestly, we don't know what language the woman even speaks. Until we have some background information, though, we're lost. Let me be clear. I'm coming here because I'm grasping for anything right now, any kind of lead that could help us figure out who these women are."

"Okay."

"Typically, human trafficking cases we're seeing are coming up through Latin America."

Selena tilted her head back and made a guttural sound that startled Josie. "Let me get this right. Because I perform licensed massages you've made the leap to massage parlor, which makes you think those women were coming to Artemis to work for me."

Josie shook her head. "No."

"Now I have a human trafficking ring running through my salon? Did some old biddy tell you that too?"

Josie raised both of her hands in the air. "No, Selena, that's not—"

"Because I thought we were beyond this. I thought we'd all grown up a little and decided it's okay to touch someone without being labeled a prostitute." Her accent became even more pronounced as her anger intensified.

Josie hadn't anticipated her reaction. "No one has complained. And no one is calling you a prostitute. I'm here because I'm trying to help find justice for these women. You've recently moved here from South America. You may have information that the police aren't aware of. Even if it's rumor. At this point, we'll take any lead we can get."

"So now every country in South America is the same? That's such an American attitude about the world."

Josie sighed openly. "Selena, I'm sorry. I'm not handling my questions well. Of course I realize Venezuela is quite different from other countries in South America. But you traveled to the U.S. from far away, facing all kinds of obstacles that I can't know about. You may have a better understanding about what this woman has gone through than I do. It seemed reasonable to ask you if you'd heard anything around town about women traveling through the area. I certainly didn't mean to offend you."

Selena turned from Josie and stretched her long legs out in front of her, staring ahead at the shelf full of hair products across the room. "I hear drama all the time."

Josie shifted to examine the woman's profile more carefully. Her arms were crossed over her abdomen and her sulky pout had turned into a frown. She looked like a stripped-down version of the model she was ten minutes before. Josie felt like she was finally talking to the real Selena.

"About what?" Josie said.

"About girls leaving their families. The U.S. is riches and happiness." Selena turned back. Her brows were drawn together in frustration. "That's what I thought I would get here. That's what I was *told* I would get here. Look at me. I'm living in the middle of the desert with no man, no riches, and no fame and fortune." She appeared to be debating whether to continue, so Josie remained quiet. "Can I tell you something, without you repeating it?" she finally said.

"Of course you can. I'm not here to make trouble for you, Selena. I just need your help."

Her expression had become softer now, absorbed in her own story. "I left Venezuela when I was twenty-two and went to San Antonio. It wasn't human trafficking. It was me, a young girl with big plans about making a name for myself in the world. I'd been told how beautiful I was my whole life. My grandma used to tell me, 'Those men in the States, they'll adore you with your big blue eyes and ebony hair.' So I came." She shrugged it off, as if it was just part of her life experience. "But there's lots of beautiful girls. You know?"

Josie lifted a shoulder. It wasn't something she thought about much.

Selena smiled and then laughed. "You're so funny. You don't care about beauty and riches."

Josie tipped her head, acknowledging Selena's assessment. "It's not that I don't care about it. It's just that beauty and riches aren't something I have much experience with."

Selena seemed shocked, and Josie figured she was mocking her.

She held up her hand, feeling the interview starting to derail. "Let's get back to San Antonio. You came here to make a name for yourself as a twenty-two-year-old. What happened?"

Selena made an exaggerated dismissive face and said, "What do you think? I traveled here through an employment service. Men took advantage of me. I learned lessons the hard way, and I escaped. The American way. Right?"

"How did you end up in Artemis?"

"After several months in San Antonio I realized the only person looking out for me was me. I eventually saved up enough money on the side to take a cosmetology course, and a kind man, believe it or not, took me under his wing and helped me get board-certified. My trip to Artemis involves two other men and a story that's too long for now."

"But it looks like your story turned out okay."

She shrugged again. "I'm okay, yes. But some of these girls are fourteen or fifteen years old when they get here. They spend years trying to find a way out. At least I was old enough to figure out the system before it destroyed me."

"Are you aware of any trafficking operations coming through our area?"

She frowned deeply and shook her head as if it were a ridiculous question. "Why would they bring them to Artemis? There's no jobs here. They take them to big cities where they can put them to work, where the girls blend in and don't draw attention. A trafficking ring here would stand out. They're smarter than that."

Josie thanked Selena for the information and asked her to call if she thought of anything else.

"If you need help with the girl—" Selena stopped and appeared to rethink what she was about to say. She finally took a deep breath and continued. "If she needs someone to talk to, and you think I can help, call me."

SIX

Josie had felt her phone buzz in her pocket while she was talking with Selena. When she walked outside she saw she had a voicemail from the trauma center.

"Josie, this is Mark. Dr. Brazen is done with the patient. He said he could talk to you if you make it over here in the next few minutes."

Mark was a trauma nurse in his late fifties, and Josie liked his easygoing demeanor. Where Vie was hardheaded and intense, Mark was laid-back and soft-spoken. Mark had a great bedside manner with patients, but no one could take control of chaos like Vie.

Josie returned Mark's call as she was getting into her jeep. He told her the doctor had agreed to wait until she arrived.

As Josie drove the four blocks across town, she called Nick to check in with him. He'd stayed at her house to get caught up on paperwork while Josie went back on the clock. Nick's job as a kidnapping negotiator in Mexico had expanded into a ten-man team, with the territory they covered each year expanding as well. As his business grew, so did the stress of taking on new cases, but it also allowed him to spend more time in Artemis. Technology provided more freedom to connect with his team remotely, a fact that made his and Josie's long-distance relationship more bearable.

He assured her he was fine and said he'd found a can of soup in her cabinet for dinner and that he'd wait up for her.

Josie arrived at the trauma center and found Mark in green scrubs with a scrub cap over his bald head, talking to a man in khaki pants and a lab coat. Mark introduced Josie to the doctor.

"I appreciate you staying to talk with me," she said.

"No problem. I'll do what I can. She'll need intensive therapy once you find out where her home is. Until then, I'd be glad to try and fit her in again over the next day or two."

"Thank you." Josie wondered about payment for this type of service but elected not to ask. The police department had been charged for services such as this in the past, and the charges were a mess to explain to the city council, which ran the city budget as if guarding the U.S. Mint. Sadly, there wasn't much money in Artemis to guard.

"We discovered her name is Isabella Dagati. She started talking with us this afternoon. Not a great deal, but we did get some basic information," he said.

"That's great," Josie said. "In English?"

"She understood English, but she is traumatized to the point that her verbal communication is almost nonexistent. Given that she spoke with us today, I think there's great hope for her recovery, but it could take weeks, even months."

"Still, that's encouraging," Josie said.

The doctor's expression changed, as if he were puzzled. "She spoke two words repeatedly this afternoon. She said the words *help* and *Josie*."

Josie was taken aback for a moment. "I found her hiding at my house. I guess she associates me with helping her."

He gave her a doubtful look. "I don't think that was what she was communicating."

"I don't understand. I helped get her to the hospital. I imagine that's what she means."

He pressed his lips together for a moment, seeming to consider her comment. "I definitely think she sees you as helping her. But when posed a series of questions, I came to understand that she arrived at your house looking for help."

Josie furrowed her eyebrows.

"She repeated your name like a talisman, like she saw you as her savior."

Josie shook her head, not liking the term. "I'm not sure what you mean."

"Keep in mind, I'm basing my hypothesis on limited conversation, gauging her facial responses and body language and so on. But when asked questions about why she came to the United States, and why she came to Artemis, her response was always, *Josie. Help.*"

She wasn't sure why the information was so unsettling, but Josie wanted no part of being a savior to anyone. "I think we should hold off on this line of thinking until we've had more time to talk with her."

"I understand. I'm only trying to provide you with information that may be useful to your investigation."

She nodded then, embarrassed by her reaction. "You're right. It's just an uncomfortable thing to hear. I can't imagine how this woman would know my name, as well as where I live. She clearly isn't from this area, so how could she have found me?"

"That I can't answer. I wasn't able to get a feel for her native language either. I suspect she speaks Spanish along with limited English." He held out his hand and Josie shook it. "I'm headed back to Odessa. I would suggest getting Isabella out of the trauma center and into a safe place where she can rest and recover. Meanwhile, I'll be available by phone if you have follow-up questions."

"I appreciate it. Just one more quick question?"

"Sure. Go ahead."

"Since I can't question Isabella directly right now, can you tell me if she was sexually molested?"

"I'm sorry, Ms. Gray. Confidentiality laws prevent me from sharing information like that."

He handed Josie a business card and left the center.

Mark raised an eyebrow at Josie. "What do you think about all that? Thinking you're her savior?"

She choked out a laugh. "Actually, I'm a bit stunned. I should be happy, from an investigative point. Information like that can lead to a break in a case."

"But you'd prefer the break in the case not to involve you," he said.

"Exactly."

Otto stood next to Cowan, pretending to look down at the dead body while instead gazing directly above the body and across the room to a poster of the periodic table. He suspected that Cowan knew he had a weak stomach, and that's why Cowan delighted in discussing the case over the top of a cold stitched-up cadaver. There was no need for Otto to see the body. Cowan could have easily explained his findings without the theatrics, but Otto couldn't figure out a way to tell Cowan he didn't want to see the body without feeling incompetent.

"You'll notice the bruising and lacerations on her inner thighs and pubis area. . . ." Cowan went on and on, finally stating what he could have said initially without the poor dead woman being laid out on the steel gurney. "The victim was most definitely raped multiple times before she was shot and killed."

"What's the time frame on the rapes?"

"Recent. A matter of a week or two."

"Was she killed instantly?"

"The gunshot wound would have killed her within minutes."

"Does it look as if there was any tampering with the body after she was shot?" Otto asked.

"No. Other than insects and animals, I didn't see evidence the body was moved or touched."

"How long before we receive toxicology reports?"

"I'd expect two to four weeks."

"Was there anything exceptional about the bullet wound?" Otto asked.

Cowan reached out to turn the body over and Otto put a hand out to stop him. "That's not necessary. Just tell me your findings."

Cowan smiled slightly and began pulling the plastic covering over the body. If Otto had been three decades younger, he would have thrown a punch at the man's smirk. He couldn't understand why Josie seemed to think so highly of Cowan. Otto found him arrogant and intolerable.

Once Cowan had replaced the body and washed up, he returned and opened his notes on the lab table. He described the time of death as the same as his initial assessment. "The bullet has been logged as evidence and it's available for you to take. Same with her clothing and jewelry. Regarding the wound, it was just as expected. The trajectory was straight, and the wound is consistent with what you would expect from a shot fired from twenty-three feet away." He paused and looked up at Otto. "Correct? The casing found at the scene was about that distance from the body?"

"That's right."

"Well, then. I've got the finger- and palm prints, dental X-rays, photographs, hair specimens, and so on. I'll post a photograph of the victim's face on the missing persons database and we'll hope for a hit. For now, I'll keep her in the freezer." Cowan clasped his hands in front of him. "In my years here working in Arroyo County, we've only utilized the potter's field a few times to bury an unidentified body. I certainly hope that won't be the case with this young woman."

———•———

When Otto left the coroner's office at the county jail, he called Josie from the jeep. For late October, the temperature was still running hot, so he cranked the air conditioner. It had reached ninety-eight that afternoon and the relentless sun was making him irritable.

"You had supper yet?" he asked.

"Nope. But I could use some. I'm just leaving the hospital. Want to meet at the Hot Tamale?"

"I do." Otto paused, knowing he was going to piss her off. "You want to swing by and grab your mother for dinner?"

She sighed into the phone. "It's after six. She's probably eaten."

"Josie. She's your mother."

"Otto. I know that."

Otto waited out the silence.

"Damn it. All right. I'll stop by the motel. See you in a few."

———•———

Manny's Motel was a six-room establishment shaped like a strip mall, with all six doors opening toward the street. Manny's office was located in the center of the building, with a green neon sign that hung crooked from the window. One afternoon Josie had stopped by with a question about an investigation and she'd asked him, "You want me to straighten up your sign for you?"

Manny had replied, "No, I like it that way. It's not pretentious. It lets people know, *Here's a comfortable place where I can put my feet up and relax.*"

Since then the crooked sign made her smile every time she noticed it. She thought how awkward it would look hanging straight in his window.

She found Manny sitting in a recliner behind the front desk reading a book. When he looked up, his expression was distraught. "What timing! She's ten feet from opening the door and ruining the rest of her life. You couldn't give me five more minutes?"

Josie laughed. "Then you'd need five more after that. Just get this over with and you can get back to your book."

Manny groaned as he got up out of the chair and smiled when he reached the counter. "For you? I would toss the book into the trash. What can I do for you?"

"I'm here to check on my mom. Can you tell me what room she's in?"

His lips drew down in a frown. "Did you have to ask? You know I will always put your mother in the best room in the motel. Right next to me, where I can make sure everything is to her complete satisfaction."

"Room One?"

"You know it."

"You're the best," she said, and walked out of the office, leaving Manny to his paperback.

Josie headed down the concrete walkway and knocked on the door to Room 1. Beverly Gray answered wearing three-inch-thick wedges, cutoff jean shorts, and a tight white low-cut scoop-necked T-shirt that Josie thought would look more appropriate on a teenager.

"Well, hey, darlin'! Did you come to take your mom to dinner?"

Josie recognized her mother's exaggerated hillbilly drawl from her childhood, but after so many years away from home it sounded foreign.

"I'm still on duty, but Otto and I thought we'd buy you supper at the Hot Tamale."

Her eyes lit up like she'd been invited to a special event, and Josie felt a twinge of guilt.

"Hang on. I'll get my purse."

Josie watched her mom take dainty steps back to the bathroom to check her makeup and her hair. Her high-heeled tiny steps had always looked completely ridiculous to Josie. There was nothing dainty about Josie; she walked tall and with purpose. At moments like this, Josie's longing for her dad caused a deep ache. She was eight when he died, and now she could only imagine what kind of physical presence he had when walking into a room.

Beverly walked out of the bathroom, grabbed her purse off the motel room desk, and headed straight for the door.

Located across from the courthouse, the Hot Tamale was a popular diner for most everyone in Artemis. The service was quick, and the owner, Lucy Ramone, made everyone who entered feel like a friend. She also served up local gossip like it was her job.

At six-thirty the diner was still hopping, with tables and chairs scattered across the place in a haphazard manner that would drive Josie crazy if she were a waitress there. Lucy made it clear to her diners that talking came first, and so people were given free rein to arrange the tables to best suit their needs.

They wove their way through and sat in a corner by the window where Otto had pulled up chairs for them. Josie and her mom sat across from Otto.

"Are you rested up from your trip, Beverly?"

"Oh, my, yes. It doesn't take much for me to liven up. Life's too short for naps."

"Do you have plans for your stay out here?" he asked.

Josie stared at the menu and listened intently.

"I guess that mostly depends on my daughter. Whether she can stand me here or not."

"Oh, I know she could stand you. I think it's more whether you could stand her schedule. I can attest to the fact that she's not around much. The job is a killer."

"Well, I don't want to marry her, I just want to visit!"

Otto laughed as Lucy hustled up to the table. "How's my two favorite cops in all of Arroyo County?"

"We're just fine," Josie said. "You doing okay?"

"Never better. Business is good."

"Lucy, this is my mom, Beverly. All the way here from Indiana."

Lucy bent down and hugged Beverly, who laughed and squeezed back. The two women chatted for a moment until Lucy finally wrote down their order and took off for the kitchen.

Otto picked up the conversation. "You were married to a police officer, weren't you, Beverly?"

"Best man that ever walked the earth," she said, and then sat her drink down to look at Otto. "Excluding present company, of course."

"Understood."

"He was a road trooper. Died in a line-of-duty accident. Ripped our lives right into two when he passed away."

"Josie said he was a great cop and a great dad. That's quite a combination."

"She's just like him. He was quiet and serious, always thinking about things. That's why we were such a good match. I made him laugh. That's just what Josie needs in her life. A man to make her laugh."

Josie felt the heat seep into her cheeks at her mom's comparison of Josie to her dad. After he died, her mom rarely talked about him. And as much as Josie would have liked to have discussed her dad, she wasn't ready to talk about her private life in the Hot Tamale with Otto while on duty.

Josie pulled the conversation back to the present. "I have some bad news regarding your visit. It may be a while before I get a normal shift so we can spend some time together. A woman was found murdered, and in a small town like this, we throw everything we have on an investigation, meaning long hours away from home."

"Meaning, you won't be taking me to the mayor's fund-raising dinner tomorrow?"

"It's actually his wife's fund-raising dinner for her mission work. And we'll still plan on going unless something comes up with the investigation to keep me from it. But I probably won't see you between now and tomorrow evening. I get off work tonight at midnight, and I'm back in at eight in the morning."

Her mom took the news well and after dinner they walked her back to the motel with no complaints. Either her mother had mellowed considerably, or she wanted something and was choosing her battles.

"Thanks," Josie said as she and Otto reached the top of the stairs at the police department.

"For what?"

"For having dinner with my mom. I know you're anxious to review the case."

Otto unlocked the office door and Josie flipped on the fluorescent lights. As he walked to his desk he said, "You know I try to stay out of your personal life as much as I can." He turned his head and grinned.

"Oh, really?"

"But I'm going to give you a bit of friendly advice tonight. This job is a tricky one. There's a fine line between devotion to your job and sacrificing your family. And I'm not really talking about your mom. I just mean in general. You're a young woman who deserves a family and a happy place to go home to at night. But if you've always got the job on your mind, you'll never find that."

Josie poured herself a cup of burnt coffee and held the pot up to Otto. He grimaced.

"I get what you're saying, but it's hard to turn it off. A woman is lying in our morgue because some monster shot her in the back. Her friend is too terrified to talk. How do I not make that my top priority?"

"Of course it's your top priority. At work. But you have other priorities at home. You have to find a way to leave it at night or it's going to eat you up. You have to develop that on-off switch in your head. I've been telling you this for years and you don't seem to get it."

"Honestly, the only way I know how to lose those visions at night is a glass full of bourbon." She knew Otto never used alcohol as a coping mechanism, but she figured he wanted candor, so she gave it to him.

"You're not listening. That's what your family is for. That's why you have to make your family and your loved ones, your man friend Nick, priorities too. They'll keep you strong enough to keep doing this insane job. They'll help you clear your head instead of filling it up with bourbon. Even if it's only a few hours at the end of your shift, you have to shut your brain down. You can't be in that fight-or-flight mode twenty-four/seven or you'll be joining that woman in the morgue all too soon."

Josie glanced up at him, surprised at the anger in his voice.

Otto sighed. "I'm sorry. I just worry about you. Somebody has to."

"You're a good friend, Otto. I appreciate your advice, and I'll give it some serious thought."

"Good enough."

"Okay, grab your notes," she said. "Let's get down to business."

As they were sitting down at the conference table they heard someone coming up the stairs, two at a time. Marta walked into the office looking like she'd waded through a mud pit. Her uniform was mud-streaked, as were her face and arms.

"We got that son of a bitch!" she called.

"Who?" Josie asked, grinning at her excitement.

"Slick Fish is in custody. I'd heard rumors that he was going to transport a large group this evening around dusk. I set up an observation point on the river along with two Border Patrol agents who knew all about him. Slick had seventeen people ready to cross, and we nabbed him with the very first one."

"Did you mud-wrestle him to the ground?" Otto asked, pointing to her muddy pants.

"That's exactly what it was. He might have been wet and naked, but he couldn't slip by three officers. And, best of all, it's BP's case. No paperwork for Marta." She grinned and brushed her hands together.

"You smell like dead fish," Otto said.

"You know I hate that river. Next time *you* get the river detail."

"Well done," Josie said. "And good timing. We're just about to debrief on the murder."

———

Marta washed up in the office bathroom and sat down with her notebook.

Josie started with Otto. "What did you find out on the autopsy?"

"No surprise with the bullet wound. Cowan said the wound was consistent with being shot from behind at twenty-three feet. The body wasn't moved or tampered with after the gunshot. The biggest news was that Cowan said she had been raped multiple times before her death."

"Recently?"

"That's what he said. Recent multiple lacerations around her groin and thighs."

"What about the other woman?" Marta asked. "Do we know if she was raped?"

"The doctor won't tell us. Patient confidentiality. We'll have to wait on her to offer that kind of information," Josie said.

"Cowan also confirmed time of death was what he originally thought. She'd been lying in the desert for two days. The official time of death is now ten p.m., but it's obviously an estimate."

Josie raised her eyebrows in surprise. "We had originally thought it happened during the day, and we were surprised Dell hadn't heard the shots." She pulled her calendar up on her phone to look at the date. "That was the night of the water meeting. Dell and I had come into town together. It was a special session that everyone in town knew was going to get heated and would probably last for hours. Which it did," Josie said.

"So maybe the killer is someone who knows you well enough to figure you'd be at that meeting," Marta said.

"And they took advantage of you and Dell both being gone," Otto said.

They sat for a moment, trying to decide if the new information changed the course of the investigation. Otto finally moved on. "Was the psychiatrist able to share anything?"

"Her name is Isabella Dagati," Josie said. "Lou is running a search for her name. We still don't know where she's from. She may be bilingual, Spanish and English."

"That's more than I thought we'd get today," he said.

"There's more," Josie said. "The doctor said she repeated the words *Josie* and *help* multiple times. He interpreted it to mean that she went to my house, seeking help."

Otto frowned. "Not that you had provided her help at your house, and she was just repeating that you'd helped her?"

"That's exactly what I thought. The doc said that considering her body language and facial expressions he thought she came to me for help." Josie paused. "He said she viewed me as a kind of savior."

Otto's eyebrows shot up.

"It makes sense to me that she would latch on to you like that," Marta said. "You *were* her savior. You finally put an end to the nightmare she'd been living for days. But it seems like a big jump for the psychiatrist to conclude that she was seeking you out specifically, if she can't even talk much yet."

"I agree. Without having been in the room, it's hard to know how he came up with that idea."

"Brazen is a respected psychiatrist. He works with PTSD. I don't think he'd make a statement like that if he wasn't confident in his assessment," Otto said.

"So let's take the information at face value. What does that tell us?" Marta said.

"Here's the way I see it. The women were either traveling with a man or a group, probably held against their will. At least one of the women was raped multiple times. We can assume things got bad enough that the women planned an escape. Someone gave them my name and told them where I live. They crossed the border and came to my house for help. Whoever they were with crossed the border, hunted them down, and killed one of the women. The men came back to the place where they killed her, searching for the one who escaped. That's when Nick and I heard the car and discovered the woman on my porch."

Otto nodded and asked, "What about security at the trauma center?"

"I'm working with the sheriff to make sure we have someone posted there twenty-four/seven," Josie said.

"Someone had to tell the two women who you are, and give

them directions. Who would do that?" asked Marta. "If someone locally had found the women, they would have contacted you. They would have helped the women to safety."

"Maybe somebody helped them from across the border. Someone in Piedra Labrada gave them my name."

"Could be a human trafficking situation gone bad," Otto said.

"I met with Jimmy Dixon from Border Patrol earlier today. He said there was a trafficking outfit that moved women from Guatemala through El Paso. It got busted last year. He's checking into recent activity," Josie said. "I also talked to Selena Rocha."

Marta nodded. "The hairdresser from Venezuela. Did she have anything?"

"She said if the girls are truly part of a human trafficking scheme, that this wasn't the destination. They would have been headed to San Antonio, Houston, Dallas."

"Sure. Makes sense," Marta said.

"Maybe the women heard about a female cop and came to you for help," Otto said, pointing at Josie.

Josie nodded. "It makes sense. I'll call Sergio and see if he has any ideas."

Sergio Pando was a Mexican Federales officer who grew up with Marta in Mexico. His wife was killed ten years ago, an innocent bystander caught in the middle of cartel warfare. His life now revolved around his high school–aged daughter, keeping her safe in a world gone crazy.

Josie put her desk phone on speaker. "Sergio, this is Josie Gray."

"Josie! It's good to hear from you."

"How are you? How's your daughter?"

"I'm good." He laughed. "And my daughter is a senior in high school now. She has turned into what you call a social butterfly."

Josie smiled. "So you're staying busy keeping up with her."

"That I am. And tell me how Marta is. She never stops by anymore to visit."

Josie glanced over at Marta, who looked away in embarrassment. Marta knew that Sergio had pined after her since childhood. When Marta married her husband, a man with alcoholic demons he'd never been able to tame, Sergio had married too, but he'd told Josie years ago that he'd never stopped loving her.

"Marta's doing well. She's sitting here with me. We're actually calling to see if you can help us with some information."

"Absolutely. What can I do?"

Sergio had heard about the two women and the fact that the surviving woman was found at Josie's home. Josie explained her theory and asked, "Does it seem plausible that two women, traveling through Mexico, would connect with someone in your town who would lead them to me rather than to a safe spot in Piedra?"

"Of course it does. Right or wrong, the general feeling is that once you've made it this close to the border, your only hope for help is to make it across. People stake everything on their trip across the border. They flee Guatemala and Honduras, trying to escape the cartels that are destroying their cities. Many of them have sold everything, their homes and their belongings, to pay for the trip north. They believe, even if you get picked up by the U.S. authorities, that they'll help you find shelter and food."

"Does it seem reasonable that someone would have sent them to me, specifically?" she asked.

"You've had two bad run-ins with the Medrano Cartel. Both times, you lived. Not only that, but you humiliated them. Your name is known in Piedra Labrada. I've heard you called *señora con muchas vidas*."

"Which means?"

"Lady with many lives."

Josie sighed audibly.

"That's it. You don't get more than one life with the Medranos. People think you have the saints on your side."

Josie winced. "It's got nothing to do with saints, Sergio. I don't want this to get weird."

He laughed. "You don't have a choice, Josie. The saints choose you, not the other way around."

"I just need to know who helped these women get to me."

He made a noise as if he was thinking. "Do you know of Señora Molina?"

"No."

"She's a hundred years old, with the heart of a lion. She's the mother to the women and children who have none. If anyone could help you, I'd say it would be her."

Sergio provided Josie with directions to the woman's home. "The local story is that she took a vow of poverty over fifty years ago, not as a Catholic nun, but as a servant of God. The locals say she trusts no one and helps everyone. She's an amazing woman, but she has no phone or anything beyond the basics. You'll have to chance a visit and hope to find her home."

Josie thanked Sergio for the information and ended the call with a promise to visit soon.

"I'll go tonight. Nick's staying at my place until we clear this up. He knows Piedra Labrada, so he can help me find the woman's home. He also speaks fluent Spanish. I might stand a better chance of talking with her if he's with me."

Otto huffed as if irritated. "You need to take him with you for protection. If he can't go with you tonight, then call it off. Sergio said you're known in town. Well, that means you're known in town by the cartel too. Play it safe."

"I got it. And Marta, can you check in at the trauma center? See if you can get anything else out of Isabella?"

Marta nodded. "I don't feel good about her staying at the center. But we don't have any victims' assistance homes in town. With the house for battered women closed down we have nothing."

"I've got an idea on that. Let me work on it for tomorrow," Josie said. "There's a sheriff's deputy posted there until eight. Why don't you relieve him and stay through your shift. I'll call the sheriff and make sure he's got someone who can cover you at midnight."

———————

Marta parked her jeep in the parking lot at the trauma center and carried her printing kit inside, where she found nurse Vie Blessings in her purple scrub suit and bright pink tennis shoes talking to Caroline Moss, the mayor's wife.

Marta had never cared for Caroline. She was rich and uppity, and Marta always felt as if the woman thought she was doing Marta a favor when speaking to her. Marta wanted to remind her, *You might be the mayor's wife, but he's mayor of a town with twenty-five hundred people in it, not exactly bragging rights.*

Rather than interrupt the conversation, Marta took a seat in the waiting room.

When Caroline left, Vie approached Marta. "You here to check on Isabella?" she asked.

"Yes, ma'am."

"She's a popular girl."

Marta frowned in confusion. "Someone's been here to see her?"

"Selena Rocha stopped by earlier and asked if she could speak with Isabella, but she was asleep."

Marta nodded, surprised at the news. "Josie talked to Selena earlier today."

Vie shrugged. "She said she wanted to offer her help. She said she's from South America and might be able to talk to her. I suggested she work through Josie."

"I'd prefer that. She may hear information we could use and not realize it's relevant," Marta said.

"And then Caroline stopped by to see her."

Marta followed Vie's glance out the window, where they watched Caroline drive away in her convertible

"She said she's having a dinner tomorrow to raise funds for the local missions and she wanted to know what the woman needs, clothes and shoes, basic necessities to help her get back on her feet."

Marta nodded, feeling a twinge of guilt for her earlier thoughts.

"She asked if she could talk with her, but Josie told me not to allow outside visitors until you know more about her background."

"Is she awake? I'd like to ask her a few questions."

Vie pointed down the hallway. "She's watching television."

Marta stopped in the hallway to talk to Sheriff's Deputy Scott Wilson, who was sitting in a chair outside the patient room. Wilson was in his early twenties, with a heavy build and a southern way of drawing out his words. He'd had a crush on Marta's daughter in high school, but Teresa had preferred the bad boys. Marta could only hope she'd passed that phase in her life.

"Hey, Marta. You here to relieve me?" he asked.

"I am. Anything to pass along?" she said.

He sighed heavily and stood. He leaned in and whispered to Marta so that Vie couldn't hear as she walked into the room. "Nothing. Hope you got a pot of coffee in your car. I ran out of things to do after I counted the floor tiles for about the tenth time."

Marta laughed and he patted her on the back before taking off.

———•———

After Vie checked the woman's vital signs and left the room, Marta pulled a chair beside the bed. She reminded her that she'd sat with her in Josie's living room early that morning, and Marta noted that she made eye contact at the mention of Josie's name.

"We'd like to help you, Isabella. We can help you get back to your home and your family if you'll give us some information."

She paused and the woman turned her head away to stare across the room at a painting. Marta took a deep breath, knowing the following request would probably shut her down.

She opened her bag and pulled out her pad and ink, smiling, attempting to lighten the task. "I've brought a kit with me. I need to get your fingerprints here on this paper. It will help us get your records in order." She set everything up on the rolling bedside table and stood, holding her hand out. Surprisingly, Isabella held her own hand out in response and allowed Marta to print her as she talked.

"Where do you live?"

Isabella remained silent.

"Are you from Mexico? Maybe Brazil?" She paused. "Guatemala? Honduras?"

Nothing.

"Do you live here in the U.S.?"

No reply.

"Can you tell me where your friend is from?"

Isabella closed her eyes and her face tensed up as if she were trying to fight back tears.

Marta dropped Isabella's hand and slipped everything back in her bag. "Can you tell me your friend's name? Her first name?"

She shook her head. "No, no, no."

"You can't tell me, or you don't know?"

"I don't know. I don't know her name."

Tears poured from her eyes until she began shaking and then sobbing. Marta pushed the call button beside the bed and a moment later Vie rushed in. She looked at Marta accusingly.

"What happened?"

"I asked about her friend and she started crying," Marta said.

"I think you'd best go," Vie said.

Back in the hallway, Marta was sorry that she'd caused such a reaction in the young woman, but she was interested to learn that Isabella claimed not to even know the other woman's name. She sent a quick text to Josie and Otto to that effect and took her position on the chair in the hallway, settling in for a long night of waiting and wondering.

SEVEN

Josie arrived home at 7:30 p.m. and found Nick on her couch reading a *True Crime* magazine and drinking a beer. He pitched the magazine onto the coffee table as she sat beside him.

"You look like you need some sleep."

She shrugged and blew air out in frustration. "I feel like we're checking tasks off a to-do list. No big breaks yet. Did you hear anything today?"

"I have feelers out about the trafficking and two missing women. Since we're in Medrano territory I have guys checking there first. There's no doubt the Medranos are involved in prostitution and trafficking, but I don't know about transportation routes. Did Border Patrol have information on routes?"

"Jimmy Dixon's working on it."

Josie watched Nick take a long swig of his beer, and again she was struck by his physical presence. When he walked into a room he filled it up; he was big and intense and couldn't blend into a crowd if he wanted to. In contrast, Josie tried to fall back and observe; she attributed this to being a cop, but she knew it was also her personality. She watched the condensation drip down the bottle and onto his jeans and took in his hard jawline. He smiled without turning to face her.

"You okay with the view?"

She laughed. "A little cocky, aren't you?"

"Just making sure you're satisfied."

"I was deciding what kind of a bodyguard you might make."

"The best."

"You busy tonight?" she asked.

"I'm your man."

She smiled as she nodded. "Good. I need an escort to Mexico."

Nick carried dual citizenship in the U.S. and Mexico and frequently made the trip across the International Bridge. Driving in his black armored SUV, they passed through customs with no issues, and within a few minutes they were driving parallel to the river, headed for desert country. Once they were out of Piedra Labrada they both rolled down the windows and let the warm night air blow through. When Josie had told Nick about Señora Molina he said he knew her. Apparently she was a legend with the young kids in the area. When somebody needed a place to crash, they could count on her.

Nick pulled off the marked gravel road and onto an arroyo that led down into a shallow streambed a half mile from the Rio Grande. The arroyo was dry, since no measurable rain had fallen in the area for several months. The monsoons should have started in September and people were getting nervous that the territory would have another fire season like the year before.

As Nick drove over the fallen boulders in the dry creek bed, Josie couldn't help smiling at the night. The sun had faded and a fresh scattering of stars cast light across the sky. They were driving along slowly enough to catch the whirring sound of the night insects in the cottonwood trees at the top of the arroyo. In spite of the unpleasant nature of the trip, she relaxed into the night and breathed in the smell of juniper and creosote, a pungent earthy scent like perfume to Josie.

She felt Nick's hand rest on her own, lying on her thigh.

"You like this, don't you? The rough desert?" he asked.

She took a minute to respond. "I do. It's strange to think back, how I grew up in the Midwest, but I never felt at home until I moved here. It's like my body was meant to be here, with the heat and the wide-open spaces."

In the failing light, Josie could barely make out the turnoff that Nick pulled onto from the arroyo.

"How could someone in trouble ever make it out here?" Josie asked. "It would be impossible to find."

"That's the beauty of Señora Molina. To get here is a feat in itself. It's not like some kid who had a bad day at school would make his way over here for help. You have to seek her out to get here. And she recognizes that. She's a pretty amazing lady."

"Have you worked with her often?"

"She's helped me with a few negotiations. She has a network of contacts that would rival any police department's."

"Why don't the police use her? I've never even heard of her," she said.

"I'm not sure how to explain her," he said. "She doesn't have allegiance to the police, or to anyone, for that matter. She wouldn't put up with the police coming to her for information, especially as an informant."

Josie nodded.

"She told me once that her life's work is heartache and trouble."

They rounded a bend and Nick pulled the SUV to a stop. Josie stepped outside and stood still to allow her eyes to adjust to the dark. She smiled and breathed in deep the sweet smell of wood smoke from a fire, and then heard the river flowing before she saw it, a dark swath cutting through the high bank on the U.S. side of the river. A jagged silhouette of rocky outcroppings and clumps of salt cedar were visible above the bank. As she turned away from the river she saw the stone house, barely visible against the low canyon wall that ran behind it. Tucked back under a narrow front porch was a door with two windows lit up on either side of it.

The house was stacked stone, with the rock most likely collected from the low-lying mountains around it. Ruins of old stone homes could be found throughout West Texas, but there were still people who fought the critters and the occasional cold winters to live in them, enjoying the centuries-old way of living. Glass lanterns glowed in the deep windowsills and let off a warm orange light.

Nick knocked on the door, which resembled an old barn door with long wrought-iron hinge straps that held the wooden slats together. Josie could see thin strips of light between gaps in the wood. Nick hollered through the door, "Señora Molina. It's Nick Santos. I've come to check on you."

Nick had said he always came with a small gift of appreciation, something to help her get by, so Josie found herself holding a loaf of French bread that she'd fortunately picked up at the grocery to have on hand for her mother.

They stood quietly at the door until it was finally pulled open. Josie realized Sergio hadn't been exaggerating about the woman's age. She was stooped over at the waist so far that she had to lift her head up to see Nick. Gray wisps of hair stuck out from under a faded blue bandanna tied around her head like a babushka. She wore a loose-fitting white smock top and long flowered skirt. She squinted up at Nick and then broke into a smile that showed a half dozen teeth.

"What you doing here so late, ole boy?" Her voice crackled with age and carried very little accent of any kind.

"I wanted to see how Señora Molina was. And you look better every time I see you." She reached her hand out and they held hands for a moment before she turned to Josie.

"And you brought a friend with you. Well, then you come inside so you can introduce me proper."

She stepped aside and Josie followed Nick into a room that held a small kitchen and woodstove to the left and a table with eight mismatched chairs around it in the middle of the room. To the right of the table, a handmade wooden couch with cushions covered in colorful afghans and wool blankets ran the length of the wall. Nick took the loaf of bread from Josie, and she watched him set it on the table and then slip money underneath it.

Señora Molina shut the door and latched it, and turned to study Josie.

"This is my good friend Josie Gray," Nick said. "She lives just across the river, not too many miles from here."

The woman put both her hands out and Josie did the same. She held Josie's hands inside of her own warm hands and looked straight into her eyes for a long time. "I know who you are, Josie Gray. You have a heart for people. And you do what's right in the face of evil."

The warmth from the old woman's hands was like a tonic. Josie felt the strength and wisdom move from the woman's hands through her own body. She was overcome by this seemingly simple woman and her strength of spirit.

"You do the work of God. Do not ever forget that. You are a foot soldier, just like me. Yes?"

Josie felt her throat tighten with emotion and she was shocked at her own reaction. All she could do was nod yes in response.

The woman finally let go of Josie's hands and pointed to the table, where Nick was sitting. When she dropped her hands it was as if a connection had been broken. Josie turned to the table, shaken by the experience. She could feel Nick watching her as she sat down, and she finally looked over at him. His face was soft and kind. He seemed to understand what had just happened. Maybe this was the effect the old woman had on people.

They watched as she went into the small kitchen area, pulled a teakettle off the wood-burning stove, and carried it over to the table.

"Can I help you?" Josie asked.

She pointed Josie toward the small bank of kitchen cabinets and a tray that sat on top of the counter with teacups and containers holding milk and sugar.

They sat down at the table, and as Josie poured each of them a cup of tea to steep, the woman asked, "Have you come to see me about the two women I sent to you?"

Josie stared at her, startled by the question. She'd hoped to find some tidbit of information, but never expected the women had actually visited Señora Molina. "I have. Yes."

"They made it to you safely?" she asked.

Josie glanced over at Nick, unsure if she should upset the woman with the news that one had been murdered.

"You can tell her. Señora Molina has watched the same story unfold again and again. It won't surprise her," he said.

The woman sipped from her cup, her expression never wavering as Josie explained how they had found the murdered girl in the pasture and the other girl hiding on her porch.

Josie was sitting next to Señora Molina, who laid her arm on the table and opened her hand for Josie to take it.

"When God calls upon you to do something important, you mustn't question. God trusts you to make decisions to help people as best you can. When you question your decisions, you weaken your resolve. If those women hadn't come to see you, perhaps both would be dead."

Josie nodded.

"Too much thinking goes on up here." She dropped Josie's hand and tapped a finger to her own temple.

Josie smiled and noticed Nick doing the same. "I've been told that," she said.

"We do the best we can, and we let the rest go," she said. She braced her hand on the table and slowly stood. "I want to show you something."

The woman walked into the kitchen and then called for Nick. She pointed to a box on top of a kitchen cupboard in the corner. "Reach up there and pull that down."

He did so, and she carried a small glass bowl to the table. Several bullets rattled around in the bowl as she placed it in front of Josie.

Señora Molina sat down beside her again and said, "When I was fifteen I married a man much older than me in my village. He was a mean man. When he drank, his anger boiled up into a volcano of hatred for me. The longer we were married, the more he hated me. But I had nowhere else to go."

Her voice was so broken and cracked with age that Josie wasn't sure she'd be able to finish her story. Nick pointed to a clay honeypot on the tray and Señora Molina nodded. He lifted the lid and twirled the dipper to gather honey onto the stick and then drizzled it into her tea. She stirred her tea and drank from it, allowing her voice to rest before she continued.

"One hot summer night he was in the horse stable and I was inside the house. I could hear banging and yelling. He'd been drinking tequila all day. He'd skipped the supper I had laid out for him. Then he started yelling my name, and I went to him. Why did I walk into that barn full of trouble and hate? I can't tell you. That's what victims do, they walk into trouble. I found him lying on his back in one of the horse stalls, pointing his gun at me. He fired as soon as he saw me. He looked right into my eyes. Six times he pulled that trigger. Time enough to stop and think, regret, feel something other than hate for me, for the woman who cooked his meals and shared his bed."

She reached up with hands crooked, probably from arthritis, and slowly unbuttoned the top buttons of her smock. She looked at Josie with eyes distant from memories, and she ran her finger from the hollow at her neck down and over to an indentation under her collarbone. She slipped her finger into the hole like a plug in a socket.

"That's where all the hatred from one man's soul buried inside me for eternity. If I push hard enough, I can still feel the lead." She reached her hand into the bowl of bullets and picked one up, showing it to Josie. "He died that night. Drank himself to death. Later I stood in the barn with his rusty pocketknife and dug the rest of these bullets out of the wood in the barn stall. I've kept them all these years."

She motioned for Josie to fix the buttons on her top. When Josie was done buttoning them, Señora Molina studied her again. "You have your own lead bullet lodged inside your heart. Don't let it poison you. That night I committed myself to doing good in the world. And I don't let the hatred inside that bullet escape." She tapped her chest where the bullet was buried. "You protect yourself with people who care about you. With good men like Nick. Yes?"

Josie nodded and felt her face flush.

Señora Molina brushed at her sleeve with the back of her hand as if brushing off a worry. "Now. I've talked too much. Tell me why you came to see me."

Josie looked at Nick. She was so overcome with the woman's story she wasn't sure she could make the right connections just yet.

Nick set down his cup and said, "We came here looking for information about the two young women. Can you tell us what you remember about them? Any details about where they came from so we can search for their families? Our problem is, we have the young woman in our trauma center, and we know her name but don't know where she's from. She speaks some English, but she's said little more than Josie's name since we found her."

Señora Molina nodded. "A rancher who lives five miles down-river from here brought the women one afternoon. He found them hiding in his barn. They wouldn't talk. His wife fed them and let them clean up. They'd been staying in the barn."

"Did they talk to you?" Nick asked.

"The first day they slept. I made them a pallet of blankets on the floor and they slept for hours and hours. The next day they talked and talked. A horrible thing that happened to them."

"Did they speak English?" Josie asked.

"Spanish. To me anyway. They are from Guatemala."

Josie looked at Nick. It was a good start.

"Did they tell you what city?" he said.

She pursed her lips in thought for a moment and then shook her head. "No. I don't remember that. They come from all over. I can't remember all of them."

"Did they tell you why they were heading to the U.S.?" Josie asked.

She tilted her head as if it were a frivolous question. "Same as all the others. Going to a big city to get a job and send money home to family."

"Did they give you any information about the men who had been transporting them?" Nick asked.

She thought for quite a while and finally said, "Two. I remember they said there were two of them. And one of them was a very bad man. He forced himself on them. They could barely speak of it."

"Were the men from Guatemala too?" Josie asked.

She shook her head slowly. "I don't know. I don't remember. All these details. They mix up with all the others. I remember I tried to get them to go home. Back to Guatemala. But their families had spent precious money on their trip. They had to make it to the U.S. I remember that. And that's when I sent them to you. To Josie."

On the way home, Josie kept thinking about how the two women saw the United States as their savior. Josie as their savior. What a disturbing idea, Josie thought. In her experience, there were no saviors on earth, just people trying to get by as best they could.

As Nick drove the SUV up and out of the arroyo, he said, "It's almost ten and you didn't get much sleep last night. How soon do you need to get home?"

She shrugged and looked at his profile, smiling into the dark. "What did you have in mind?"

"It would be better in the daylight, but I'll show you one of my favorite places in Mexico. A fishing hole on the Rio."

"You go there often?"

"I own some land. I have a fishing cabin on the river. Actually, when you first called me about your old boyfriend being kidnapped, I was headed to the cabin for a weekend. I was surprised how close your house was to my place. And I heard the desperation in your voice." He glanced over at her. "It didn't take much convincing to get me to take the case when I heard you were the cop that tangled with the Medranos."

"At first, taking on the cartel might have been bragging rights. But now? I'm over it. I want to live my life. I want to do my job and not worry about looking over my shoulder twenty-four/seven."

"Doesn't work like that," he said.

She felt her blood pressure spike, and while she regretted the path the conversation was taking, she couldn't stop herself. "If they want me, then come and get me. Let's get this over with."

"You don't use bravado with these people. They don't have the same moral code you do. They will one-up you every time. You will *never* outbrave them."

"It's not about that! Don't you see? I want my life back."

"You aren't even talking sense. You know better. Nobody's dealt a fair hand in life. If you're born in the slums, you work your ass off to get out. If you're born into wealth, you work your ass off to make your own name in the world. If you work as a cop, you—" He stopped talking, apparently sensing her growing anger.

She glared at him, and after a moment he laid his hand on her thigh. She instinctively tensed her leg muscles.

"We're arguing over words right now," he said. His voice was quiet. "Let's stop."

He drove another five minutes along the river and finally pulled down a narrow path lined with cottonwood trees and then stopped abruptly in front of a wooden shack.

He looked over at her and smiled. "This is my mansion. My house in Mexico City? I'd take this little shack over that monster any day."

She got out of the SUV and he moved around to her side and grabbed her hand. "Let me show you what makes me happy."

They walked side by side along a dirt path that led to the wooden porch. He unlocked the door and she could smell the earthy wood and stone as they stepped inside. He turned on the lights and she smiled.

"This is you," she said. Mismatched wool blankets hung from large windows that faced the river. A stone fireplace was located between the windows with a massive split log for a mantel. On top of it was a mantel clock and what appeared to be family photos. The living room was small, with a couch, love seat, and coffee table filling it up, but the ceiling was open to the wood rafters above and gave it a spacious feeling.

"How come you never mentioned this place?" she asked. "It's a perfect hideaway."

"Exactly. It's a hideaway. I've had this place almost ten years now and I've never brought another person here. This is where I decompress. Not even my brother knows about it."

"Why did you bring me?" she asked, turning to face him.

"Because this isn't enough anymore. When I want to relax and get away from the job, I want you with me. You quiet the noise in my head."

She smiled at his description. She couldn't quiet the voices in her own head; she couldn't imagine how she could quiet his.

He cradled her face in his hands and kissed her forehead. "I love you, Josie."

"I love you too," she whispered. She kissed him, a slow sweet kiss that was uncomplicated and perfect.

He ran his hands down her back and she shivered. He put his mouth close to her ear and whispered, "There's one more room I need to show you."

She followed him into the bedroom, where he pushed back the curtains and opened the window. She stood beside him and they listened to the Rio Grande rush by, watching the water glint from the moonlight's reflection.

"It's beautiful," she whispered.

"And so are you."

Nick moved behind her and gently pressed his thumbs into her shoulders, making her sigh and smile. She took a slow deep breath, smelling the clean river air, feeling her senses come alive.

She turned around and they undressed one another slowly, dropping their clothes onto the floor. She ran her hands over his arms and chest, her fingertips sensing the soft skin covering the hard muscles underneath.

Nick bent his head and kissed the hollow of her neck and then drew his finger down to her heart and left it there.

"You don't need to keep that lead bullet in your heart, Josie. I don't want you to keep hate trapped inside of you. I want to be the one who protects you, so you don't worry all the time. I want to make you happy and keep you safe. Will you let me do that?"

She wrapped her arms around his neck and pulled her body

into his, as close as she could get, and whispered into his ear, "I love you so much that my body aches with it. I didn't even know I had this feeling inside me." But she couldn't answer his question. She didn't know if she could let him be her protector, and she wouldn't lie to him.

"We'll just take this slow," he said. "I'll do my best, and you'll do the same, and somehow I think it'll all work out."

He bent his head and kissed her until the words fell away, and the worries drifted out the window, and there was nothing left but two people in love.

EIGHT

Back to reality the next morning, Josie sat at her computer to email her contact from Immigration and Customs Enforcement about Isabella Dagati, whom they now believed had resided in Guatemala. Like so many customs issues, it wouldn't be a simple deportation, especially with a murder connected to the case. The case could take months of sorting through policy and procedures with Homeland Security and ICE. Josie had just finished summarizing the situation for Prosecutor Tyler Holder when Lou buzzed and asked her to come downstairs. As the dispatcher, and the only employee working on the first floor, Lou spent her full shift at the PD, only getting out for lunch if one of the officers took her place.

Josie found Lou in front of her computer.

"I've been thinking about the girl at your house, and how you said there's been a car driving by your place. This probably isn't anything, but I thought I better mention it."

"I'll take anything."

"I just remembered a man called here a few days ago and asked about your schedule. I thought it was odd, but it's not like your schedule is confidential. I asked who he was and he said he was a police officer, but he didn't give me his name. He wasn't friendly. Didn't seem like he wanted to talk, so I just told him."

"You're right. Nothing confidential about my schedule. He didn't say what agency?"

"No. I thought that was a little odd too. Most law enforcement people state their name and who they work for up front. I didn't ask, and he didn't offer. I figured, none of my business."

"I'd like you to track down the phone call. Get me the phone number as soon as possible. Somebody knew my schedule well enough to shoot a girl in the pasture beside my home when I wasn't there."

"I've already been thinking it through. I'm pretty sure it was five days ago. I remember because I got the phone call, and then a few minutes later I went off duty early for a dentist appointment. I should be able to pull the digital recording up pretty easy."

"Thanks, Lou. Anything you can give me. Date, time, number, name, address."

"I'll work on it. Also, Marta just called. She said to get ahold of her this morning on her cell."

When Josie was back at her desk she called Marta, who answered on the first ring.

"What's up?" Josie asked.

"Let's talk about Isabella." Marta took a few minutes to recount her contact with the woman at the trauma center the night before. "She speaks English fluently. She opened up a bit last night. She wouldn't tell me her family's name, but she told me a few stories about her town in Guatemala. I think she's ashamed to tell her family about the mess she's in, but that will come."

"That's good to hear."

"I just think it's odd she said she didn't know the other woman's name, the woman who was shot. Maybe they weren't friends. Maybe they didn't even know each other, and we're way off with the trafficking theory."

"You think it was a translation issue? Maybe we're interpreting something totally different than what she meant," Josie said.

"I don't know. I couldn't make sense of it."

"Anything else?"

"You said the psychiatrist thinks she'd be better off out of the trauma center, in a home, where she can heal."

Josie knew Marta well enough to know where the conversation was headed.

"With Teresa gone away to college, I have an extra bedroom."

"Marta, we can't do that."

"Just hear me out. I speak Spanish, so I can communicate with her. And she's already established a relationship with me. I posted outside her room at the trauma center last night. I talked with her several times about Guatemala and her family. Nothing about the case, but I'm building trust."

"That's great. Meet with her again today. We need to find out who they contracted with to come to the U.S. But bottom line, she's a suspect in a murder investigation."

"She's been traumatized!"

"Marta, come on. She is the only personal connection we have to the murder victim. At this point, we believe she knew about the body for days. We don't know what happened, so we can't clear her as a suspect." Josie paused. She knew Marta wouldn't like her next comment. "And, something else. She clearly wants help, but she's not giving us anything. That may be an indication she's hiding something. We just can't tell."

Marta took a second and said, "I think that's a horrible stance to take. She's most likely been raped and mentally terrorized for who knows how long by these men. And we're going to treat the victim like the criminal?"

"That's not what I said, and you know it."

"I'll see you at three-thirty," Marta said, and hung up.

Otto drove twenty-five minutes to Presidio, the town nearest to Artemis, to meet Trooper Dan Haspin, a twenty-year veteran with the Texas Department of Public Safety. Otto had worked with Dan through the years and knew he was active with the Texas Human Trafficking Task Force. Otto called Dan and filled him in on their suspicions, and Dan had offered to meet Otto to share intelligence.

A black man in his early forties, he wore the khaki uniform, blue tie, and hard felt cowboy hat of a Department of Public Safety trooper. He was bulked up around the chest, with a narrow waist that made Otto wonder if he had to work to maintain his physique. Otto blamed his belly on Delores, forty years of Polish comfort food. But he'd take his satisfying suppers over a tightened belt any day of the week.

Otto walked into the sandwich shop and found Dan in the corner booth with his back against the wall, his sandwich sitting untouched in front of him. He waved and smiled, and Otto bought his lunch and joined him.

They discussed Otto's goat herd and the price of meat at the market, and Dan's woodworking hobby, making toy trains and trucks. Both men knew the benefit of a hobby to occupy a cop's off-duty mind.

Midway through their sandwiches, the conversation turned to work and Dan finally said, "You've got a dead woman in her early twenties, and a traumatized woman in her early twenties who speaks Spanish. The women are apparently from Guatemala, but they don't show up in the missing persons databases. And the traumatized woman doesn't want to share information about her family."

Otto nodded. "That's it."

"It sure as hell fits the description for a human trafficking case."

Otto cocked an eyebrow at him. "Without knowing any other details, you'd make that statement?"

"Here's how widespread it is. Texas has a trafficking guide for teachers now to help them identify and report signs of trafficking in school-age kids. And it's not just our state."

Otto shook his head in disgust.

"Look. I'm not saying it's rampant, but there are more cases than people would like to admit. It's not just massage parlors and crappy hotels. So I'm not surprised to find that small-town Artemis has been affected."

"That's not the answer I was looking for," Otto said.

Dan considered him for a moment. "You're sure they came from Guatemala?"

Otto nodded.

Dan frowned. "From Guatemala to West Texas?"

"The surviving woman told someone who was providing her help, as well as one of our officers, that they were from Guatemala. I can't imagine why she would lie about that," Otto said.

"Here's my issue. We have known groups coming up out of that country. No doubt. But it doesn't make sense that they'd come to this part of West Texas first."

Otto shrugged, not sure what he was getting at.

Dan took out his cell phone. "Let me pull up a map and you'll see."

A moment later Dan handed his phone to Otto with a route map drawn from Guatemala in Central America, up the eastern coast of Mexico, to Houston and San Antonio. Artemis, in West

Texas, was hundreds of miles to the west. He nodded, instantly understanding.

"It's a sixteen-hundred-mile trip from Guatemala to San Antonio. Even farther to Houston," Dan said. "I can't see them driving another six hours to West Texas, only to turn around and head back toward San Antonio."

Otto was taken aback. "Why would you automatically assume traffickers would head to San Antonio?"

"I just don't have much intel about this area. Houston, San Antonio, and occasionally El Paso, sure. But not Artemis, out in the middle of nowhere."

Otto passed a card across the table. "Make sure you give me a call if you hear anything that might help us out."

Dan nodded and stuffed the card in a wallet packed full of business cards. He was a typical cop, Otto thought—his wallet packed with more work-related notes than payment options.

———

Josie found Lou at her computer, her arms crossed at her chest. "You will not believe this." It was two o'clock and Lou had just buzzed her desk and said to come down.

"Did you track down the caller?"

"I did."

Josie waved her hand for Lou to get on with it.

"Josh Mooney."

Josie pulled back at the name, smiling like she'd heard wrong. "Seriously?"

"Josh Mooney wanted to know your schedule for the week. Told me he was a law officer. And we have it on tape."

"You are a saint."

———

Back in the office, she called Otto and explained Lou's findings.

"That's the creep that hangs out with his sister all the time?" he asked.

"That's him. Macey is his sister's name. We busted them for meth about three years ago."

Otto laughed. "Oh, hell. I remember that bust. We found both of them in a house trailer. With an afternoon soap opera blaring on the TV."

"While they were cooking up a batch of meth in the kitchen," she said.

"Matching Mickey Mouse pajamas."

"I was afraid to touch anything, even with gloves on. A hazmat suit was in order."

"How much time they serve?" Otto asked. "Two years?"

"Probably half that."

He shook his head, obviously disgusted. "You headed to Mooney's house now?"

"Can you meet me?"

"Yep."

"I checked the address. They're renting from Cici Gomez. They're living above the pawnshop."

"Well, there's a shocker. See you there in ten minutes."

Josie drove two blocks to the San Salbo Pawn Shop, located next to the Family Value Store. The pawnshop was owned by Cici Gomez, a longtime drug dealer with multiple arrests on his record for a variety of offenses. Josie had arrested him several years ago for abusing his elderly grandfather, a sweet old Navajo with a heart too tender for his own good. He had refused to press charges against his grandson because of an intense family loyalty that Josie had found maddening. Regardless, she thought Cici was a piece of crap;

he'd been out of jail for less than six months and was most likely already up to no good. She wasn't surprised to hear he had a brother/sister meth duo living above his shop. There were people who were literally too stupid to deserve a place on the planet. She'd probably fry in hell for thinking that way, but it's how she felt when she had to deal with people like the Mooneys.

The San Salbo Pawn Shop looked like a cheap version of an old western movie set from the fifties, including a fence out front to tie the horses to and a wooden porch with rocking chairs.

But Cici's good-ole-boy image was nothing more than that. Cici knew the game; he knew how to move in and out of places without being seen. When she thought about Cici, the line in the old *Scarface* movie with Al Pacino came to mind, the scene when he calls someone a cock-a-roach. That's how she imagined Cici, crawling along the floorboards in the dirt.

And now Josh and Macey Mooney were running game above Cici's shop. Parked in front of the store was a banged-up eighties-era orange Chevy Camaro that she recognized as Josh's drugmobile.

Otto pulled up beside Josie and she got out of her jeep. She felt for the latex gloves in her back pocket, a precaution against whatever nastiness the Mooneys might have inside their apartment.

"Any good news from Dan?" she asked.

"News, yes. Not sure if it's good yet." He explained the geography of the transport from Guatemala to West Texas.

"Remember, that's what Selena said too. She said there wouldn't be any reason to bring trafficked victims here. And the BP says there's no reason to even drive through here."

"So why would the transporters bring the two women on a five-hundred-mile detour from the major cities in Texas to travel through this part of Texas? This doesn't work as an efficient route," he said.

"I don't know. Let's go jack up Josh and Macey. See why Josh wanted my work schedule."

"You don't think they're out working? At two-thirty on a bright sunny afternoon in the middle of the week?"

"Your sarcasm is getting worse, Otto."

"Hazard of the job. It's sarcasm or wild women. I have to get rid of the stress somehow, and you know Delores wouldn't put up with wild women."

The narrow wooden door facing the street was located between the Family Value and the San Salbo. Josie entered first, then Otto, and they walked up a dimly lit stairwell that led to two apartments at the top of the landing. Josie knocked on the door with the number two painted in black on it. There was no peephole. The trick was getting them to open the door and allow entrance.

Josie knocked a second time, louder and faster, and a few moments later she saw a thin strip of Josh Mooney's face appear in the crack of the door.

"Yeah?" he said.

"Josh, this is Chief of Police Josie Gray. I'm here with Officer Otto Podowski. We'd like a minute of your time."

The door remained cracked and the eyeball unblinking.

"No trouble for you. Just a couple questions and we'll be on our way," she said.

"About what?"

"It would be a lot easier to talk about this if we weren't out here where your neighbors can hear everything that's said."

The eyeball flitted away for a moment, probably glancing around the room for paraphernalia, and then focused on her for another few seconds.

"Hang on. I have to get dressed."

Otto shuddered.

Several minutes later a wide-eyed and panting Josh Mooney again opened the door a crack to look at them and then shut it. Josie and Otto looked at each other as they listened to voices from inside the apartment growing louder. They finally heard the fortunate sound of a chain being pulled against the latch, and the door swung open. Josh stepped back and Josie and Otto entered to find Macey standing closely beside Josh, their arms touching. Macey was clearly out of breath as well, probably from hiding their stash. She clutched her hands in front of her and pressed her lips together in a thin line.

Josh and Macey reminded Josie of the Who characters in the Grinch movie. They both stood about five feet tall, with big blue eyes and yellow hair and a perpetually shocked look in their eyes. Although they all clearly knew each other, Otto went through the formality of introductions while Josie scanned the apartment.

She'd been here less than two years ago when the former tenant had been murdered. The man was Mexican, working in the U.S. to send money back to his family. The apartment had been almost bare. Now every square inch appeared filled: photos, piles of magazines and mail, shoe boxes filled with who knew what stacked ten high in the corners of the room, bookshelves filled with knick-knacks against the wall. The bookshelf to her right, just inside the entryway, was filled with snow globes and dozens of ceramic ashtrays. It smelled musty, with the underlying odor of stale pot smoke.

Macey wore a short dress with combat boots, and her hair was in pigtails.

"We're reorganizing. That's why it looks so bad," she said, without any introduction. "We just need another week."

"We're not here about your apartment," Josie said. She glanced at the couch and had no desire to sit on the cushions. She then saw that even though the kitchen table was piled high with papers, its chairs were empty. "Can we sit in your kitchen for a few minutes and talk?"

"Sure. We can do that," Macey said. "We're organizing. Gonna have a garage sale. Make some money. Give some to Mom. That kind of thing." She spoke with a clipped manic rhythm to her words.

The four of them sat around the table, and Josie looked at Josh. "I hear you've been asking about me at the police department."

His unbelievably big eyes opened farther and he peered at Josie over the stacks of junk mail. "What?"

"You called the police department, asking about me. Why'd you do that?"

"I don't know what you mean."

Josie saw Josh glance at Otto, who was shaking his head as if disappointed in his answer.

"Here's the deal. You just lied to me. Strike one. You tried to impersonate a police officer when you called to ask about my schedule. Strike two. You know what strike three is?"

He shook his head.

"We have your impersonation of a police officer all on tape. Strike three."

He leaned back against his chair and looked to his sister as if she might know what to say.

"Why did you want to know my schedule?" Josie asked again.

"I was going to come talk to you."

"About what?"

He shrugged. "I forget now."

"No, you don't."

"I do!"

Josie looked at Otto. "I don't have patience for this."

Otto tipped his head toward Josh. "Let's take him in. Arrest him for impersonating an officer. Give him some jail time so he can remember what he wanted to talk to you about."

"I am not going back to jail! That place is a hellhole filled with a bunch of gagbags."

Macey seemed as if she was going to start crying.

"Why did you tell the dispatcher you were a police officer?"

He considered her for a second, like he wasn't sure if the truth was a good idea or not. "I didn't think she'd tell me your schedule if I said I was me."

"You needed to talk to me so bad that you pretended to be a cop, and now you can't remember why?"

"That was a long time ago."

Josie started to nod her head slowly and gave him the knowing look of someone who just caught on to the game. "I know what it was. I bet you wanted to talk to me about the two women you transported from Guatemala. Was that it?"

"No! We had nothing to do with that!"

"Macey, help us out here," Otto said. "We know about the trafficking. We just need some information from you."

Again, wide-eyed innocence.

"Tell us about those two women. How did they end up here in Artemis?" he said.

"It wasn't our fault!" she said. Her voice was a high-pitched whine. "You need to go talk to Ryan Needleman. He's the man you need. Not us."

"How do you know him?" Otto asked.

"We know him from around town," Macey said.

"What does he have to do with the women from Guatemala?" he said.

"We just heard he was driving some people up. He asked us to help but we didn't want to get involved."

"You mean, you didn't want to get involved with the woman's murder?" Otto asked.

"With none of it," Macey said.

Her facial expression didn't change at the word *murder*. Josie had no doubt the two were involved.

Otto stood, moved behind his chair, and gripped the back of it. He scowled angrily at both of them. Josie was always surprised when Otto took this role in an interview. He was such a kind, generous man; to see him turn dark and angry was unsettling.

He stared at one, and then the other, finally landing on Josh. "Let me tell you something." His voice dropped an octave and landed into a quiet threatening zone. "We found a young woman, shot in the back and left to die. Her friend slept in Chief Gray's shed for days and is terrified now. I will catch who did this. So you can either stay out of a lot of trouble now and come clean with us, or you can wait and pay full price with jail time later."

Josh cleared his throat and Macey looked at him in a panic.

"We'll think about—"

Macey cut him off. "We got nothing to say because we did nothing wrong."

Josie stood and laid her business card on top of a piece of mail. "You think it over. Our deal stands until ten o'clock tomorrow morning. After that? You're on your own."

Back outside, Josie motioned for Otto to climb into her jeep instead of taking his own vehicle.

Otto slammed the door and said, "I wish we had something more recent on him. I'd love to take that kid to jail."

"You know Ryan Needleman?"

"The name's familiar," he said.

"He just graduated high school last year. Played sports. He was a hothead, got into trouble for fighting. His dad told me he got thrown out of college the first week of school for beating up some kid in the dorm. Still hard to figure how he'd go from college in August to transporting women from Guatemala to Artemis two months later."

"How would the Mooneys connect with him?" he asked.

"He probably bought dope off them. Now he's their scapegoat."

"You got something in mind?"

"Let's get to him before somebody tips him off. His dad told me he's working over at the landscape place," she said. "Maybe he can give us something on the Mooneys."

Turf and Annuals was a landscaping company that specialized in helping West Texans grow grass and flowers that normally weren't seen in a desert climate. When the economy tanked, so did its business, but it had started to pick back up again. Josie had been a customer for years and knew the owner, Lisa Spinner, well.

Driving down the gravel lane, Josie pointed to the variety of pine trees on either side.

"Lisa got a research grant and uses some kind of experimental underground irrigation system that taps into groundwater supply."

"They got a heck of a place here in the middle of the desert," Otto said.

They parked in a gravel lot that fronted five large greenhouses and a log cabin office. On the other side of the lot, several Bobcats and backhoes were running, scooping mulch and digging trees. Josie parked in front of the office and found Lisa inside on the phone. She told whoever she was talking with to hang on and covered the receiver with her hand. "What can I do for you, Chief?"

"I'm looking for Ryan Needleman. He working today?"

Lisa frowned and drew her eyebrows together. "He is. He in trouble?"

"No. I just have a couple questions. You care if I talk to him for just a minute?"

"Not at all."

The woman ended her phone call and radioed Ryan to come in off the Bobcat to talk to Josie.

Josie and Otto stood outside the office and waited for Ryan. He parked the Bobcat and was wiping his hands on his jeans as he reached them. It was almost four in the afternoon, but the sun was still bright, and he squinted at them. Josie thought he looked wary, like he was waiting for the handcuffs to appear, but she figured it wasn't often that a uniformed cop pulled you off your work duty simply to talk.

She put her hand out and he shook it as they introduced themselves.

"I talked to your boss, so she knows we're here to see you. I let her know you aren't in any trouble. We just have a few questions for you. That okay?"

He shrugged.

What had happened to a polite *Yes, ma'am*? Or even a plain yes or no? After all these years she was still shocked when someone treated a visit by the police as an inconvenience.

"Have you heard about the two women that were found in Artemis this week?"

He shrugged again.

"Okay. How about you drop the shrug routine and answer the questions. I'll be more specific for you this time. Tell me what you've heard about the woman who was found shot in the back out in a ranch pasture this past week," she said. It wasn't the best way to start an interview, but his insolent stare and shrug were pissing her off.

This question at least produced more than a shrug. His eyebrows rose and he reeled back like she'd asked something distasteful. "Same as anyone else. I heard about it on the radio. Figured she was some illegal crossing the border."

"Who would shoot an illegal in the back for crossing the border?" she said.

He turned up his lip like it was a stupid question. "Who would shoot anyone in the back?"

She felt the sting from his response. She wasn't handling the interview well. Otto obviously noticed and stepped in. "Okay. Let me be even more blunt, Ryan. We heard from a couple people that you were involved in transporting two women from Guatemala to the U.S. Were you?"

His expression carried the expected measure of shock, but there was an element of fear as his eyes darted from Otto to Josie and back again in a way that made Josie believe the Mooneys might actually have sent them in the right direction.

"No! I was at college!"

"But you got thrown out for assault and battery. Right?" Otto said.

The shock gave way to full-on fear. "No! I mean, I came home. I got in a fight and all, but I came home because I hated it."

"Hated getting thrown out of college?" Otto said.

"Why are you asking me about this? Those charges were dropped."

"What do you know about Josh and Macey Mooney?" Josie asked.

He leaned his head back and groaned. "Seriously? Is that what this is about?"

Josie said nothing.

"They are inbred freaks. If they told you anything about anything you can count on it being a lie."

"How do you know them?" she asked.

The question obviously caught him off guard. He stammered and said, "Everybody knows them. They're weird as hell."

"But you said they lie. What have they lied to you about?" she said.

He grinned and tilted his head as if he were being misunderstood. "I just meant in general. Everybody knows they're freaks and they're liars."

Josie looked at Otto. "Did you know they were liars?"

Otto seemed to consider the question. "No. I didn't know they were liars. Did you?"

"Nope." She faced Ryan again but said nothing. *Let him hang himself,* she thought. People watched cop shows on TV and figured investigations turned on some clever piece of evidence, but nine times out of ten, the case was solved by dogged police work and whittling down witnesses, one question at a time. Just the right question, at just the right time, to make the vulnerable witness falter and break. That was the goal—a crack in the story.

Ryan's shoulders slumped, and he looked at Josie as if she was messing with him. She was surprised by his general composure, given he was only eighteen or nineteen years old.

"You know what I mean. That's their reputation," he said.

"I know that Josh and Macey both said you were involved in transporting those two women from Guatemala to the United States. And now one of those women is dead." Josh started to reply, and Josie put one hand on the butt of the gun sticking out from her belt, and the other hand in the air to stop him. It did the trick. "Look. We have enough intelligence to know that you're involved with the transport. You help us figure out who we need to talk to, and you'll have some room to bargain."

He kicked the dirt and pressed his fists into his eyes. Barely out of high school, and yet the cops were already talking to him about murder. He was one of those kids that people loved to gossip about because his parents were nice, upstanding people in the community. As if nice parents kept you insulated from making bad decisions.

"It's those two idiots—the Mooneys! They knew I was trying to pay my parents back for flunking out of school my first semester." Ryan paused and Josie wondered if he was gauging her reaction to his lie about flunking out. "I met them both one night at a party at Cici Gomez's apartment."

Otto made a face. "If that's where you're hanging out, we may as well arrest you right now."

His hands rose again in a conciliatory gesture. He clearly realized his excuses were getting him in deeper, not providing the alibi he was moving closer to needing.

"I'm just saying that I was at the party with another guy, and the freak brother and sister came up to me. They were like, *Hey, we heard you got kicked out of school. You want to earn a few bucks driving a van full of girls from Guatemala to the U.S.? We'll teach you how to drive the van, and that's it. The trip should take a week total and you make two thousand bucks.*" He shrugged, as if saying, *What else was I supposed to say? Easy money.*

"So you drove to Guatemala, just like that?" she said.

"Well, no, it was more detailed than that. Macey explained everything a hundred times. Who, what, where, and when. She drilled it into my head. And then she'd say, 'And you don't need to know why. MYOB.' I'd think, *Really? Is this junior high? You're paying me two thousand dollars and telling me to MYOB?* Whatever. The money was good and I needed it. That's all I know."

"You know a lot more than that," Josie said. "You transported two women who endured horrific crimes."

"I don't know anything about any crimes. I just drove the van."

"What kind of van?"

"One of those ugly ones with bench seats. Me and Josh took turns driving. We drove sixteen hours a day. Those were the rules. I drove eight and he drove eight."

"What city did you pick the women up in?"

"I don't know. All I know is we were in Guatemala. I don't speak Spanish. I couldn't read the signs. There were guys driving in trucks with machine guns wearing face masks. It looked like a war zone. It was like nowhere I've ever been. And Josh is a complete idiot. I was sure we were all gonna die before we got out of there. I just drove where he told me to."

"How many people were you transporting?" she asked.

"There were five women. And Josh and me."

Josie felt nausea well up in her stomach. Five women. So where were the other three?

"Josh drove too?" she asked.

"Yeah, he did! And then he tries to sell me out. The guy is an idiot."

"So you and Josh were the only men on the trip?" she asked, surprised at the implication of that.

"Yes."

"Where are the other three women you transported?" she asked.

He put his hands up in the air. "I don't know. I swear. I drove to Piedra Labrada, and Josh took it from there."

"Why didn't you finish the trip with him?" she asked.

"I didn't have my passport to get back in the country. Josh had it and we got into a fight. He wouldn't give it back to me, so I just crossed on my own."

"Help me out here, Ryan. We're talking about five women. One of those women is dead, the other is traumatized. We need to find out where those other three women are."

"I swear, I don't know. When I left, the five women were all with Josh. He was going to get the van across somehow. I don't even know how. He wouldn't tell me. I just hiked out of the city and crossed the river by foot on my own."

There were several issues they could have pushed with Ryan, but she wanted the leverage for later. No sense showing her hand just yet.

Josie held out her card and Ryan took it, seeming shocked that the meeting was ending.

"You go home and think about all of this. You may decide you want to come talk to us before this gets much further. You might do yourself a big favor in the end."

They walked away at that point, leaving him standing there with Josie's card, completely unstrung. When they got into Josie's jeep, she started it but didn't move.

"That's a shocker," Otto said. "I don't see Josh as a rapist."

"That just leaves Ryan."

"You think we ought to take him in now, while he's nervous? He may get counsel and freeze up," Otto said.

Josie watched him climb back up on the Bobcat and turn the machine away from them. "I don't know. It's a gamble. I'd like to think he may realize the trouble he's in and offer up Josh. We can play one against the other before the attorneys take over."

"Or he'll talk to his parents and get an attorney tonight and we'll get nothing. We could go over and ask him to take a ride with us to the station, Mirandize him, and hope he talks because he's so worried about everything."

"We don't have anything concrete to bring him in on. The rape? I think it's a stretch between knowing the dead female was raped, and attaching that to Ryan. Who knows what else may have happened on that trip?" she said. "Maybe Josh brought someone else in to help after Ryan left."

"We need a statement from Isabella. Immediately."

"And we need to find out what happened to those other women."

Josie sent Marta a text asking her to meet them at the PD. She said she was already there typing a case report, working a swing shift. When Josie and Otto entered the office, Marta sat down at the conference table with her notepad. It was obvious from her lack of friendly chatter that she was still angry with Josie over not allowing Isabella to stay at her house.

Josie recapped the conversation they'd had with Ryan Needleman and Josh and Macey Mooney. Marta quickly warmed to the conversation, asking questions about the major break they'd had in the case.

Otto finally said, "Have you talked with Isabella today? Or the doctor?"

"No. I've been working another case. But I think the psychiatrist was supposed to work with her again this evening. He was hoping to be at the trauma center by six."

Josie looked at her watch. "Damn. I have that charity dinner the mayor expects me at for his wife."

"I can explain the situation to the doctor. Let him know we desperately need her to open up about the trip and her attacker," Marta said. "I'll see what he thinks."

"I appreciate it. It's five-fifteen now. I'm going to stop by and talk to Manny and see about getting Isabella a room at the motel for the next week. I'll see what the sheriff can offer, but we just don't have the manpower to continue dedicating an officer to a room twenty-four hours a day right now."

Marta nodded.

"If the doctor agrees, can you talk with her tonight? Explain that we're trying to help make her safe by arresting the men that abused her? But she has to help us locate those other women before this gets even worse. And we have to find out what happened in the pasture when the other woman was shot."

"I'll do that. Hopefully with the doctor in the room with me."

"And will you talk with the doctor about moving her into Manny's tomorrow morning? At least for a few days, until we can figure out how to relocate her with her family?" Josie said.

Marta nodded.

"Otto, can you get online and look for a couple photos of Ryan?"

"Won't he have a mug shot from the fight at college?"

Josie shook her head. "They kicked him out of school, but no charges were filed. I'm guessing you'll find some photos of him from playing sports in high school. We'll have Josh's mug shot. Put together a photo lineup. Get at least six photos, nine if you can. Get them to Marta so she can take them with her tonight. We'll see if Isabella can identify Josh and Ryan."

"Will do," he said.

"Okay. I have to go change into something other than a uniform. We're all good?" She glanced at Marta.

"We're good. I understand," she said. She frowned and nodded once, indicating the argument was over.

"Once we confirm with Isabella, I'll brief the prosecutor and bring both men in for questioning," Josie said.

———•———

Josie got into her jeep and called Nick to let him know she was headed to the charity event with her mom.

"Hanging out with the rich and famous tonight?" She could hear the smile in his voice.

"Neither. I'm hanging out with the do-gooders."

"What's wrong with people trying to do good?" he said.

His question made her pause. "I don't know. Nothing's wrong with them. They're good people."

"Then why call them do-gooders? Why do they irritate you?"

"It's the self-righteous people who throw their good out there for praise that irritate me."

"So give them a little praise. What's wrong with that?"

"I think you're trying to harass me."

He laughed. "I'm not. I'm just trying to understand you. You're a complicated person sometimes."

She sighed. She couldn't explain her reasoning to herself at times, so how could she expect Nick to understand her? She changed the subject. "What are your plans tonight?"

"I'm on stakeout. We had a big breakthrough this morning. We know where the victim's being held. We hope to close in tonight with a rescue. I won't see you tonight. Maybe tomorrow if everything goes well."

"That's great. Just be careful, stay safe. And let me know what happens."

NINE

After a quick shower and change into a yellow sundress and sandals, Josie pulled her hair up into a clip and left the house in a rush to pick her mom up at Manny's by 5:50. Her mom was standing by the curb and had the jeep's door open before Josie had reached a complete stop. She hopped in, smelling like a mixture of perfume and hair spray and deodorant and lotion and all the other cosmetics she had no doubt applied.

"Lord have mercy, Josie. I'd have thought after all these years you'd have figured out how to get somewhere on time."

Josie pulled away from the curb, drove to the stoplight, and turned left, heading a half mile out of town to the Artemis Fellowship Church.

"I have a job to do, Mom. I can't just leave an investigation because I have a dinner date. It doesn't work that way."

"You know I hate walking into somewhere late."

If there was one thing Josie could say about her mother, she was punctual, preferably ten minutes early to any function. Josie preferred to walk in on time so she could avoid the inevitable small talk that came with early arrival.

After they parked, her mother chattered all the way through the parking lot and down the stairs to the large fellowship area and kitchen. At least fifty women were sitting in metal folding chairs around a dozen tables, smiling and talking amicably. Josie spotted two empty chairs, side by side near the middle of the room, so she and her mother wove their way through and took a seat, smiling at the women across from them.

Her mother put her hand out to the woman sitting on her left and introduced herself as Josie nodded and smiled to the vaguely familiar-looking woman on her right. Then she glanced across the table to find Melissa Chang looking awkwardly away, like she was searching for someone in the crowd. Josie had tangled with her about a year ago when the twenty-something-year-old woman had called the police to report a tree down in the middle of the road. Josie had driven right over and found a limb that she easily dragged off to the side of the road. Melissa still hadn't left her car, and Josie had asked her why she hadn't moved it herself.

Melissa had looked at Josie, obviously shocked by the question. "I'm wearing my work clothes! That's why we have city employees. My taxpayer dollars pay your salary so you can take care of these issues. I did my civic duty."

"Your taxpayer dollars pay employees to take care of things that other citizens can't take care of. Your civic duty would have been to get out of the car and move the tree branch yourself."

The altercation ended in a summons to Mayor Moss's office and an official reprimand in her employee file. Now here the woman sat in front of her, looking everywhere but directly across the table in Josie's direction. This was exactly the reason she hated public functions.

Fortunately, Caroline Moss was introduced a few minutes later.

In a form-fitting little black dress that showed her curves without being inappropriate for a church setting, she graciously accepted the room's applause. Tasteful gold jewelry glinted off her neck and ears and wrists, and her blond hair fell softly around her shoulders as she thanked the "fine women of Arroyo County" for coming.

Caroline talked for the next thirty minutes about the "good works" taking place in Artemis and Arroyo County, much of which was being conducted by women "just like you," she said to a rousing round of applause. Josie smiled and clapped and wished she could text Marta to see how the doctor's visit was going with Isabella.

"She's not much of a speaker, is she?" her mom whispered into her ear.

Josie turned and glared at her mom. "Wait till we're in the car."

"I'm just saying. She needs some humor or something. I'm about ready to nod off."

Josie wondered if this was her future: sitting through interminable mother-daughter banquets with a mother who'd lost her filter.

Caroline then introduced half a dozen speakers, each of whom conducted charitable works through her umbrella group, Arroyo County Missions and Outreach. Supper was finally served and another round of speakers took the podium, this time people who had received funding of some kind from the group. By the time Josie had eaten her chocolate cake, she'd decided on a plan to keep the evening from being a total washout.

———

When Marta arrived at the trauma center at six o'clock, Dr. Brazen had already been meeting with Isabella for over thirty minutes. When he was done, the nurse led them to the staff lounge for a quiet place to discuss the case.

"How is she?" Marta asked.

"She's come a long way in two days, given she has no family or friends here."

"I realize you're limited on what information you can provide me in terms of her recovery. But we're desperate to get information on the two men that transported her. A woman was murdered and we discovered three other women are missing. And every day that passes makes it more difficult to catch the killer."

He nodded once, his face in a deep frown. "What do you need from me?"

"Your professional opinion and your presence." Marta held up the photograph lineup Otto had given her, which included photos of Josh Mooney and Ryan Needleman. "We believe we have photos of the two men that drove the women from Guatemala. We believe at least one of the men raped the woman who was killed, and possibly Isabella. We haven't asked her that question yet, but it's important information for us to move forward with the case."

"Would you like to ask the questions with me present in the room?"

Marta sighed with relief. "I would. I feel very uncomfortable asking these hard questions, considering her state of mind."

"I understand. With the progress she's made over the last twenty-four hours, I feel confident she can handle the conversation. Let's go have a word with her."

"One more thing. You mentioned moving her into a home until we can contact her family." Marta went on to explain the lack of agencies in their small town to help with something like that, and Josie's refusal to allow her to stay with an officer. "But we do have a small motel in town. It's clean and run by a good man who will keep an eye on Isabella. We'll have officers checking on her frequently."

"I think it's an excellent idea. Physically she's fine. And I don't see psychological harm in moving her. The sooner she sees herself as recuperating, the better. Assuming the conversation we're about to have goes well, I'd move her this evening."

Marta smiled. "That's good to hear." She knew the importance of keeping an emotional distance from victims, but young people, especially a young woman so close to her own daughter's age, pulled at her heartstrings. Through the years, Teresa had made some horrible decisions, and Marta thanked God every day that she'd come through them unbroken.

The doctor knocked on Isabella's door and entered. He was inside with her for about five minutes before he beckoned Marta into the room. With the overhead light off and the light outside the window fading, gray shadows played across their faces. Marta was glad when Dr. Brazen turned on the bedside lamp.

She reached out her hand and Isabella took it and smiled slightly, but her eyes revealed the dread of what was to come.

Dr. Brazen stood next to Marta and spoke quietly. "You've come a long way, Isabella. I feel confident you'll recover from the terrible things that happened. Once you're reunited with your family, and you continue talking to a doctor, you'll come through this a stronger person."

She nodded, her eyes focused intently on him.

"You understand that Marta's job is to put the men that hurt you in jail? She wants to lock them away so they can't hurt you or anyone else."

"I know that," she said. Her voice was soft but strong.

Marta was shocked at the difference, even in her appearance, from last night. Her long black hair was clean and pulled back in a headband, and her pale cheeks now had a little color. Marta was struck by how innocent she appeared, sitting in the white hospital bed in the cotton gown.

Marta felt the doctor's eyes on her and she realized he was giving her the signal to proceed.

"Let's start by talking about your family," Marta said. "We want to get you back home. If you can give me a phone number and an address, I'll make contact. We can start making arrangements to connect you."

Her expression turned cold and she shook her head. "No."

"I'll be glad to talk with them, explain what's happened."

"No. I won't talk about this."

Marta sighed. She had no idea what the issue was: the shame of taking family money and not achieving the goal, the shame of rape, the fear of returning. Marta had hoped to break the ice with talk of her family, but it hadn't worked. She hoped the girl's resolve would soften.

"Isabella, the doctor explained that we want to help you. We want you to be safe."

The young woman pursed her lips and jutted her chin out in a brave gesture.

"I'd like to show you some photographs of several men. I'd like you to tell me if you recognize any of them. Can you do that?"

She glanced down at the photos in Marta's hand and nodded.

Marta held up the sheet of photos and Isabella nodded and pointed to the photo of Ryan Needleman and turned her head away. "Yes. He's one of them."

"What do you mean by that?" Marta didn't want to put words in her mind, so if it ended up at trial, she wouldn't be accused of leading a witness.

"He drove us. From Guatemala to Mexico."

"Can you tell me where in Mexico?"

"In Piedra Labrada. That's where Renata and I ran."

Marta tried to keep the surprise from her expression. "You told me you didn't know her name. Why didn't you tell me before when I asked?"

She looked away, a sign that told Marta she was acknowledging the lie, or still not telling the truth.

"I was just afraid," Isabella said.

"Can you tell me her last name?"

"She never told me."

"Do you have any idea where the other women are that didn't leave with you?"

She took a deep ragged breath, obviously trying to hold back tears. "They wouldn't come. We begged them, but they said they had to make it to the end. We ran the night we were going to cross the border into the United States. We'd checked into a motel for a few hours' sleep. Ryan was taking a shower and Josh lay down on the bed and fell asleep. They'd quit being so careful with us. They never imagined we'd run. But I couldn't take one more night with him."

"Who do you mean?" Marta asked.

"The man named Josh. He was a monster. So Renata and I left. We opened the door of the motel room, quiet as we could, and then we ran." She swiped at a tear falling down her cheek. "I don't know what happened to the rest of them. I'm sorry."

"You say you couldn't take one more night. Why is that?"

She looked at Dr. Brazen, who nodded for her to continue. "Josh, he made Renata and me do terrible things. He said he would kill us and our families if we ever told anyone."

"When you say terrible things . . . can you be more specific?"

"He raped us." Her face was stoic, as if she'd planned these words and committed to saying them.

Marta held up the photographs again. "I'd like you to look at this group of photos again and tell me if you see the person who hurt you."

Isabella studied the photos for several seconds when her composure suddenly broke. "That's the one," she said, her voice barely a whisper as she pointed to Josh Mooney's mug shot from his meth-amphetamine arrest. "He looks different now, not so skinny as that picture. But that's him."

When she shut her eyes against the image, Marta worried she'd just obliterated all of the progress the woman had made, but the doctor stepped closer to her and said, "It's okay, Isabella. Seeing them again is terrible. It's completely normal to feel scared and angry. But they're gone now. And you're safe."

Marta felt horrible for pushing further, but she had to ask one more question. She patted the girl's leg and sat down on the edge of the bed as Isabella wiped her eyes with a tissue.

"I need to ask you one more question. We want to find the person who shot Renata. Can you tell me what happened?"

She started crying again, shaking her head no. She finally managed, "It was dark. We were hiding in the little shed beside the house and we saw the car stop. We knew they were coming for us, so we ran for the pasture, away from the light. Renata and I got separated in the dark. I heard the gun and kept running."

"Can you tell me how many men there were?"

"I don't know."

Marta let it go. If Isabella knew more, it was clear she was still too frightened to share the information.

———

At eight p.m., donation buckets were passed around the room and guests were encouraged to mingle with the women who'd shared their stories. Josie made a beeline for Caroline before she got caught up in the small talk that would no doubt last far longer than Josie wanted to stay.

"I'm sure you've heard about the female victim who's currently staying at the trauma center," Josie said.

"I have. That's such a tragedy. And the other young woman dying? I can't understand how something like that can happen here," she said.

"I'm sure the mayor has told you we're working hard to reunite the two women with their families. The women are from Guatemala and we're trying to find a way to help them back home. The flight will obviously cost quite a bit, plus some meals and incidentals. The police department doesn't have any kind of discretionary funds available. Is this something your organization would consider supporting?"

"Absolutely. You tell me what you need in terms of travel money, and I'll see what I can come up with. I'm glad to help."

Josie had always thought of the mayor's wife as someone who got involved at the top end, but rarely got her hands dirty. So her answer now was a nice surprise and it solved a major problem for Isabella. Returning home the body currently in the morgue was another issue altogether, but that would have to wait.

※

Josie found her mom chatting with several other women. They finally left the function at eight-thirty, and Josie drove her mom back to Manny's.

She parked along the street in front of her mom's room and turned the jeep engine off.

"You coming inside?" Beverly asked.

"No. I've got work in the morning," she said. "I'm sorry your trip hasn't turned into much time to visit. That's the lousy part about police work. When something like this breaks open, you can't put it on hold."

"Josie. Give me some credit. Your dad was a cop. I know the drill." Her mom opened the door and climbed out. Before she shut it she said, "I don't expect you to babysit me or spend every minute with me. I just want to get to know you again. You're my kid and I barely know anything about your life." She paused and sighed. "I know I sucked being your mom after your dad died. But it was a long time ago. People change. I just thought it was worth giving it a shot again."

Josie watched her mom walk up to her hotel room and unlock the door. Her thoughts turned to Isabella, and how she had fled her country and her family in search of something better. It made Josie realize that what she had all those years ago might not have been what she wanted or needed at the time, but it was a hell of a lot better than others had it.

The evening had left her feeling small and lonely, and she wanted nothing more than to climb into bed and curl up next to Nick, who was in Mexico trying to reunite a man with his family. She checked her phone before pulling away and saw a text from Marta.

Interview went great. Isabella confirmed both Ryan and Josh. She's checked into Room 2. Can you check on her? Told her I'd be by at 9:00 to check in but I'm working an accident and can't get away yet.

Josie sighed and texted back. *Will do.* She didn't like the idea of leaving Isabella alone in the motel room, but Josie was out of options. She didn't have an officer she could dedicate to the hotel that night. All they could do was check in on her and make sure she kept the door locked to anyone but the police.

———————

Josie got back out of her jeep, walked one door down from her mom's room, and knocked, but there was no answer. She could see light filtering around the curtain. She waited a minute and knocked again, this time calling Isabella's name and announcing her own name to reassure her.

Thinking she might be in the shower, Josie turned to go to her mom's room when Beverly stepped outside with a cigarette and lighter in her hand to sneak a smoke. Josie was too preoccupied to chastise her.

"I need to check on the woman staying next door to you, but she's not answering the door," Josie said. "Can you hear when water is running in the room next to you?"

Beverly made a face like it was a ridiculous question. "The walls are like paper. I can hear Manny humming in his apartment on this side." She jerked her thumb toward the opposite wall.

Josie walked to the back of her mom's room and into the bathroom, where she placed her ear against the wall shared with Isabella's room. She heard nothing.

"Have you heard any noise from that room since you walked in?"

"No. But I've only been here a few minutes."

Heading quickly back toward the door, Josie said, "There may be a problem. I need you to go back inside your room and lock the door. Don't leave until you hear from me. You promise?"

Her mom's forehead tensed into worry lines but she nodded, put her cigarette out, and shut the door.

———·———

Josie ran down to Manny's apartment and asked for the key to Room 2. He followed her down and they knocked again but heard nothing.

When they entered the room, she could tell where the bed had been lain in. A towel lay on the floor by the bed, but nothing else. The bathroom light was off, and when Josie checked she found it empty. The sink and shower were both still wet from use. She found the closet empty and nothing under the bed.

"Do you know if she came in carrying a bag?" Josie asked, pulling her phone out of her pocket.

"Yes," Manny said. "She kept thanking Marta for the clothes

and things. She had two bags. I think one was maybe a purse, and the other was a black duffel bag."

"Did she say anything to you about leaving?"

"No. Nothing. Marta said she'd be back to check on her, and she smiled and thanked her. I don't understand."

Josie glanced at her cell phone: 9:04 p.m. She dialed Marta's number, and she answered immediately.

"Marta. I'm in Isabella's motel room and she's gone. There are no bags here. It looks like she showered and left."

It took Marta a beat to respond. "It's just now nine. That's when I told her I'd be there."

"Did she say anything to you about leaving? About taking a walk, maybe?"

"No. Absolutely not. She's still terrified. She didn't want me to leave, but I explained I had work to do. I said I'd be back later to check on her." Josie heard a car door slam. "The tow-truck is here at the accident. I'm on my way."

Josie turned to Manny. "Has anyone come by here today asking about rooms? Or called about rooms?"

"No one came by. Lawrie Small called earlier today about having rooms ready for her family coming into town, but that's it. It's been a slow week."

She glanced over at the bedside table, and then around the room. "Is there a phone in the room she could have used?"

"No. With cell phones everywhere I took the room phones out. They weren't worth the money."

Josie called Marta back. "Did she have a cell phone yet?"

"No. She knew I was working on getting her one. One of the churches in town was helping with incidentals. They were going to get her a disposable one with minutes."

"Okay," Josie said. "When you left the trauma center, did you notice anyone watching? Think back to when you walked outside with Isabella. Anything stand out in your memory?"

As Marta thought for a moment, Josie told Manny to stay in his apartment until he heard otherwise and to call if he heard anything from Isabella. Josie got in her car.

"No. I didn't pay attention to the parking lot. I should have, I just didn't think about it. I was worried about trying to make her feel safe."

"Who all knew that we were moving Isabella to Manny's?" Josie asked.

"The only people I've talked to about it were Dr. Brazen and Mark at the trauma center. Unless they told someone, no one else knows."

"Okay. Don't come here. I'm headed to the trauma center. They have security cameras on the parking lot. I'll talk to Mark and see if we can pull something up. Can you check Josh and Macey's house, check for their car, ask Cici if he's seen them? Also, call Otto and ask him to check for Ryan, for his car, and check with his parents. Tell him it's critical we find Ryan. I'll call Lou to notify the neighboring districts. When you're done, drive the neighborhood to scout for her. I'll check in as soon as I'm done at the trauma center."

Marta let out a breath as if she'd been holding it. "This is just horrible."

"Marta. This isn't time for second-guessing. Focus on the job, not the person. Don't get caught up in the emotion. That's how details are missed."

"I know, I know. I'm at the stoplight now. Stay in touch."

Josie drove to the trauma center, searching the dark streets for pedestrians, but saw only a couple in their fifties walking hand in hand and a couple of boys on bicycles. Parking in the emergency lane, she ran inside and found Mark at the nurses' station.

He looked up and smiled when her saw her, but his expression fell serious as Josie explained the circumstance. "Have you heard from her or seen her?"

"No. Nothing. I think Marta was going to meet her tonight."

"She was. I showed up instead and found her missing," Josie said. "Did you tell anyone she was being moved to the motel? Maybe even mention it in passing to someone?"

"No! Of course not. I knew her situation," he said. "Do you think the men who brought her here took her?"

"If they did, we need to find a link immediately or we'll lose her. Is there someone who can pull up your security cameras and look at today's footage?"

"Sure. Same-day footage is a snap. I can pull it up on this computer. We use it occasionally for a dementia patient or someone who walks off." He sat down behind the desk and began typing. "What time frame are you looking at?"

"Can you look up the discharge time for Isabella? I want to see who was parked in the parking lot when she left."

He ran his finger down a chart on the desk. "The exact time was seven thirty-five p.m. I can pull that right up. Come on around here so you can see."

As she walked around the desk, Josie's phone buzzed in her pocket. Her mom had texted asking if everything was okay. Josie had forgotten to call her back. She sent a quick text that everything was fine, and that she'd check in with her in the morning. She felt guilty for having forgotten her, and she realized how unaccustomed she was to thinking about family and their needs.

Josie watched Mark drag a bar at the bottom of the computer touch screen along a time continuum. He stopped it at seven o'clock and they looked at a static recording of the west side of the parking lot. The picture was clear and in color, nothing like the old grainy black-and-white shots businesses used to have.

Mark pointed out his car, Dr. Brazen's car, Marta's jeep, and two other cars that might have been the vehicles of the two patients currently staying at the center. It was still bright enough outside to determine the cars were all empty.

He switched to the view from the second camera and before he'd had time to identify any other vehicles, Josie knew she'd found what they were looking for. Josh Mooney's orange Camaro had been backed into a parking space so that the front of it was facing the trauma center entrance. The location gave Josh a better view of the entrance, but it also gave Josie a better vantage point to see who was sitting in the car. She wondered if it was the same car that had been driving by her house in the middle of the night.

"Can you zoom in on that car? I want to see who's in the driver's seat," she said.

Mark focused in on the windshield. There were clearly two people in the car, but a glare made it impossible to make out their faces. He fast-forwarded to 7:40 and watched as Isabella walked out of the hospital with Marta. The light from the parking lot illuminated her face as she paused before getting into the jeep. She looked around the lot, smiling, as if noticing her surroundings for the first time, the trees and the homes, finally letting down her guard a little.

After Marta's jeep pulled away from the trauma center, ten seconds later the Camaro followed. As the Camaro drove closer to the security camera mounted on the front of the building, a clear shot of the driver's face came into view. Josh Mooney.

Josie thanked Mark, and as she drove back to the department, called Marta to fill her in.

"This is awful," Marta said. "Josh's car is gone. No one answered the door at the apartment. Cici of course played dumb."

"Come on back to the department. We'll talk next steps."

Josie hung up and called Otto, explaining what she knew. "Did you find Ryan?"

"I called his number, but no answer. It's almost nine-thirty, so hopefully he's at home. I'm on my way to his parents' house now. That's where he's been living."

"Hang tight for a minute. I'm ready to go to the prosecutor. Let's bring Ryan in on charges. I think we'll get more out of him if he's facing jail time."

"Will do. I'm just a few minutes from the house. I'll wait to hear from you."

Back at the department, Josie issued a BOLO alert, both online and for all area dispatch, to be on the lookout for Isabella Dagati and an orange Chevy Camaro. Josie had hoped that Caroline Moss's community group could rally around Isabella and help relocate her to a safe place where she stood a chance at a happy future. Now she was back in the custody of the man who had raped and stalked her, and possibly murdered her friend.

Josie dialed the prosecutor's office, doubting anyone would be in so late in the evening, but hoping nonetheless. She was surprised when his secretary, Ramona, answered the phone.

"Tyler Holder's office."

"Ramona! I thought the office would be empty."

"Big trial tomorrow. What can I do for you?"

"I need to speak to Tyler. It's urgent."

"He's headed out the door. Want me to grab him?"

"Please. Can you get him to swing by the PD for ten minutes?"

Josie heard the phone clank down on the desk, and a minute later the secretary came back on and said he was on his way.

"You're a saint, Ramona. I owe you one."

The county prosecutor's office was located in the courthouse across the street. Tyler Holder was in his early forties and had garnered the respect of the local law enforcement officers with a fair and heavy hand at trial. Josie didn't always agree with him, but she never got the sense that he was taking the easy way out.

She gathered her case notes and took them to the table. A few minutes later she heard Tyler take the stairs two at a time and enter the office looking wired. He wore a light gray suit and red tie and smelled faintly of cologne. Josie shook his hand and he took a seat beside her at the conference table.

"I appreciate you coming. I know you're on your way out."

"Can we do it in ten?" he asked.

"You bet."

Just then Marta walked into the office, looking frantic. Josie motioned toward the table and she said hello as she pulled out a chair.

"Here's where we're at," Josie said. "Isabella Dagati is the name of the surviving woman who was transported here from Guatemala. We've only identified the woman who was murdered with a first name, Renata. We provided photos to Isabella, who confirmed that Josh Mooney and Ryan Needleman transported her and the murder victim, as well as three other women, from Guatemala."

"Ryan Needleman?" He squinted at Josie as if he didn't believe it.

"I've talked with him. He's already admitted it. He got thrown out of college for fighting this fall and was looking to make some quick money. Josh Mooney set it up."

"His family will be devastated. How'd a kid from such a good family go so wrong?"

"The situation got much worse about an hour ago. A psychiatrist from Odessa, who's been working with Isabella, agreed to moving her out of the trauma center into a more relaxed environment until she can go back to her family. Marta moved her over there at seven-forty this evening. When I went to check on her at the motel at nine o'clock, she was gone."

"She left?"

"I don't think so. We pulled up surveillance tape of the trauma center parking lot and found Josh Mooney sitting in his orange Camaro, parked in the back of the lot. There was a passenger who we believe to be Macey, his sister."

Tyler winced. "No surprise there. You don't think Ryan's with him?"

"I doubt it. I think Ryan realizes what a mess this is and wants nothing more to do with it. As soon as I give Otto the word, he's ready to bring Ryan in," she said. "We believe Josh and Macey were watching the hospital for Isabella's release. The video shows that as soon as Marta pulled out of the lot to transport Isabella to Manny's motel, Josh and his passenger followed."

Tyler was typing something into his phone, presumably a note about the case.

"To make it worse, Isabella also identified Josh as the man who repeatedly raped both her and the woman who died."

He made a disgusted noise. "I'd not heard about the rape."

"I don't believe Ryan was involved in the rapes, but I want to bring him in. Charge him with transporting an illegal into the U.S. I need to scare him into giving us everything he knows about Josh and Macey, and where they might be taking Isabella."

Tyler had started nodding his head in agreement as Josie explained. "You want to grill Ryan on Josh and Macey's whereabouts?" he asked.

"Immediately. Not only do they have Isabella, but the other three women from Guatemala are still missing. They were last seen in Piedra Labrada, just before they crossed the border. That's where Isabella and Renata ran for it."

"I have no problem with bringing Ryan in. They broke a federal law through the Immigration and Nationality Act. Skip the warrant in the interest of time, but keep me posted."

Tyler left and Josie felt a huge surge of relief. He generally drilled her with questions. She had neglected to tell him that Ryan had had a falling-out with Josh, and at least two of the women escaped before the van ever made it into the U.S. Technically, Ryan hadn't done anything that Josie could charge him with yet, but he didn't know that. Josie was using the prosecutor and the fear of arrest to scare the hell out of Ryan. Ryan was her best chance at finding the missing women, so she was willing to risk the wrath of the prosecutor.

She dialed Otto's cell phone. "Tyler's clear on the investigation and gave his blessing." Josie summarized the conversation and asked Otto to bring him in for questioning.

"I would Mirandize him in the car. He may be so flustered on the way into the jail that he'll offer up information before his dad can get an attorney set up for him."

"Will do. Meet me at the jail in about thirty minutes."

TEN

Josie and Marta drove to the jail separately and pulled into the parking lot as Otto was walking Ryan in through the prisoner door at the back of the jail. He didn't have cuffs on, but Otto was holding his upper arm and Ryan had his head ducked low as if trying to conceal his identity.

Once Ryan was in an interrogation room, the three officers met in the hallway.

"Did he open up on the way over?" Josie asked.

"Not a word. But his dad's not supplying an attorney. His parents were ready to blow. I explained the criminal charges in front of them. They had no idea about the trip to Guatemala. He'd given them some story about helping a friend move. His dad basically disowned him on the spot. I read Ryan his Miranda rights in the kitchen. When we got in the car I told him he could have a court-appointed attorney but he didn't respond."

"Good enough," Josie said. "I get first dibs."

"Have at him."

"Do me a favor. Go ask the dispatcher if she has a Texas map with highways. Maybe Ryan can help us figure out where Josh might be headed."

Ryan was dressed in blue jeans, work boots, and a black concert T-shirt featuring some band Josie had never heard of. The graphic on the front of the shirt showed a giant snake's mouth, opened wide with overextended fangs dripping blood. Sweat poured down Ryan's temples, and a sour odor came off his body. As he used his forearm to wipe away the perspiration on his forehead, Josie noticed the insolent stare from earlier in the day had been replaced with a look of fear.

Marta positioned herself in one corner of the room to observe while Josie handled the questioning. She sat down across from Ryan and placed a digital recorder on the table, went through the formalities, and then asked again if he wanted an attorney present, for which he shook his head no.

"Please speak out loud for the record," she said.

"No. I don't need an attorney. I already told you what I did. I didn't know I was doing anything wrong."

"Do you know that it's illegal for a person from another country to cross the border into the United States without proper documentation?"

He nodded once.

"Please speak out loud for the record," she said.

"Yes."

Otto walked into the room and laid a folded road map on the table, and then sat down next to Josie.

"So you understand that transporting women from Guatemala into Mexico was illegal?" Josie avoided mentioning transport into the U.S.

He shrugged and then said, "Yes."

"Do you also understand that knowingly standing by while a rape is taking place is a crime?"

His jaw tightened as he clenched his teeth. He finally said, "I didn't know that was happening."

"The rapes took place multiple times, against multiple women. You can't hide from this. Not only will you have an arrest warrant for the federal crime of transporting across an international border, but you'll be labeled a sexual predator. Your name will be added to the registry for sexual offenders. Your parents will have to notify your neighbors that you live in their house. That's assuming they don't throw you out after you serve your jail time."

Ryan pushed his thumbs into his eyes as if trying to keep from crying, but he eventually gave in, trying to hide behind his hands as he sobbed. Josie grabbed a tissue box off a corner table and shoved it over to him. He finally stopped, taking ragged breaths and blowing his nose into a handful of tissues.

Josie had interviewed enough people to know the breakdown was a very good sign. But she worried the whole process was taking too long. She needed Josh and Macey's whereabouts, but she couldn't afford to spook Ryan into silence.

Ryan took a long deep breath and shuddered as he exhaled.

"Isabella is gone, Ryan."

He looked up at her, apparently caught off guard at the statement.

"Josh and Macey are gone," she said.

Again, confusion in his eyes.

"I want to know where they are," she said. "No games. No lies. You have too much on the line to screw with me right now."

He nodded and his expression grew earnest as his breathing returned to normal. "I understand, but I don't know where they are. I haven't talked to either one of them since I got back to Artemis."

"We'll get your phone records. You know that, right?" she said.

He leaned his head back and groaned. "Okay. Seriously, Josh called a few times, but not about leaving with her. He just called freaking out because they were missing. He kept telling me that he had to get them delivered. That someone would come after him if he didn't get the women before they went to the cops."

"Who was coming after him?"

"He never said. I never asked. I didn't want to know."

"So what did you do about the missing women?" Josie could feel the acid burn in her stomach.

"Nothing. He called the first time and he was like, *You have to come with me. You have to help me find these two women. I was like, Listen, I did what you asked. You still haven't paid me the other half of the money you owe me. I'm done with this. I should have never gotten involved.*"

"Did you go with him to search for the women?" she asked.

"One night. We drove out by the river."

"By my house?" she asked.

He nodded.

"How did you know to look for them there?"

"Somebody told Josh that Isabella and Renata hitchhiked out to stay with some old lady in Mexico, and that she told them to go see you. That's why he kept driving by your house. I swear. I drove out with him one time and that was it. I told him I was done."

"Who gave Josh this information?"

"I don't know. He didn't tell me."

"What day did you drive out looking for the women?" she asked.

"It was Saturday." He wrinkled his forehead and said, "Actually it would have been Sunday morning, at like two. We never saw them, though."

"Did Josh shoot Renata?"

He put his hands up. "I have no idea. I swear."

"Do you know if Josh ever made contact with Isabella or Renata after they escaped in Piedra Labrada?"

"I have no idea. After I drove out to your house with him I told him I was done. He hasn't called me since. Check my phone records."

"What about the other women?" she asked. "Where are the other three?"

"I told you, I left them in Piedra Labrada, but what I said wasn't totally true. I didn't leave because of my documentation."

He paused, and Josie glanced at Otto. She could feel the tension rising in the room as they approached the truth of what had happened on the trip.

"Could I get a drink of water?" Josh asked. Josie noticed his sticky voice and nodded. Marta left the room.

Ryan continued. "When we got to Piedra, we rented a cheap motel room to sleep a couple hours before we'd cross the border that night. We were all tired and hungry and pissed off. I just wanted it all to end. Josh lay down to sleep, and I took a shower. When I got done, I walked out of the bathroom and Isabella and Renata were gone. The other three women were huddled in a corner crying. I yelled at Josh, who'd slept through them leaving, and he jumped out of bed. Then all hell broke loose. He was yelling and screaming like a maniac. I was afraid the police were going to get called on us. He pulled one of the women up off the floor by her hair, and he started kicking her and kneeing her in the stomach. He said it was her fault for letting the other women go. I knocked Josh on his ass, and I left. I just walked out."

Ryan bent over at the interrogation table and placed his head in his hands, and Josie saw tears fall onto the table under him. "I left because I couldn't take one more night of Josh. I keep thinking about those other three women, though. I don't know what's happened to them."

"When you drove out by my house with Josh, what did he say about them?" Josie asked.

Marta walked back in and placed a Dixie cup in front of Ryan, who gulped noisily until it was empty. "He said they were staying somewhere together. He kept saying it was cool. He was going to get them delivered." He looked at Josie, and she thought he'd finally reached the point she was striving for. "Maybe that's where Josh and Macey went. Maybe they took Isabella to finish the trip to Albuquerque."

"New Mexico?" she asked.

"That's where we were headed."

"Why New Mexico?"

"Josh just said he had work for the women. They were going to get jobs. He said life in their country sucked, and he was going to set them up right in the U.S." Josh made a face like he was disgusted. "He made it sound like he was doing them some big favor, and then he—" Ryan stopped, as if he didn't want to recall the memory.

Otto broke in. "Ryan. This is critical for the investigation. You know what happened isn't right. Josh did horrible things to innocent women. This is your chance to make it right. If you saw him force those women into having sex with him, then you need to tell us now. Someone is going to pay for attacking those women. We want to make sure the right person goes to jail."

"When we stayed in a motel, we always got one room to keep everyone together. He said it was safer and cheaper. Josh got the bed and I had to sleep in front of the door to make sure nobody tried to leave. Then he'd make one of the women sleep with him." He clasped his hands in front of him on the table to try and stop the trembling. "The rest of us, we had to turn the TV up as loud as it would go, and sit on the floor and act like we didn't know what was going on. It was awful."

"Why didn't someone stop him?" Josie asked.

"Because he was the only one that knew anything! He had all our documents, our identification. We were in a foreign country with no ID. He took mine too. I didn't even know where I was. The women had fake passports that he kept. He told them once they got dropped off in Albuquerque, they'd get all their stuff back. And he'd say things about killing their families all the time. He had their addresses written on a piece of paper, and he'd read the girl's name and then her family's address. He let them know, *If you don't do what I say, your family will pay.* Then he'd be like, *Come take care of me.*" Ryan shook his head like he wanted to clear the memory out of his head. Josie wanted to tell him to imagine the nightmares the women who were raped were now having.

"When we're done here, I need you to write down the women's names, as much of their addresses as you can remember, and a description of each woman who was on the trip. Hair color, size, and any distinguishing marks. Everything you can think of."

He nodded.

"You need to do this right," Josie said. "You need to cooperate, in part to counter the mounting case we have against you. But you also owe these women something in return for the hell you helped put them through."

"I'll do it. I'll write down everything I can remember."

"Who's running the transportation ring?" Otto asked.

"I don't know. While we were on the trip Josh always made it sound like he was the boss. Like he was the mastermind, hooking women up with jobs all over the U.S. I was like, *Seriously, dude, I've seen the crappy apartment you live in. I know you're not rich enough or smart enough to do half of what you're saying.*"

Josie put a hand up so she could ask a follow-up question. "Hang on. You said, 'while we were on the trip.' Does that mean at other times he made it sound like someone else was his boss?"

"Not him. Macey did. She's smarter than him, but she gets all coked up and her mouth runs constantly. I can't stand her."

"Did she mention someone else?"

"Sort of. She was always talking about somebody being pissed off at them. She never really mentioned anyone in front of me, but she was always freaking out like they were doing something wrong, and someone was going to be pissed. Josh was always trying to talk her down."

"Talk her down?" she asked.

"Yeah, like, calm her down."

Josie glanced at Otto and Marta, then at her watch. They were losing critical minutes.

"Here's the deal. You give me everything you can think of that might help me figure out where Josh and Macey are taking Isabella and those women?" Josie paused and stared at him for a moment. "And I'll cut you loose."

He swallowed hard and sat up straighter in the chair. "I'll do it."

"I think you finally figured out lying isn't going to help you. It'll cause you more trouble. You'll be intentionally hampering a murder investigation. And you don't want to go there."

"I understand."

She looked at her watch again and then turned to Otto. "It's almost eleven o'clock. Marta left Isabella at the motel a little before eight. She showered and dressed, even lay down on the bed for at least a short while, because the covers were slightly messed up. I'm guessing she was picked up from the motel at approximately eight-thirty, because when I got there at nine she was gone."

Josie pointed a finger at Ryan. "Every minute that ticks by means that Josh and Macey are farther down the road with those women. I'm going to give you five minutes to tell me everything you know about where Josh is taking them. If you hold back, I'll make your life hell."

"That's fine. I get it."

"Let's start with where they're headed," she said.

Otto unfolded the map in front of Ryan. It was a Texas road map the dispatcher had in her files for transporting prisoners.

"I can tell you. I don't need a map. He said we were going to take the interstate the whole way. He made a big deal about driving the speed limit so we wouldn't get pulled over. Driving that junked-out van you couldn't go seventy anyway."

"What kind of van?"

"One of the big white ones. It had benches in the back. It holds twelve people."

"An Econoline van?"

"That's it," he said, nodding.

"How fast will it go?"

"Sixty max."

Josie had pulled up a map application on her phone and said, "From here to El Paso takes about four hours. It's another four hours from El Paso to Albuquerque. You think Josh would drive all night?"

Ryan nodded. "If he went and picked up Isabella, and he had those other women with him, he'd want to get rid of them. He's freaked out right now. And Macey has to be driving him insane."

"Why do you say that?" she asked.

"When anything happens that's not according to plan, she just can't handle it. When she found out Renata was killed, I bet Macey's brain about exploded. She has to know you guys think Josh did it. And now they're driving that crappy van with all those women in it."

Josie looked at Otto. "Josh was driving his Camaro when he picked up Isabella."

"After what he did to her, I'm sure he knew she wouldn't get into that van with him again," said Ryan. "I can't believe he got her to go with him at all."

"Macey's probably the one who approached her at the motel.

She probably gave her some reason why she had to leave. Once she was in the car, they had her," Otto said.

"Where's the van parked?" Josie asked.

"Josh said he parked it behind the rock quarry."

Josie faced Marta who was still observing from the back of the room. She had already picked up on Josie's intent.

"I'll go now. The quarry's a good thirty-minute drive from here. I'll call you as soon as I check it out."

"Thanks, Marta." As she left, Josie turned her attention to Otto. "Let's assume Josh and Macey got Isabella at eight-thirty and drove her out to the quarry. It's a thirty-minute drive. They'd have been there by nine."

Otto broke in. "There's an old contractor's shack out there that hasn't been used in twenty years. I bet that's where the other women were being held."

Josie nodded, feeling like they were finally hitting their stride. "The earliest they could have left the quarry was nine oh-five. It's southwest of town, so that adds another thirty minutes to their trip to El Paso."

Otto picked it up. "They left Artemis at nine thirty-five. They've been on the road a little over an hour. There's only one decent route to the interstate. So they've already made it through Marfa. They have to be on their way to Van Horn to catch Interstate 10 to El Paso before I-25 to Albuquerque."

Ryan started nodding his head. "That's what he said. Interstate 10 to 25."

Josie left Otto and Ryan in the room and went to talk to the dispatcher for the sheriff's department.

Juan Smith was standing at the copy machine when Josie entered the dispatch room. He was in his late twenties, married to a local schoolteacher, and was a loyal, dependable employee. She was glad he was on duty. Josie quickly brought him up to speed.

"Can you get with DPS to get state troopers, Border Patrol,

local cops, anyone who will respond, set up around the Van Horn entrance ramp?"

"I'm on it."

Juan sat down at the dispatch console and took down Josie's information about the van and the driver and passengers they were looking for. A few minutes later she was back in the interrogation room.

"Let's talk about your situation," she said, sitting down again across from Ryan.

Josie always hoped at this point some good might come out of this kind of tragedy. Maybe Ryan would get his life turned around before jail terms became a way of life.

"I'll do anything you want," he said.

"That's a good answer."

An attorney would point out that Ryan didn't actually cross the border with the women, but Ryan didn't know that technicality was in his favor. And he was currently so thankful not to be sitting in a jail cell with a sexual predator sign hanging over his head that Josie was sure he would continue to cooperate.

"I'd like to cut you free. I won't file charges tonight if you can promise me a few things."

"Anything you want. I swear."

"First. No contact with Josh or Macey Mooney."

"Okay."

"However, we may ask you to contact him if things don't go well tonight. Will you do that?"

"Yes."

"But if he calls you tonight, don't answer the phone. If we find you tipped him off about what's happening? I promise you jail time."

"I get it."

She pushed her business card across the table. "Other than that, if you think of anything, no matter how small it might seem to you, call or text me. Promise?"

"I promise."

Josie stood and put her hand out. "We're done here."

Ryan shook her hand, but awkwardly stayed standing behind the table.

"Was there something else?" she asked.

"I just want to say thanks. I'm going to get my act together."

Josie patted him on the back and led him down the hallway.

———

After Ryan left, Josie and Otto walked back to the dispatch station for an update.

"Border Patrol has two vehicles en route. Both are northbound on Interstate 10. Two state troopers are posted just before the Van Horn entrance ramp to the I-10."

"That's awesome. Quick work, Juan."

He grinned. "If he's on the interstate, we'll get him."

Thirty-five minutes later, they listened as dispatch near Van Horn fired up. Border Patrol stopped a white twelve-passenger Econoline van with Texas plates. Josie and Otto listened to the dispatch traffic as Josh and Macey Mooney were arrested for transporting four female passengers with no documentation. Twenty minutes into the episode, Josie called one of the officers and received confirmation that Isabella Dagati and the other three women in the van appeared to be unharmed.

ELEVEN

At ten the next morning Josie and Otto arrived at the Arroyo County Jail, where Texas state troopers had transported Josh and Macey Mooney after capturing them just outside of Van Horn, Texas. The four women were now patients at the trauma center undergoing thorough medical examination, three of them getting treatment for dehydration.

The jailer already had Josh Mooney sitting in the interrogation room next to his court-appointed attorney. The attorney had met with Josh at eight that morning to discuss the case against him. Josie was surprised that meeting had been pulled together so quickly, but a looming murder charge usually speeds the process.

The attorney was Oliver Greene, a public defender from Presidio. Greene was an expat with a dignified bearing and a soft British accent. He managed every client as if their case were the most important of his career, but he never resorted to unnecessary drama. He was one of Josie's favorite attorneys to work with.

Josie and Otto sat down across from them. After the preliminaries were finished, Greene gave his standard verbal warning to Josh.

"I expect you to consult with me about anything that might be considered incriminating. That may not always be clear. If you aren't sure, don't answer the question until you've checked with me first. Do you understand?"

Josh nodded his head vigorously and Josie glanced at Greene, who looked weary. She wondered how he tolerated most of the people he dealt with. At least when Josie arrested someone she could stick him in a jail cell and move on. Greene had to have extended conversations with lowlifes like Josh Mooney.

Josie began the interview with a list of charges brought against him, which included rape, the federal charge of kidnapping across a national border, and the threat of a potential murder charge. The prosecutor wasn't yet sure how the rape charges would be handled, since the rapes occurred in a foreign country, but he had assured Josie he would pursue the steepest penalty under the law, including extradition if appropriate.

At the word *murder* Josh slapped both hands down on the interview table and tipped his chair forward like a little kid. "Okay. I might have done some things wrong, but I *never* killed anyone. You have got the wrong man."

"You were looking for her. You spent several nights outside my home searching for her. When you couldn't catch her, you shot her in the back."

"Someone else was looking for her too," he said.

"Who?"

"I don't know her name."

"*Her* name?" Josie asked.

"Yeah, the lady I work for."

"What's her name?"

"She won't tell me."

"Does she live in Artemis?"

He hesitated a moment and shifted in his seat. "Maybe."

"Do you think your boss killed Renata?"

"I don't know. I swear I don't know what happened to her."

Josie paused and looked at Josh for a long moment before continuing. "I'm going to ask you something that I already know the answer to. If you answer truthfully, then I'll be more inclined to think I can trust you. If you lie to me, your credibility drops to zero."

Had the subject matter not been so serious, Josh's wide-eyed stare would have been comical.

"I have two different witnesses who gave me your name, and one who identified you in a photograph, as being responsible for repeatedly raping both Isabella and Renata on the trip from Guatemala to the U.S. Do you admit to that?"

Greene cut Josh off before he could speak, as Josie assumed he would. "I would suggest you not answer that question until we've had a chance to talk."

Josh looked at Greene, and then back at Josie. He shrugged, as if to say, *What can I do? He won't let me answer.*

"How many times did you drive out to the pasture where Renata's body was found?"

Josh looked at his attorney, who nodded for him to answer.

"A couple times."

"I need exact dates."

"Okay, sure." He held a hand up, staring at his fingers as he ticked the days off, mumbling to himself. He finally said, "It was Friday, Saturday, and Sunday."

"What time did you go out each night?"

"It was about two in the morning. Something like that. So I guess it would be Saturday, Sunday, and Monday at about two in the morning."

"Who went with you?"

He hesitated and Josie sensed a lie formulating in his brain.

"Don't do it, Josh. Don't start telling me lies. I want the truth."

Greene said, "If you aren't sure about an answer, we can stop the interview. We'll chat for a moment, and then reconvene with Chief Gray again when you feel more confident."

Josh looked confused. "Sure."

"Who went with you each of those nights?" Josie asked.

"The first night, Ryan came with me."

"That would have been Saturday night, into early Sunday morning?" she asked.

"Yeah. Then I went by myself."

"Why didn't Ryan go back with you?"

"You can't trust him. He signed on for the trip. Then things got tough and he quit."

"Who went with you on Sunday, into Monday morning?"

"Nobody. I went by myself."

Josie was getting frustrated. She looked over and saw Otto scowling at Josh.

"Let me get this straight. You drove out *alone* to the location where Renata was murdered, on the *day* that she was murdered, and you're telling me you had nothing to do with her murder later that night?" she asked.

"That's what I'm saying. I didn't *want* to kill her. I wanted to *deliver* her. I don't make money off dead girls. Right?"

"Here's the way I see it," Josie said. "You wanted to capture both women and deliver them both, but you couldn't. You tried several different days and couldn't catch them. So you panicked. You were afraid these women were going to get to me and tell me what happened to them. Which of course is exactly what happened, and look at the trouble you're in now. So you decided, if you couldn't catch them, you'd kill them."

Greene broke in, "That's enough."

Josh cut him off. "That's not what happened! I wasn't worried about that at all! They don't have any documentation. No ID.

They're too afraid of getting deported to go to the authorities. I just wanted to get them in the van so I could make the delivery and keep my job. I did not shoot that woman!"

"When did you tell your boss that the two women had escaped?" Josie asked.

"I sent her a text message the day after it happened."

Josie jotted a note on the pad in front of her to get a subpoena for the phone records. "Did the police take your phone as evidence last night?"

"You don't see it on me, do you?" he said, looking down at his orange jumpsuit.

Josie ignored his sarcasm. "I need to know who your boss is. I'm finding it hard to believe you don't at least have an idea who she is."

"Go talk to Ryan. He seems to know who she is."

Josie gave Josh a skeptical look. "Ryan told us you set him up for this trip. He said he met you at a party at Cici's place."

"That's where we met. That's where I told him the details. The drive, how many days it would take, what he'd be doing. But it was the boss lady who told me I'd be working with him. I'd never met the guy before."

"How did she tell you about him?"

"She sent me a text. Told me Ryan's name and told me to contact him. She said he'd be expecting my call. So I called and told him to meet me at Cici's."

After the interview, Josie completed the proper paperwork to keep the chain of evidence clear and retrieved Josh Mooney's cell phone. She and Otto walked out to the parking lot, clear on their next move without needing to discuss it.

"I'll drive," Otto said.

As he started his jeep, Josie called Turf and Annuals and asked for Lisa.

"This is Lisa. Can I help you?"

"Hi, Lisa. It's Josie Gray."

"Hey, how's it going?"

"Can you tell me if Ryan's working today?"

"He is. You want to talk to him?"

"I do. But I want to talk in person. Will he be leaving for lunch soon?"

"No. He always eats here. Brings his lunch."

"Okay. Please don't mention our visit to him. We'll be there in a few."

On the drive to Turf and Annuals, Josie opened Josh's phone and discovered he'd wiped it clean before the police had gotten to it.

"How'd that bastard get his phone clean as he was driving down the interstate with a van full of Guatemalan women?" Otto said.

"I hear there's an app that'll wipe everything on your phone clean with one click."

"Bastard."

"I talked to the prosecutor this morning about the subpoena. We'll get his records."

Otto parked in front of the office, and Ryan walked out with his head hung low. Lisa stood in the office doorway, arms crossed over her chest, obviously irritated. Josie couldn't blame her. The cops showing up twice in one week didn't look good for business.

Standing in the shade of the office building, but out of earshot from Lisa, Josie said, "I thought you were being straight with us last night. That was the deal we made. It's why we cut you loose. Remember that?"

His eyebrows shot up. "I was! I told you the truth!"

"I don't think so. I think you left out a big piece of the puzzle for us."

"I don't know what you're talking about."

"You told us Josh set you up for the transporting job."

"He did. I met him at Cici's party. Lots of people saw us there together."

"But he didn't tell you about the job. Someone else did."

Ryan became very still. Josie thought how similar people were to animals in the way they reacted to fear, as if remaining motionless might somehow hide their guilt.

"Who told you about the job?" she said.

His gaze shifted across the parking lot to the greenhouses, but he said nothing.

"This is a bad idea," Otto said. "You cooperated last night and you saved yourself a lot of trouble. You don't want to hold back now."

The corner of Ryan's mouth lifted in a humorless smile and he shook his head slowly. "This all started by somebody offering to help me out. Somebody I thought I could trust."

"How'd that work out for you?" Josie said.

"Not good."

"Then you'd better come clean with us before this person takes you down with her."

He looked at Josie then, and she knew she had him. He'd caught the reference to the female.

"She said she'd destroy me if any of this ever got out. That was the exact word she used. Destroy."

"She's a criminal, Ryan. Why do you care what she—"

"She's not a criminal! That's why I can't say anything! No one would believe me anyway."

"If you're straight with us, it won't matter who she is. If this woman is transporting women from Guatemala to Texas for a profit, then she's clearly breaking the law. It's that simple," Otto said.

Ryan glared at him and said, "Caroline Moss."

Josie felt like she'd been kicked in the gut. The mayor's wife. The woman voted Citizen of the Year for Arroyo County. The same woman who offered to pay for Isabella's plane ticket to Guatemala.

"You're saying that Caroline Moss approached you about driving the van to transport those women?" Otto asked.

"See! You don't believe me! I told you."

"This is a serious allegation," he said.

"No kidding! It was serious when she said she'd destroy me too."

"Why don't you back up and start at the beginning. When did she contact you? Where were you? You tell us everything you can think of," Josie said.

He leaned his head back and groaned. "It doesn't matter what I do. I am so screwed."

"What did you just tell me last night? You were going to get your act together. This is how you start."

He blew out air in frustration and kicked at the dirt before he finally opened up. "I've known Caroline since I was a kid. She and the mayor are friends with my mom and dad. They do some wine-tasting thing every month together. We've been on vacations with them. So when I got in trouble this fall at school she sent me a card and basically told me to hang in there. That it would all work out."

"When was this?" Josie said.

"A month or two ago. After I left school. Then she stopped by here one day like she was looking around for plants. But I think she came to see me. She said she knew I was having a bad time, and that she had a way for me to earn some extra money to help pay back my parents. I was like, *Yeah, that'd be great.* It was weird, though. I could tell she was nervous about talking to me. Then she was like, *Listen, if you do this, you can't tell anyone what you're doing.* She told me to come up with a story about helping a friend of mine to move here from Mexico." Ryan crossed his arms and leaned against the building, his expression unbelieving. "I thought she was shipping dope from Mexico. Then she says it's girls. She's helping these girls from Guatemala who have these terrible lives, and she's figured out how to help them get jobs here."

"When she was explaining this, did it surprise you that she would ask something like this from you?" Josie asked.

"Not really. I mean, she's always doing some charity thing. That's how she described the whole thing. She said the girls didn't have the money for passports and all that. She was going to get them here first, and then help them get paperwork and all that. She wanted to help them become citizens and get jobs."

"Legally it doesn't work that way. You get the documents first," Josie said, trying to figure out if Ryan was that naïve.

"I don't know how it works. I didn't care either. I mean, it was Caroline. She wasn't going to do something that could get us into trouble."

"But she said she'd destroy you if you told anyone?"

"That came later. After the girl got shot. She came to the house when she knew Mom and Dad were gone. She was shaking, had tears in her eyes. She kept asking me what happened, and I kept telling her I didn't know. The girls just escaped, and now one of them was dead. Then she got mad at me, like the screwup was my fault! I was like, seriously? I was driving a van with a lunatic who wanted to have sex with anything that moved, and *I* screwed up?"

"Do you think she had anything to do with the murder?" Josie asked.

He curled his lip at the question. "No. She was freaking out. I think she thought she was helping those girls, and Josh just fouled it all up."

"Do you think Josh shot Renata?" she asked.

He shrugged. "I don't know. I've been thinking about it constantly. I mean, he's the only one who makes sense to me. But I don't know for sure. I wasn't there."

"Have you been in contact with her since she came by your house?"

"No. She made me promise I wouldn't tell anyone about anything. That's when she put a finger in my face and said she'd destroy me if I talked about it to anyone, including my parents."

Josie glanced at Otto, who shook his head once, signaling he was done. "We'll be in touch," she said to Ryan.

"Are you going to tell her that I told you about this?" he asked.

Josie considered him for a moment and realized she wasn't able to offer him any reassurance. "I just don't know at this point."

When they'd gotten to the jeep, Otto slammed his door and looked over at Josie. "What the hell are we going to do?"

"This is gonna get ugly."

TWELVE

Josie called Marta and asked her to have burritos from the Hot Tamale delivered to the police department. Otto dropped Josie by the jail so she could pick up her jeep. By the time she arrived at the department the delivery kid was just pulling up with a paper bag full of food.

Upstairs, they spread out their lunches around the conference table and popped the tops of soft drinks while Josie dropped the bombshell.

"Caroline Moss."

Marta's jaw fell open and then snapped shut. "You're putting me on."

"I wish I was."

Marta dropped into the chair in front of her burrito. "I just don't know if I can believe that. I mean, I never liked the woman, but I always thought she was basically a good person. That her heart was in the right place."

"Maybe her heart *is* in the right place," said Otto. "The way Ryan talked, she was trying to help those women."

Josie gaped at Otto. "You don't seriously believe that, do you?"

He talked around a massive bite of burrito. "I'm just repeating what Ryan said."

"Human trafficking is a federal offense. She knows that. And even if she somehow twisted her participation into something humane, she hired Josh Mooney, who apparently raped at least two of the women he was hired to protect. That goes way beyond irresponsible."

Otto began nodding and raised his hand to stop her. "Calm down."

"What do we have, beyond Ryan's word?" said Marta.

"Nothing," he said.

"I'll subpoena Josh's, Macey's, and Caroline's cell phone records, but they'll be throwaway phones. We may ping one in her cell phone area, but that's about it. We won't connect Caroline to Josh and Macey," Josie said. "Unless Caroline paid for a throwaway phone with a personal credit card."

"She'd be more careful than that," Otto said.

"Unless she figured it was a throwaway number that would never be traced back to her. It's hard work covering your tracks. People get bogged down in the details and forget about the never-ending paper trail," Marta said.

"Meanwhile, we've got the testimony of an eighteen-year-old kid versus the mayor's wife, who is also a philanthropist and well-respected senator's daughter," said Josie.

"And we have three displaced women, a murder victim, and a witness to the murder who refuses to talk about it," Otto said.

"Then let's go to the source," Marta said. "Yesterday, when I dropped Isabella off at the motel, I pressed her to give me contact information for her family. She confided that she didn't want to tell us who her family was because Josh had said their families would be killed if any of them left before reaching their destination. She finally gave it up, but she didn't want to. He played terrible head games with those girls."

"He's a sick bastard," Otto said.

"It gets worse. She said he would read one of the girls' names off a list, and then read her family's address as a threat. Letting the women know how much control he had."

"That's the same story that Ryan told us," Josie said.

"What are you getting at, Marta?" Otto asked. "Are you suggesting we call the women's families and ask who they contacted to organize their trip to the U.S.?"

"Sure. What could it hurt? I have Isabella's information. I should be able to get the rest too."

"Make the call," Josie said. "Just let them know the women are safe, but in custody. They should receive a phone call with more information within the next few days."

———•———

Marta spent the next thirty minutes on the phone with Isabella's mother. The conversation took place in Spanish, so Josie and Otto had to wait for the recap after the call ended.

Marta hung up looking worn out. "If there was any doubt about this being a truly humanitarian effort, the phone call just put that idea to rest. Each one of those women's families paid twelve thousand dollars for the trip to Albuquerque. That amount included the travel cost, food and lodging, and a finder's fee for getting the women high-paying jobs in the hotel services industry, as well as their room and board until they were hired."

"Lodging? Seven people shared a motel room each night." Josie choked out a laugh. "Twelve thousand dollars times five women is sixty thousand dollars for what probably amounted to a couple weeks' work. Ryan said he got two thousand for helping. Josh may have gotten five thousand, which probably included gas and expenses for the trip."

"That means Caroline clears about fifty thousand dollars on this delivery," Otto said.

"And our Border Patrol contact, Jimmy Dixon, claims she'll get an additional payment from the so-called hotel services industry when the women are delivered somewhere in Texas." Josie shook her head at the amount of money that was being made. "When Ryan explained how Caroline involved him, I couldn't imagine why she would risk getting caught over something like this. But what if this isn't her first delivery? She could be bringing in a couple hundred thousand a year." She let the thought hang.

"Here's something else," Marta said. "Isabella's mom said she found out about the deal from a Web site. I have it written down."

Josie and Otto stood behind Marta as she pulled up the Web site.

"She says a variety of transporters have Web sites to basically broker deals with families," Marta said.

"Sounds like the traffickers are taking a cue from the Internet call girl industry," Otto said.

The title at the top of the Web page read Jobs Without Borders. Underneath the title was a rotating banner of glitzy photographs of young women dressed in stylish clothes smiling and laughing, dancing, eating in fancy restaurants, holding the hands of well-dressed men. Underneath the photos was a paragraph that started with, "The United States is more than the land of opportunity. It is the land of wealth and happiness. It is the land of hope and the land of unlimited prospects. The hotel services industry in the United States is a booming industry in need of young women from across the globe looking for excitement and a new life!"

Marta mumbled something under her breath and clicked on the menu tab "Contact." There were no phone numbers or addresses, just a form to fill out with a promise that someone would respond within forty-eight hours.

Josie went over to her desk and started her own computer. "I'll call DPS and see if we can work with their cybercrimes unit. Maybe they can track down the domain address to a city."

"There aren't enough typos or grammatical errors for me to think that was written by someone in Guatemala," Otto said. "It sounds like it was written by an English major."

Josie talked with one of the cybercrimes techs at the Computer Information Technology and Electronic Crimes Unit, referred to as CITEC. A technician named Josh pulled up the Web site. He offered to do some digging, and within thirty minutes he called back and said he had some "unofficial" information.

"Let's have it," Josie said.

"This won't be admissible in court. We need to go through proper channels," the tech said.

"Absolutely. Just get me started and then I'll file the paperwork."

"The domain is registered by a U.S.-owned Web hosting company. A John Davis registered the company four years ago as a private company. The name is not associated publicly with the Web site, and it's probably a fake name. However, file the paperwork to get the records for payment. If you find out how John Davis paid to register the domain name, you might find out who owns the site."

"I got it. I'll file with the judge."

Josie hung up the phone, summarized the call, and stared across the conference table at Otto and Marta.

"What the hell are we going to do?" she said.

"Take it to the prosecutor," Otto said.

"I think I owe the mayor a conversation about this first."

Otto frowned. "I don't think that's wise. He may be involved, for all we know."

"Come on, Otto. His wife is a political barracuda. She comes from money and power, and she's hungry for it. She wants her husband in the senate. But the mayor? I don't like the man, but I don't see him in this. Not at all."

"Okay. Let's just assume she does rake in two hundred thousand dollars a year, or even fifty thousand. You think she could be making that much money and he doesn't know about it? Even if she only did it once, she can't just hide that kind of cash." His tone was incredulous and he was looking at her with a smile, as if he couldn't believe her explanation.

"Of course she could hide that kind of cash! Spouses have bank accounts their partners don't know about. You aren't that naïve."

"You sound like you're taking up for him."

"Otto, he's my boss. It has nothing to do with taking up for him. I just think I owe him the professional courtesy of telling him what we're going to the prosecutor about. I'd do the same for you."

He laughed and looked at Marta, who shrugged in response, like she wasn't getting involved.

"What happens if you tell him and he does something stupid? What if he tells her and she takes off? We lose the person who's behind all of this."

"Come on. You know she's not a flight risk. She's too public, too proud. She'd fight to defend her name before she ever ran."

Otto finally threw his hands up to concede the fight. "I think you're making a mistake, but I've said my piece. You do what you have to do."

The meeting broke up and Josie filed the paperwork with the judge to subpoena the phone records and to get a warrant to access the Web site payment information for John Davis. When she was finally alone in the office that evening she pondered Otto's comments for some time, and tried to put herself in the mayor's position. As much as she disliked him, she thought he deserved to hear this from someone other than the Marfa public radio station.

When Josie arrived home that night it was almost eleven o'clock and Nick was lying on the couch watching a rerun of some show about living in the Alaskan outback. He sat up when she walked in and patted the seat next to him.

"You look whipped," he said.

"It was one hell of a day," she said.

"Want to talk about it?"

She thought for a moment. "I don't think so."

He nodded. "I figured as much. Why don't you go put on something comfortable. I have something to show you."

Josie kissed him on the cheek and got up, thinking how nice it was to come home to someone who understood she didn't want to talk through a nightmare most nights. Occasionally, talking helped. Other times, it made a bad day worse.

After she put on a pair of jeans and a T-shirt, she walked through the living room, then the kitchen, and finally found Nick bent over a dozen candles he was lighting on the back porch. She walked outside and he handed her a tumbler of bourbon.

"Woodford Reserve," he said.

"Wow. No Old Crow?"

"Only the best for you, baby."

They clinked glasses and she took several long drinks, enjoying the burn.

They sat on the porch swing and Josie swung her leg over his thigh.

"What's the occasion?" she asked.

"You are."

She smiled and realized it was probably the first time she'd smiled all day.

"Why am I an occasion?"

"You've had a tough few days. When I didn't hear anything from you today I figured things got crazy."

"Without going into the whole mess, I'll just tell you that the mayor's wife is who's behind the trafficking ring."

He leaned his head against the back of the swing. "Son of a bitch. The mayor?"

"He doesn't know yet. We just found this out."

"Think he's in on it?"

She shrugged off the question. "We'll know more tomorrow."

He nodded slowly. "So, speaking of tomorrow."

"Yeah?" She looked over at him. She could see his tentative grin in the candlelight. She wondered suddenly if there was more to the candles than her bad day.

"Your mom called me today."

"Called you?"

"When she didn't hear from you this evening, she called Lou and got my number."

Josie frowned. "Lou shouldn't have done that."

"Don't get mad at her. It was your mom she was talking to."

"What did she want?"

"I think she just wanted some reassurance that things were okay. I checked in with Lou and called her back. It was all good."

"Thanks for doing that," she said, feeling guilty that she'd not done it herself.

"She also mentioned that you were really busy. And that she was getting stir-crazy sitting at the motel."

"Ah. And she wants you to entertain her."

He shrugged. "I don't think entertain is quite it. But I told her I'd drive her over to Marfa tomorrow and we'd eat at the Food Shark for lunch. I'll show her some sights."

Josie found herself nodding, not sure what to say.

"You okay with that?"

"Sure. Yeah. Thanks for offering to do that."

"If something breaks and you have a minute to get away—"

Josie dipped her head and said, "Come on. In the middle of a murder investigation?"

He drained the rest of his bourbon and didn't say anything.

"I'm sorry. I'm not being very grateful. I do appreciate you offering to take her out. It's really nice of you."

"But?"

"I just never know what's going to come out of her mouth. And I won't be there to intervene or explain." She paused and finished her thought. "Or hear what kind of BS she's feeding you." She tipped her own glass back and let the burn slip down her throat.

"Josie. I've heard enough stories about your mom to take it all in stride." He stood from the swing and put a hand out for her, taking her glass and placing it on the table before turning back to her. "I love you. I want to make your life better, not more stressful. If you don't want me to take her, I'll make up an excuse."

She put her fingertips on his lips. "I want you to do what you planned. You're a good man, and I'm glad you're here with me. Right now I just want you to blow those candles out and take me to bed."

———•———

Josie started the morning at the office following up on phone calls and media requests for information regarding the murder and the displaced women. Otto had two domestic calls he had to respond to, and Marta wasn't scheduled in until three that afternoon.

At eleven o'clock, Josie received warrant approval from the judge and called a customer service specialist employed by the Web hosting company, Host Post & Go. Josie spoke with a woman who introduced herself as Linda Spellman. Josie briefly explained the purpose for the warrant.

"I specialize in liability and law enforcement issues," Linda said. "While we make it clear to our clients that their information is protected and secure, we also state clearly that we're bound by law enforcement and government regulations. And we state that illegal content will be removed immediately under the penalty of law."

"I appreciate your cooperation," Josie said.

"Absolutely. We don't want criminals on our books any more than you do. Let me put you on hold while I take a look at your paperwork."

Josie listened to recorded music for over ten minutes and was then greeted again by Linda.

"I've confirmed your warrant for information and have the requested documents ready to email at this time. I'll email as confidential documents, accessible with the encryption code I'll provide you at this time."

Josie wrapped up the conversation thoroughly impressed with the woman's professionalism, and a little surprised at how smooth the transaction had gone. Fortunately, Josie had found that criminals tended to believe the Internet was more anonymous than it actually was.

Thirty minutes later, Josie opened the encrypted email to reveal the payment history for the Internet Web site owned by John

Davis. Her pulse quickened as she reviewed the information. She called Otto.

"You have a minute?" she asked.

"I'm in my car, headed back to the department. What's up?"

Josie explained her conversation with Linda Spellman. "Get this. The initial payment to set up the Web site four years ago was charged to a Visa credit card owned by Caroline Moss."

"Why would she do that?" he said.

"That was four years ago. Maybe back then she was still trying to convince herself this was a humanitarian effort. The renewal payment a year later was an automatic withdraw from a bank account in Guatemala. That's probably when she got worried and decided to cover her tracks."

"Little late for that," he said. "Any idea who John Davis is?"

"The woman I spoke to said it was probably just a fake name to set up the Web site. She said the person registering the Web site, and the person paying for the account, don't have to be the same."

"Good enough. I'll see you in ten."

The new information sealed the case for Josie. It was no longer one kid's word against a well-respected woman. Josie forced herself to step away from her desk. She headed next door to the Artemis City Office to visit Mayor Moss. She was ready to talk to Holder, and contrary to Otto's beliefs she felt strongly that she owed Moss an explanation before going to the prosecutor about his wife. She would expect the same professional courtesy if the situation were reversed.

The mayor's secretary, Helen, was a stout woman in her fifties who guarded the mayor's office like a sentinel. She was pleasant until crossed, or more specifically until the mayor was crossed, whereby she defended him like an overprotective mother.

Josie opened the door and a bell announced her presence. Helen looked up from paperwork and smiled broadly.

"Chief Gray! It's a pleasure to see you."

Josie smiled, thinking that her next visit would most likely not be met with the same enthusiasm.

"What can I do for you?" Helen asked.

"I'd like to see Mayor Moss, if he has a minute." Josie hoped Helen would say, *No, sorry, he's out of town for the week.*

"Oh, I imagine I can hook you right up. One minute." Helen picked up her phone and spoke quietly into the receiver. She turned and faced Josie, smiling as if she had fantastic news. "Go right on in. He'll be happy to speak with you."

As Josie walked down the hallway, for the hundredth time she imagined how she would approach the subject. She had made love to Nick the night before, but her impending conversation with the mayor had nudged at her brain, interrupting the only joy she'd hoped to squeeze out of the day.

The mayor flung his reading glasses onto his desk as if she were interrupting an important task.

"Good morning," he said, frowning and gesturing to the pleather chair in front of his desk.

The dark paneling, large mahogany desk, and fake leather furniture gave the office the feel of a cheaply decorated men's club. Josie had the urge to open the curtains, which were always drawn, most likely because the wall faced the alley at the back of the office.

"Good morning, Mayor. Thanks for seeing me."

He faced her, clasping his hands on the desk in front of him. She focused her attention on his eyes, took a deep breath, and stepped into it.

"I have some disturbing news to bring to you."

"Well, you're a cop. Most of the news you bring me is disturbing. Bring it on."

"It's about the human trafficking case. We've identified the two men responsible for transporting five women from Guatemala to the U.S. as Josh Mooney and Ryan Needleman."

He put a hand to his ear as if he'd heard wrong. "Bill's boy?"

Josie nodded. "He's admitted it, and cooperated fully."

"His dad know yet?"

"He does. He's obviously upset, but he refused to pay for an attorney. Meanwhile, Ryan opened up and explained the entire operation to us."

"Son of a bitch. I've known that boy since he was a baby. We gave that kid a hundred dollars for graduation last year, and then he got thrown out of college for fighting before he even got through the first semester. I thought about asking for a refund." He leaned back in his chair and stared at Josie, clearly shocked at the news. "He's a little rough around the edges, but I never figured him for a bad kid."

"He was asked to work with Josh Mooney to drive five women from Guatemala to New Mexico, where the women would work for the hotel services industry. Most likely as maids."

"How the hell did Ryan get mixed up in a shitstorm like this? What'd Bob have to say about this? I bet he's ready to kick that boy's ass all the way to the river and back."

"That's actually why I'm here, Mayor," Josie said. She felt the acid bubbling up in her stomach and knew with sudden clarity that Otto had been right. The following information would never be viewed as professional courtesy.

"He didn't want to share the information, but Ryan finally said that it was Caroline who asked him to participate."

The mayor cocked his head. "What did you say?" His voice was low and quiet.

"He said that Caroline asked him to transport the women from Guatemala. She asked him to drive the van."

He tilted his head and smiled like he'd just heard an absurd joke. "This is bizarre, Josie. Even from you. It's just absurd."

"Ryan explained that Caroline was trying to help these women. He said she was helping them come to the U.S. so she could find them jobs and help them get citizenship."

Moss looked at Josie as if she'd lost her mind. "What the hell is wrong with you? This is my wife you're talking about! You just attended her charity dinner, and now you bring me this?"

Josie laid a paper that contained a screenshot of the Web site from Jobs Without Borders on his desk and pushed it toward him. "We've traced this Web site back to Caroline. We believe she is behind the trafficking organization. I wanted to tell you first before I go to the prosecutor with this. I didn't want you to hear it on the radio."

He stood suddenly, knocking his chair over behind him. "I don't give a good goddamn what you believe, Chief Gray. You are completely out of line!" He placed his fists on the desk and leaned forward toward Josie. "You're going to take the word of a kid who got thrown out of college this fall over the work of a woman who has shown herself to be a pillar of this community? Is that seriously what you're doing right now?"

Josie stood, intending to walk out. Talking the situation through was obviously not an option at this point.

"Give me your badge and your gun," he said. He spoke so quietly that she barely heard his words.

It was Josie's turn to look shocked. "Excuse me?"

He tapped his desk with his fingertip. "Right here. I want your badge, and I want your gun. You are officially on administrative leave until further notice."

"You're making a mistake," she said.

He threw his arm out and pointed toward the door. "I will have your job over this. Now get the hell out of my office!"

Josie glanced down, unclasped the badge that was pinned above the pocket of her uniform, and pitched it onto his desk. She pulled the gun from her holster, checked the safety, and placed it on his desk, averting her eyes from him. Without another word, she walked out of his office and past Helen, who was standing in the hallway with a hand over her mouth.

THIRTEEN

Lou started to speak and then stopped after seeing Josie's clenched jaw as she stepped into the PD. She walked into the office and found Otto typing on his computer. He turned when he heard her enter and sighed when he saw her expression.

"Damn it, Josie. You went to talk to him, didn't you?" He noticed the bare spot above her breast pocket and his eyebrows rose in shock. "Did he strip you of your badge?"

"I've been suspended until further notice."

"Damn it. I told you not to talk to him!"

"That's not helpful right now."

He stood and pointed to the conference table. "I'm sorry. Sit down."

Josie sat and Otto went to the back of the office and poured them both a mug of coffee.

"I'll go talk to him," he said, sliding the mug across the table to her.

"Why? So we can all be suspended together?" She sipped the coffee and considered him for a long time. "He's wrong, Otto. I know it. Caroline is guilty. I was trying to give him a heads-up so that he wasn't blindsided when this breaks open."

"Guilty people walk free every day. If we can't tie her to the crime that took place? You're screwed. I'm sorry, but it's a fact you need to face."

"She's the one who paid for the Web site! She founded the group that transported those five women to Artemis," she said. "One of the transporters not only fingered her, but is a close family friend."

"Big deal! Just because she paid a bill for a Web site doesn't mean that she knew it was to be used for human trafficking. Any defense attorney could prove that. And it doesn't mean Caroline killed that woman. It doesn't mean she had any knowledge of the rapes. Even if she paid Ryan to go pick those women up, unless there's physical proof, a check or paperwork, it's his word against hers. And once she gets ahold of him, you think he'll stick with the story he told us?" Otto made a face. "Not a chance. We got nothing, Josie."

Lou appeared in the door of the office. She rarely left the front office unattended; instead she would push the conference button and call upstairs if she needed someone. But here she was, standing at the door, obviously shaken.

"What happened over in the mayor's office?" Lou said.

"What do you mean?" Otto asked.

"I just got a news release emailed to me saying that Chief Gray has been suspended without pay until further notice for breach of contract. What's going on?"

Blood rushed to Josie's face.

"This just happened ten minutes ago!" Otto said.

Josie rose and moved to the back of the office. It would be all over Artemis in a matter of hours. Suspended. She heard Otto's words replay in her head. *We got nothing.*

Josie heard Otto sigh and a chair scoot across the floor behind her. "Have a seat," he told Lou.

Josie's chest tightened as she listened to Otto recount their conversation with Ryan Needleman, and Josie's decision to tell the mayor about his wife before going to the prosecutor.

Josie liked to think of herself as someone whose core values propelled all of the major decisions in her life. If people in the community wanted to believe whatever trash the mayor wanted to sling, then screw them all. But now, faced with the public humiliation of getting stripped of her badge, she realized she cared a great deal about what people thought. Without a doubt, even if she was completely exonerated, there would be those who would use the suspension to question her ability to lead. Her reputation would be forever tarnished over someone else's crime.

The blood inside her body seemed to be pooling in her legs, leaving her light-headed. Perspiration covered her forehead and she felt as if the room were closing in around her. She turned from the window and grabbed her car keys from her desk as she walked to the door.

"I'm going home," she said, and opened the door to leave.

"Josie. Come sit down so we can talk this through," Otto said. His tone of voice was calm and reasonable. "Breach of contract? How does that even apply to this situation? We'll call the county attorney and get some guidance. It's not as bad as it seems."

With her hand still on the door, she wasn't able to turn and face him. "I'm going home."

Nick parked his SUV in front of Manny's Motel and found Beverly Gray sitting on the wooden bench with her purse in her lap. She smiled and waved as Nick watched her approach, trying to see Josie in her mom. Where Josie was tall and agile, her mom was short and thin, with a careful way of walking, like she was prone to falling. Josie's expression was guarded, while her mom's face was a wide-open smile. She opened the door and climbed in, already chattering about her day, and Nick grinned, amazed at how different the two women were.

"Good gracious," she said, pointing at the onboard computer. "Looks like an airplane cockpit in here."

"Helps me track the bad guys."

She buckled her seat belt and turned to face him. "Where you taking me?" she asked.

"I thought we'd drive over to Marfa. I'll take you the back roads, if you want slow driving but amazing scenery, or we can take the faster route on the highway."

"Faster! I had enough scenery on the drive from Indiana to Texas to last me a lifetime. Get me some shopping!"

Nick laughed and drove away from the curb. Josie would have said back roads and avoided shopping at all cost. "You know, we're not known for shopping around here. We got the basics and that's about it."

"So what's the appeal?" she said. "I can't figure out how Josie ended up out here in the middle of nowhere."

Nick glanced at her and saw she was serious. Josie had lived in Artemis for more than ten years. He found it hard to believe that they'd never had that conversation.

"Most people either love the desert or they hate it. If you love it, once you settle here, it's hard to leave," he said.

"But why settle here in the first place? How the hell did she even find this town? It's just a speck on the map."

"That's the appeal. That's what Josie was looking for. She looked for law enforcement jobs out West. She told me it was the ghost towns at the end of the road that travels through Artemis that convinced her to move. She wanted to be away from people."

"Well, that's what she got."

Nick pulled onto River Road and waved his hand out in front of him. "See all that wide-open desert land? You can breathe here without other people getting into your space."

"There's no trees. And the ones you have look like dwarfs."

He grinned and pointed to a grove of cottonwood trees along the Rio Grande. "There's trees. But there's enough space between them so that you can see for miles on end. It opens your mind up."

"I don't know. I just don't get it," she said. "When she left, I knew she hated me. But I figured, lots of young people hate their parents. Right? It's part of growing up. But I never figured it'd last this long."

Nick held himself back from reassuring her. He was inclined to say that Josie didn't hate her, but he didn't really know what Josie felt.

"She's pretty independent," Nick said, hoping to move to safer territory.

Beverly let the conversation go and they spent the rest of the afternoon shopping and talking about whatever random topics seemed to pop up. At lunchtime, Nick took her to his favorite lunchtime hangout in Marfa, the Food Shark. She'd never heard of falafel, so he ordered them each a different variation and they ate at picnic tables under a giant awning. Nick got a kick out of her candor, and the idea that no question was off-limits, a trait he figured drove Josie crazy.

On the way back to Artemis, she peppered him with questions about West Texas and adapting to the desert environment. It became clear to Nick that she was seriously considering moving to Artemis. When he pulled in front of the motel to drop her off she said, "You think Josie could get used to me living here?"

He grinned at the question, but saw the worry lines on Beverly's forehead.

"I've been with Josie long enough to know I'd better not answer for her. That's a question you'll have to ask her yourself."

Josie parked her jeep in front of her house and saw Chester loping down the lane from Dell's house, his ears flying out behind him like a little girl's pigtails. He tumbled into her, whining and wagging his tail like he'd not seen her in weeks. He followed her inside the house and she went to the pantry to get his rawhide chew, even though it was only lunch and not yet time for a chew. Chester settled onto his rug in the living room, and she slipped it between his paws.

Back in the kitchen pantry, she took off her gun belt and hung it on its designated hook, staring at the hole where her gun should have been holstered. She shut the door and wandered through the house doing all the things she did every day when she came home, but she was operating on autopilot.

In the bathroom, she stood in front of the mirror and ran her fingertip over the tiny holes where her badge had pierced her uniform that morning. *Who am I if I'm not a cop?* she wondered. Otto's words played through her mind again and again. *We got nothing.* She realized this went beyond a stupid move on her part, and could end with her losing her job. It was no secret the mayor didn't think a female should hold the job of chief, and he seemed to especially dislike Josie.

Losing the one constant in her life, the part that gave her a sense of purpose, was unthinkable. Gazing in the mirror, she watched her fingers unbutton the uniform shirt and then she dropped it on the floor. She looked at her weary eyes in the mirror and tried to identify some emotion inside of her that she could latch on to. All she felt was numb. *We got nothing.*

She finally picked up the shirt and hung it in her bedroom closet. She put on shorts and a T-shirt and a pair of hiking boots. Staying inside wasn't an option. She'd lose her mind staring at the walls, waiting for Nick to come home from his lunch date with her mother.

———

Chester followed Josie out the front door and out of habit headed back toward the pasture and Dell's house beyond. She smiled when he realized she wasn't following him, and he circled back to see what she was doing out by the road.

"Let's take another route today," she said, patting his back as they took off walking along the side of the road.

Josie had removed the yellow crime scene tape in the pasture where they had found the murdered woman so that it wouldn't draw the attention of gawkers looking for a cheap thrill. But she had left the foot-high wooden stakes that had held the tape as a visual for herself until the case was solved. She stopped on the gravel road, in a direct line of sight with the stakes.

Standing on the side of the road now, facing the pasture, she estimated her house was about a quarter of a mile to the east of where she was standing. Dell's house was straight back down the lane from her house, about a half mile northeast. Josie scanned the path that the women probably took from the toolshed, behind the house, across the lane leading to Dell's cabin, and into the open pasture.

From the bits and pieces Josie and Marta had collected from Isabella about the night Renata was killed, it sounded as if the women had been hiding in the toolshed. They had been watching through a knothole in the wall as a car drove slowly down the gravel lane, searching for them. Isabella had told Marta that they had heard the car and ran for the pasture, probably thinking they would be safer in case someone came searching for them.

She imagined them running, but realized it would have been far from a run, in the dark. Clumps of prickly pear cactus and

Spanish daggers with knife-sharp edges dotted the ground and would have stopped them immediately, causing incredible pain, if they'd run into one. The women would have had no choice but to cross the pasture carefully.

Josie and Nick had found Renata's body lying prone, with her head facing north toward Dell's house, instead of the westward direction they had been running. Josie imagined the car might have stopped where she was now standing on the side of the road, next to the pasture. Someone could have jumped out of the car and run into the pasture, causing the women to veer toward Dell's house, rather than running parallel to the road.

Josie continued walking alongside the road, trying to imagine various scenarios with the two women and the man or men chasing them. About a mile from home, she turned and walked the same route back again, keeping her mind focused on the case while trying to avoid the toxic thoughts about her current suspension. That wound was too raw to touch just yet.

Chester had been walking just in front of her, sniffing along the road, when he paused and lifted his head toward the pasture as if he'd seen something in the distance. Josie stood still, scanning the pasture from the road back to Dell's cabin, and beyond to the mountain range, but she saw no movement. She walked backward about a dozen steps, and then moved forward again when a glint of silver caught her eye. She took her cell phone out, snapped a quick shot, and took off toward the shiny object, which appeared to be about two hundred feet away from the road.

Ten feet from the object, she stopped, shocked at her discovery.

FOURTEEN

Josie knew better than to process the scene. She called Chester away from the area and got Otto on the phone.

"I found the gun," she said.

"What gun?" he said.

"I'm in the pasture beside my house, so most likely it's the gun used to kill Renata."

"I'm on my way," he said. "Don't touch anything until I get there."

Josie sighed into the phone, annoyed at the remark.

"Sorry. Give me ten minutes."

Josie walked slow concentric circles around the gun, starting at ten feet and moving out to about fifty, checking for anything else that might have been missed. Ten minutes later, Otto met her in the pasture. She described her theory that the women were hiding in the shed when the car stopped in front of Josie's house and someone got out to search for them.

"I think the women took off running and the person either got back into the car and drove down the road farther to catch up with them, or what makes more sense is a second person in the car."

He pointed across the pasture to the toolshed behind Josie's house. "So the driver stops the car and a passenger gets out. The person is walking around, searching for the women. Maybe the women see a flashlight getting closer to the toolshed, and they panic. They leave the toolshed and take off running behind your house toward the pasture. The driver moves down the road to directly where we're standing in the pasture and stops. Maybe even turns the car to point the headlights into the pasture here, trying to illuminate the women."

"Exactly. So they stop running parallel to the road, and they take off toward Dell's place," she said.

"And Renata is shot in the back," Otto said.

"Isabella hears the gunshot and runs out of the beam of the headlights and escapes into the night." Josie scanned the pasture, pointing to the stakes where the dead body was. "Then the shooter freaks out and wants to get rid of the gun immediately. He flings it as far as he can and it lands here."

"Pretty stupid move," he said.

"Look at our suspects. Assuming we have two people, we're looking at Josh and Ryan. One's basically a kid, and the other an idiot."

Otto cocked his head. "Ryan said he only went one time. Maybe he was telling the truth. It could have been Josh and Macey."

Josie nodded. "I like it. Macey's the driver. I can see Josh flinging the gun in a panic."

"What did Isabella say when Marta asked her about what happened out here?" he said.

"She'd just opened up at the trauma center. She hadn't provided a lot of details. Marta planned on talking to her again. And then Josh took off with her."

"So we need to get back with Isabella again."

"Assuming she'll talk with us. We didn't exactly provide the security that we told her she'd get," she said.

For a few more minutes, they threw around ideas about other ways the shooting could have gone down, but Josh and Ryan, or Josh and Macey, made the most sense.

Josie walked Otto back out to the road where his jeep was parked. He got inside and talked to her through the open window.

"What are you going to do?" he asked.

"Right now I'm going to hope like hell you and Marta can connect those two morons to Caroline Moss and get me out of this mess."

He offered a slight smile. "I'd like to go talk to the mayor. I think I can get him to reconsider."

"I don't want you to do that. I'll work from behind the scenes for a day or so and see what shakes out. For now, get the prints from the gun and the ballistics and keep me posted."

"You got it, Chief." He waved good-bye and took off.

———————

Josie retrieved a pair of creek shoes from the back of her jeep and whistled for Chester, who ambled off the porch where he'd been napping away the hottest part of the day. He followed her across the road and they walked on public land for a quarter mile and then down to the Rio Grande, where she took off her boots and slipped on the mesh creek shoes to protect her feet. She kept her pistol in her shorts pocket. She'd given her duty gun to Moss, but her backup pistol was her own property.

She waded into the river with Chester, who was happy to cool his paws and belly. Josie walked along the rocky side of the river in thigh-high water scouting for signs of illegal crossing, keeping Nick's admonition to be watchful in her mind. She thought about the kayaks that she and Nick had found a few miles upriver. The Mexicans had clearly been using them to cross into Texas. She and Nick had found trash and pop cans along the bank on the U.S. side, and followed foot tracks up to the paved road. That had been several months ago. Since then, Josie had kept a closer eye on the area. The Medrano Cartel had a vast network of narcos who would stop at nothing in their efforts to push their cocaine, heroin, pot, and meth northward.

Her phone buzzed in her pocket with a text from Nick saying he was on his way home from town and did she need anything. She responded, *Nothing but you*, and meant it more than he could have known.

When she and Chester reached the driveway, Nick was already there and pulled her in for a hug and kissed the top of her head. She held on too long, and he finally pulled his head back to get a look at her. His expression changed to worry when he saw the tears in her eyes.

"What's wrong?"

"It was just a bad day." She sniffed, embarrassed at her reaction.

"Why are you home so early?"

She took in a chest full of air and blew it out slowly, forcing herself to stop the emotion. Avoiding eye contact, she said, "Mayor Moss took my gun and badge."

He pulled back from her and placed his hands on her arms. "What happened?"

She closed her eyes for a moment, feeling sick with the memory of the conversation. "I was ready to go to the prosecutor over Caroline. She's behind the transportation ring that funneled through Artemis. Or she's at least a major player. I went to Moss to warn him."

"Why would you go to him about that?" He gave her a look like she'd lost her mind.

"Would you not expect the same treatment? When you're in

law enforcement, you at least have the decency to give your fellow officers a heads-up before you destroy their world. You know how it is for a cop, or a lawyer, or anyone in the public eye. Imagine serving as mayor of the city and finding out after the fact that the local police were going after your wife. People expect anyone in the public eye to be above reproach."

"He should be above reproach in his position!"

"It was his wife. Imagine hearing about her arrest from the radio station." Josie sighed. "Look. I don't know why I'm sticking up for the bastard. I'm just trying to explain why I went to him in the first place. Obviously it was a horrible mistake. But I thought I was doing the right thing."

He put an arm around her shoulder and they headed toward the house. "I'm sorry. I'm sorry you got sacked for trying to be a decent person."

They sat down on the couch and she turned so she could see him better. She rested her hand on his thigh, glad for his physical presence, and realized suddenly how much she was starting to need him. The thought worried her as much as it made her happy.

"How was my mother?" she asked.

He grinned. "Where do I begin?"

She leaned her head back against the couch and groaned.

"Not in a bad way. She was fine." He laughed at her expression. "She didn't say anything that would have embarrassed you."

"Come on, Nick. Now I know you're lying to me. My mother doesn't ever have a conversation without embarrassing me on some level. And you spent all morning with her."

He laughed again and looked guilty for enjoying her discomfort. "Look. She was your mom. She spent a lot of time trying to figure out your motivation for coming here. To West Texas and Artemis specifically. I don't think she understands that some people find the desert and the isolation beautiful. It didn't ring true to her."

"And did she talk about her motivation for being here?"

He pursed his lips and nodded slowly as if he had an answer that he would rather not share.

"Well?" she said.

"I think she wants to move here. I think she wants to have some sort of relationship with you." Nick put his hand over the top of hers and squeezed it. "And just to be clear. I gave nothing away. At one point she made an offhand remark about you hating her, and that's why you moved away. I didn't correct her. I let it go."

"I don't hate her. I feel lousy that I gave you the impression that I might. I just can't say that I suddenly want to work on a relationship. I feel horrible about that. I have a lot of guilt over it but I have reasons that I don't want to spend a lot of time with her."

"You moved two thousand miles away from home. That says something."

"And now she wants to be neighbors."

FIFTEEN

Too much was riding on the ballistics evidence to chance anything but a personal delivery. Otto called the state police crime scene lab in Springville to make sure Ernie Mays was working. He wanted to place the gun Josie had found, as well as the bullet from Renata's body, in Ernie's hands and beg for quick results if necessary.

Otto found Ernie bent over a microscope. He leaned back a few inches when Otto entered and called hello, but it took Ernie a while to stretch his six-foot body out to its full length. He reached around to rub his lower back and smiled when he realized it was Otto. "Just turned seventy-one this month. And all I'm good for is bending over this blasted desk of mine looking at small stuff."

"You could retire and fix watches."

"Better yet, I could retire and do nothing but watch bad TV." He grinned and winked. "Now. What rates high enough for you to drive all the way here from the hinterlands just to see me?"

"How backlogged are you?"

Ernie snorted. "Weeks. Months."

"Even for murder cases?"

"That's what I'm referring to."

"This case involves a cop, who's investigating a mayor's wife, who may be peripherally involved in a murder."

Ernie raised his eyebrows.

"The cop is now suspended by the mayor."

"Let me guess. The cop's a friend. So you're here asking favors."

"That's about it."

Ernie sighed heavily. "Us old-timers have to stick together. What do you need?"

"A few things. First, latent prints and DNA from the gun." He held up a plastic bag with the pistol. "I'm after one clear chain of evidence from the scene of the crime to your lab. The police officer in question never touched any of this, so we're looking at good evidence. I don't want any reason for someone to cry foul later."

Ernie waved it off. "No problem. I understand. What else?"

Otto held up another plastic bag, this one holding a bullet and casing. "I need to know if the bullet found inside the woman's body, and the casing found at the crime scene, match the gun found at the crime scene."

"All right. Unless I run into problems, I'll get you an answer by tomorrow."

Otto smiled and then laughed, feeling a huge sense of relief. He'd expected at least a two-week turnaround. "Next time I make it up this way, I'll buy you a steak dinner."

Ernie patted Otto on the back and told him there might not be a next time, that retirement was indeed looming. But Ernie had been saying that for a decade, and still kept showing up at the microscope.

As Otto drove back to Artemis he saw that it was just after five o'clock and decided he had one more stop for the day: Selena Rocha.

He knew Josie liked her and valued her input, and Otto thought she might be able to offer some additional piece of information. Through the years, he had discovered that hairdressers, garbage collectors, and mail carriers were some of the best sources for information in a small town.

At quarter after five Selena turned the dead bolt on the salon door and opened it for Otto to enter. When he introduced himself she smiled pleasantly and said that, yes, she knew him and she hoped everything was okay.

She closed the door and turned back to him. "Would you like coffee or tea?"

"No, no," he said, feeling nervous talking to this woman with long legs and big brown eyes and a bright white smile. For a brief moment he couldn't remember why he had thought it important to visit her.

They sat in the waiting room and Otto cleared his throat, organizing his thoughts.

"Chief Gray came by and talked to you a few days ago about the woman who was murdered."

"Yes."

"She suggested that you have a good feel for what's going on in town. And that you have some knowledge of the trafficking industry." He paused and she frowned, but nodded once to acknowledge the statement.

"Things have gotten complicated since she last spoke with you. I'd like to talk with you in confidence about the case. Can you give me your word that you won't talk about the case with anyone?"

Her expression altered somewhat, her eyes focused and brightened. She was getting interested now. "You have my word."

"Good," he said, settling into the conversation. "Did you hear today that Chief Gray has been suspended due to breach of contract?"

"We heard it on the radio this afternoon. I couldn't believe it."

"You won't share this information with your coworkers?" Otto asked. If she did, it wouldn't put the case in jeopardy, but he preferred to keep the information quiet as long as possible.

"Just because I hear gossip doesn't mean I spread it," she said.

"Good enough. Chief Gray's suspension is tied to the trafficking case. There are some things that make us believe Caroline Moss may be connected to a trafficking ring. That she may have set up the transport of the women who came here from Guatemala."

She shook her head slowly and murmured, "Unbelievable. The Citizen of the Year."

"Remember. She's not been arrested. This is conjecture."

"I know, I know. You made that clear." Selena squinted at Otto as if she were putting the pieces together. "I also heard they picked up Josh Mooney for driving the van. The word around here is that Josh kidnapped the woman at the trauma center, but he was arrested before he could get her delivered."

Otto put a hand in the air and wavered it. "Something like that."

"Now you think the mayor's wife got Josh to drive the women from Guatemala up north?" Her eyes widened and she placed a hand across her heart. "It was that bastard mayor who suspended Josie, wasn't it?"

Otto pursed his lips and decided to avoid that part of the conversation as best he could. "Something like that. But here's my question for you. We suspect Caroline's involvement, but we have little to go on. I'm wondering if you've heard anything about her being involved in any kind of transporting of illegal immigrants."

She stretched her legs out in front of her and slumped back into her chair. "No, just the opposite. I thought she helped people in trouble, especially women. Did you talk to the women who Josh was transporting?"

Otto explained that the police had spoken with Isabella and the other three women, but that they'd learned little new information.

Selena stood. "I'll help you. Chief Gray stood by me when people were questioning my business. She didn't allow a bunch of gossips to ruin me. So I'll stand by her now."

Otto stood too, having no idea where this woman thought they were headed. "How do you propose to help?"

"Who do you think those women want to talk to right now? The police?" She made a face. "They don't trust you any more than they trust the men who brought them here. They want you to save them, but they don't trust that you will."

Otto started to speak and she stopped him with a hand in the air.

"Don't get defensive. I know what these women are thinking. It's exactly the way I felt." She considered him for a moment. "It's because there's this mixed message we get. Sometimes the media loves the immigrants and wants to do everything they can to help people like those women. Other times the media says, 'Send them all home. We don't want them!'"

Otto crossed his arms and tried not to look skeptical.

"Go home tonight and turn on your TV. Watch one channel and you'll hear about the illegals ruining the country. Taking all the jobs, committing crimes, running the country broke, turning to terrorism. Watch another channel and the immigrants are hard-working people wanting better for their families. Some towns help us settle and find work. Other towns throw us in jail the first chance they get. It's no wonder we don't trust anyone!"

He hadn't considered this angle, but she had a point.

"Then this woman, Isabella, comes to the U.S. to find work and is raped and humiliated and the police say they'll help her find safety. And *then* she's kidnapped by the man who attacked her and maybe even murdered her friend. She doesn't want to talk to you."

Otto studied her for a moment. "You said she was raped. That's not public knowledge."

"It is now. Macey spread it all over town that the police were accusing her brother of rape. How he was getting ripped off." She made a dismissive noise and rolled her eyes.

Otto sighed. "Okay. How is it you think you can help?"

"I'm from Venezuela. And I know they're from Guatemala, but I know what these women have gone through to get here. I can talk to them as someone who made it. I can help them understand that you don't want to send them to jail. You want to help."

"We need to find out what happened the night Renata was shot. I need Isabella to talk about that night. What she heard, and what she saw."

She nodded.

"The other three women too. They're all at the trauma center under observation. You'll be able to talk with them all?"

She nodded again.

"And we need to find out who's behind this ring."

"I'll get my purse and lock up."

Otto walked outside and raised his arms slightly to allow a breeze under his armpits. He wondered how it was that a man of his age could still be nervous around a well-put-together woman less than half his age. It was an embarrassment. He got in the jeep and blasted the AC, pointing the air vents toward his sweaty forehead. Even if a genie in a bottle granted him one guilt-free night with that woman, a night Delores would never know about, he'd turn the genie down. He had no interest in that young hairdresser woman, so why the fluster? He thought of Delores in her soft cotton dresses and house slippers, taking apple chunks out to the goats in the field for a snack, saving stray cats, and making homemade dumplings to die for, and he was overcome with love for his wife of forty years. He called Delores.

"Delores?"

"Yes, Otto. Who did you expect to answer the phone?"

He smiled. "I'll be a bit late. I've got to run over to the trauma center."

"Roast and potatoes are in the oven. They'll wait till you get home."

"I love you."

The line was silent for a moment and he could imagine her looking shocked, and then smiling, her cheeks blushing. "Well, I love you too," she said.

———

Selena climbed into the jeep and placed a hand on his forearm.

"Before we go. Can we just agree that you won't talk about this to people?"

"What do you mean?" he asked.

"I've had to fight to get people to take me seriously as a hairdresser. As someone who can successfully run her own business." She scowled at Otto when he continued looking confused. "I'm more than just a skirt and a pair of legs. I don't need the massage parlor rumors started up again."

"Ah," he said. "Understood."

He pulled the jeep away from the curb and started across town. When she remained quiet he glanced her way, noticing her erect posture and the worry lines stretching across her forehead. "I appreciate you doing this. I'm sure it takes you to a place you'd just as soon forget."

Selena shrugged. "I grew up knowing there were things I had to do for my family. Even as a kid I knew my looks were part of who I was. They would take me places other people couldn't go. Some people have brains. Some people have looks. You use what you have."

Otto pulled into the trauma center parking lot and thought

about his own daughter, Mina, married with kids. He'd not raised her to value looks over brains. But he wondered if this young woman didn't have a point. You took your gifts, whatever they were, and you used them. He turned off the engine, thinking about Josie and her take on this conversation. Had she been here, he was fairly certain she'd be lecturing him about some part of his thinking. He smiled at the mental image of her scowling face and realized how much he appreciated her perspective. He hoped like hell he could get her out of her current predicament.

They walked through the sliding glass doors of the trauma center and Otto turned to Selena, worrying suddenly that the plan was too off-the-cuff. "Would you like to go over questions? Talk about the information we're looking for?"

"No. I don't want to sound like a cop. I want them to know I'm here to help them."

"Right," he said, nodding, hoping it would work.

Otto asked the receptionist if Vie Blessings was available. Ten minutes later she bustled into the lobby wearing her bright purple scrubs and pink glasses. She extended her hand to Otto, and he introduced her to Selena.

Vie pointed to her own spiked hair and smiled. "I know Selena well. She keeps me looking good."

"Nice to see you," Selena said.

"We're here to check on the young women from Guatemala," he said.

"Physically, they're okay. Dehydrated, mostly, but nothing serious. Mentally, I can't begin to think how horrible this has been for them."

"I'm trying to balance their need to recuperate with our need to catch the bastards who are behind this."

Vie nodded. "Absolutely. I understand."

"Selena has offered to talk with the women, to get a different perspective. Can you allow that at this point?"

"I think that would be fine. The doctor from Odessa can't be here until tomorrow. It may do them all some good to talk about their situation." Vie narrowed her eyes at Otto. "The women are two to a room. I'm not sure how you want to meet with them."

"Do you have a lounge or empty staff room that they could meet in all together?"

She looked uncertain. "We don't usually allow patients into the lounge, but I can just let the staff know it's off-limits for an hour. Do you think that would be enough time?"

Otto nodded. "That would be much appreciated."

———

Fifteen minutes later, Selena found herself entering a nurses' lounge where four women in hospital gowns sat around a table looking dazed. Vie had entered first and introduced Selena in English, but two of the women clearly couldn't understand her.

Selena sat down at the table and took a long calming breath. The expressions on their faces took her back several years, and she realized the officer had been right. She did not want to relive the feelings she'd put behind her, but as she looked into the terrified eyes of the four women staring back at her, the fear grabbed hold and closed her throat so that she could barely speak. She felt a hand on her shoulder and turned to see Vie smiling kindly at her.

Selena cleared her throat and spoke in Spanish. "I'm so sorry for what's happened to you, to all of you. I'm here to try and explain things. So you know what's happening. So you won't be so frightened." She stopped, suddenly aware she had no idea what was going to happen to them. No one had any idea what was going to happen to them. They were one more casualty in a world where monsters preyed on the desperate.

They stared at her, probably too tired to hope she could really help, but also too desperate to turn away.

"I'm from Venezuela," Selena said. "I came here like you did. I paid my way. People lied to me. Stole my money and my dreams. Men treated me like an animal. My life was gone." One of the women shifted in her seat and looked away as if she didn't want to confront the subject matter, but Selena continued. "I learned that when people said they wanted to help me, it was usually a lie. The police. Other girls. People who said they wanted to find me a job and place to live and food to eat? They took advantage of me. Made me do things that made me ashamed to even be alive."

A woman whose long black hair was in a loose braid down her back swiped away tears.

Selena leaned into the table. "But I want you to know that I made it. I'm okay now. There are people who are good, who want to help you. The man who drove you was a devil who should burn in hell. But the people here?" She gestured toward the door. "The nurses and doctors and the police? They aren't bad. They want to help."

The woman with the braid sniffed, blinked away her tears, and sat up straighter. Selena recognized her attempt to put on a strong front when everything around her was crumbling. She herself had been there too many times to count.

The woman said in Spanish, "The police told me they were there to help. They gave me a clean bed and room to stay in. And that monster came and took me. He took all of us. How do we know he won't be back?"

Selena recognized the woman speaking must be Isabella.

"Because he's in jail. When the police stopped the van, they took him and locked him away. It's partly why I'm here." She paused and looked directly at Isabella, who stared back, her eyes filled with worry.

"How do we know he'll stay there?"

"If you can tell me what happened, we can make sure all of the people who hurt you go to jail and stay there. But we need your help."

One of the women sitting at the end of the table hugged her arms around her chest and said, "What's going to happen to us?"

Selena sighed. "I don't know. I wish I could say, but I won't lie to you. I do know that you need to tell someone what happened. Someone needs to stop the people who put you through this." She paused. "And you need to put the people who shot Renata in jail."

Selena watched Isabella turn her head away as if she'd been slapped. She closed her eyes and put a hand to her mouth.

"Will you tell me what happened?" Selena said, lowering her voice to barely above a whisper, wishing she didn't have to drag the woman through the terrifying memory.

Isabella shook her head no.

"Do you know who killed her?"

She continued to shake her head no.

"Was it Josh?"

She began to cry, her body shaking. One of the other women wrapped her arm around Isabella's back.

Selena stood and walked over to the sink and ran cold water. She found a plastic cup in a cabinet, filled it with water, and handed it to Isabella. She drank the water and eventually settled down again.

Selena sat down next to one of the women who'd remained quiet. Selena asked her name.

"Maria." Her eyes were bright and clear.

Selena said, "I promise I'll do whatever I can for all of you. But I want someone to pay for what happened."

Maria shook her head, looking intently at Selena.

"People think there's a woman who's behind getting you here. Did you ever hear about a woman working with Josh and Ryan?"

Maria nodded, her eyes widening in recognition, as if someone had finally understood her.

"Did you ever hear her name?"

She finally began to open up. "No. They never called her anything but boss, or boss lady."

———————

Selena spent another half hour with the women, but they wouldn't talk about the trip any longer. They were more interested in Selena and her life in Texas. She could see that her story at least provided some hope. But she knew there were most likely years of struggle ahead before any of them found a life anywhere near what they had imagined when they left Guatemala behind.

———————

An overnight surveillance detail took Nick back to Mexico after dinner, and left Josie sitting on the back porch watching a lonely sundown, sipping a juice glass filled with bourbon, trying not to imagine the next day, trying not to wander around her house considering the odds she was going to get fired. She watched Chester nose around a mesquite bush, most likely on the scent of a jackrabbit. Her phone buzzed and she pulled it out of her back pocket and saw Otto's name.

"What's up?" she asked.

"Are you sitting?"

"Yep. Good or bad?"

"I'm not sure. I took the gun, bullet, and casing up to Ernie at the state police lab and called in a favor. He agreed to run ballistics and get me something, hopefully by tomorrow. I also asked him to check for latent prints."

"Yeah?"

"He just called. He's not started on the ballistics, but he ran the fingerprints and got an exact match in AFIS."

"Yeah?"

"Isabella Dagati."

Josie drew in a sharp breath. The possibility of her being the killer was so remote it hadn't even registered. She may have been technically a suspect due to her proximity to the body, but she'd never been seriously considered.

"What the hell?"

"That's about what I said. I'd even forgotten Marta had printed her at the hospital. Ernie said there's no doubt on the print. He hopes to run the bullet and gun tonight so we'll have something more conclusive tomorrow."

"That doesn't make any sense," Josie said. "Why would Isabella shoot her?"

"You want to bring her in tonight or wait until we get ballistics in the morning?"

She paused. "It's your case."

"Come on."

"If this wasn't such a screwed-up mess with Caroline and the mayor I'd say get her tonight. But I think we get it all together first and go to Holder with everything."

"Good enough," he said. "I coordinated with the sheriff. We still have an officer posted outside the women's rooms twenty-four/ seven. Phillips is there tonight. He has strict orders not to let Isabella leave. I made contact with Homeland Security, but with all the red tape I don't know what kind of time frame we're looking at to get the other women sent home. I'm hoping they can continue where they are for now."

"Any new information about Caroline from the women?"

"Selena Rocha talked to them. She asked if they knew anything about a female running things. The women agreed that Josh and Ryan talked about a woman they called boss lady, but they never mentioned her name. That's as much as we got about that. Selena also asked Isabella if she could tell her who killed Renata and she broke down. Refused to talk."

"Damn, Otto. You realize we're probably going to lose this case before we get it all pulled together?"

Otto said nothing, but she knew he understood.

"We have crimes crossing state and national lines. FBI and Homeland Security will be all over this before we're through," she said.

"Then we better work like hell to figure something out before we lose control."

Josie heard a car coming down her road and walked around to the front of her house, where she saw Smokey Blessings pulling up her driveway. She hung up with Otto and waved as Smokey got out of his truck wearing a Stetson, cowboy boots, and a western shirt. Smokey was married to Vie Blessings, his polar opposite in life. For all the vibrancy she displayed, Smokey showed none of it. The cowboy hat was as splashy as he got, and his demeanor was as low-key as his clothes.

He walked up to Josie to shake her hand and she noticed the worry lines across his forehead. "What the hell's going on?" He had a slow drawl to his words, which somehow intensified their effect.

Josie didn't have to ask what he meant. As the city council president, he was elected to work with the mayor to supervise the chief of police. Josie knew that, without the support the council had given her, the mayor would have fired her years ago.

"There's not much I can tell you," she said.

"You better tell me something. There's a group carrying signs outside of the courthouse about police brutality, and another group across the street on the corner with posters, chanting, 'Save our Chief.'"

She laughed in spite of the subject matter. "Where'd the police brutality come from?"

Smokey looked frustrated. "Hell if I know! The mayor refuses to talk about it. We've called an emergency council meeting and demanded answers but he's stalling. I want you to tell me what the breach of contract is over."

"I can't tell you. It concerns an ongoing investigation."

"I don't need to know the particulars of the case. I need to know what you did to be considered in breach of contract."

"I can't tell you that. You can talk to Otto about the case. He's the investigator and knows the particulars. It'll be up to him if he wants to share details." Josie almost smiled at the irony. She shouldn't have shared details with the mayor, who was now out to fire her, but she was refraining from telling the person who was most able to help her.

He rubbed his hand across the back of his neck and tilted his head from side to side as if trying to release tension.

"I'm here to help," he said.

"I know you are. And you have no idea how much I appreciate it. But I'm not giving the mayor any fuel to burn my ass. Someone else can, but not me. As much as I despise that man, I love my job more. And I want it back."

SIXTEEN

Chester ran to Dell's house several times a day, visiting him anytime Josie left home, in constant need of companionship. Josie made the walk to Dell's house when she needed to hear a sane voice.

She found Dell in the tack room of his barn, bent over his workbench, tooling a design into the side of a saddle. He wore a pair of ancient blue jeans and a navy T-shirt that was so threadbare his skin was visible through the cotton around the shoulders. This was a man who Josie suspected had several hundred thousand dollars squirreled away, most likely in coffee cans buried behind his house, but she knew in Dell's mind a new T-shirt was an unnecessary extravagance.

He looked up when Chester ambled in, and smiled when he saw Josie.

"How's tricks?" he said, and pitched his leather punch onto the workbench.

"You haven't heard?"

He pointed at the radio on a shelf above him, his only source of daily news. "Got tired of the drama. Gave it up for a day or two. What's happened?"

"I got suspended this morning. The mayor took my badge and gun."

He jerked his head back. "What?"

"I accused his wife of something. And he views that as breach of contract."

"How can he get away with that kind of crap? Why do people keep voting that ass into office?"

Josie shook her head slowly. "He's all we've got. No one runs against him."

Dell seemed to have caught what she had said. "What'd his wife do? I thought she was an uppity-up. A big senator's daughter, helper to the poor. All that nonsense."

"She may be an uppity-up, but I'm not so sure about a helper to the poor."

Dell motioned out into the walkway between the horse stalls. Josie sat on a bale of straw while he leaned against one of the stalls with an angry expression on his face. "What did she do?"

Josie didn't hesitate to tell Dell. Confidentiality was critical, but so was sanity, and Dell had been a trustworthy confidant for years.

She described how Josh Mooney and Ryan Needleman had transported five women up from Central America based on the orders of Caroline Moss. She also described how a haul of five women could net Caroline fifty thousand dollars' profit if all went well.

"What are you going to do about it?" he asked.

"That's why I'm here."

He grinned. "I'm ready."

"You don't even know what I'm going to say."

"I know enough. Let's go kick some ass."

She laughed at the wicked look in his eyes. "It's a good thing I'm a cop and not a criminal."

"What do you have in mind?"

"I need to get some legwork done, then I'll fill you in. We'll leave first thing in the morning if things come together."

"I thought you were suspended from the case."

"We'll leave quietly."

It was almost nine o'clock when Josie and Chester walked back down the lane from Dell's place. The temperature had dropped into the lower seventies and Chester was loving the cool weather, tracking scents from bush to bush, zigzagging through the pasture in bloodhound nirvana.

Josie pulled out her cell phone and dialed Sheriff Roy Martinez's number.

"You hanging in there?" he asked.

"I've seen better days," she said. "Sorry to call you so late at home."

"Not a problem, you know that."

"Thanks, Roy."

"Anything you need, you name it."

"It's sort of a big one."

"Bring it on."

"I need to talk to Josh Mooney."

He laughed. "That's a big one. The mayor called me this afternoon to make it clear you were off-limits at the jail."

"I wouldn't ask if I wasn't sure Caroline was all over this. I need to put that woman out of business."

"I'm thinking we never had this conversation."

Josie said nothing, hoping the silence on the other end of the phone was a good sign.

"Meet me at the prisoner entrance to the jail in twenty minutes. I'll see what I can do."

Josie drove her S-10 pickup truck and parked in the back lot, which at nine o'clock was empty aside from two pool cars and the sheriff's SUV. Roy waved to her and she entered, feeling uneasy about the situation she was putting Roy in.

"I appreciate this," she said.

He patted her on the back and pointed to a small unused office space that connected to the kitchen, deserted at that time of night.

"I put the fear of hard time into Josh Mooney," Roy said. "After sitting in that cell for two days it didn't take much. He's ready to talk."

"His attorney?"

"He didn't want one. Josh thinks he's got this all figured out. Thinks he's a wise guy, smarter than the rest of us. We're just going to leave it at that."

"The perfect criminal."

"The prosecutor's dream boy," Roy said, laughing and shaking his head.

"Excellent. Give me ten minutes. That's all I need."

The sheriff opened the door of the office and she found Josh sitting in an orange jumpsuit, his hands lying limp in his lap, the handcuffs dangling on his thin wrists like bangles. His bleached hair looked oily and he smelled of body odor, like he hadn't showered in a week.

"Got yourself in a real mess," she said.

"Like I don't know that?"

"I'm glad you're clear on that. Then I'll get right to the important stuff. I need to know exactly where it was that you were supposed to deliver those women. I need the address and the contact person."

He gave her a vacant look, but she knew his brain was spinning at warp speed.

"What if I tell you? Can you help me?"

"What if you don't tell me? Not a chance in hell that I'll help you."

He lifted his hands a few inches off his lap and dropped them, the handcuffs clinking. "I just feel like I should get something for being good. You get things in jail for good behavior. That's what I want."

Josie pursed her lips and nodded. "Okay. I get that. Then I will talk to the prosecutor, and I will let him know that you cooperated fully in this conversation. That you gave the information freely. That will definitely hold weight with Mr. Holder. Deal?"

He nodded his head. "And my own cell until I get out of here. I don't want to share a cell with someone anymore."

"I'll talk to the sheriff."

He narrowed his eyes, looking at Josie like he wasn't sure if he could trust her. "We were going to Albuquerque. In the South Valley. Have you been there?"

"I know the area vaguely."

"There's two blocks they call the Maid's Quarters. It's where the apartments are for the girls that work in the hotels."

"You have an address?"

He nodded and Josie slid a pad of paper over to him with a pen on top. He held his hands up with the handcuffs and she shook her head. "You can write with those on. You keep telling the truth and you might get those off one day. But you have some work to do first."

He picked up the pen with his right hand and rested his left hand on top while he scrawled out the address.

"Write the name of the contact person on there too."

He looked at her for a moment. "It's not really a name. They call him Big Ben."

She motioned toward the paper. "Write it down. Just make sure what you're giving me is accurate."

He nodded again. "Totally accurate. I swear."

"Now the phone number."

She watched as he wrote down a number.

"So how do I connect with Big Ben?"

"Nobody calls. You send a text message that says the word *ready* with a question mark. He texts back for the date and time and you send it to him. He says okay. That's it."

"Then what?"

"You go to that address. It's like a crappy apartment building. Go to the office on the first floor and ask for him by that name. You tell him you have a load and he says meet me in back. That's it."

"Then what?"

"You drive behind the apartment building and unload the women."

Like cattle, she thought. "You've done this before?"

"I made a few trips."

Josie nodded and decided to address that issue at a later time.

"It's not hard. They aren't really very careful. It's not like there's a secret handshake or whatever. You just give him the women and their fake passports and IDs, and he gives you an envelope with a check in it."

"Who's the check made out to?"

He shrugged. "I don't know. I wasn't allowed to look."

"Who's your boss?"

"I told you. I don't know. She never said."

"Will this Big Ben be expecting the delivery at any certain time?"

"Not really. It's not like we're the only ones delivering girls to him. And he knows they're coming from far away. That's why you text him when you're ready to deliver."

"Won't he question when someone other than you delivers the girls?"

Josh gave her a dismissive sneer. "He doesn't care who delivers. As long as you send the text that says *ready*, he'll know you're legit."

"You don't think he'll be wary about the women from West Texas being found? It'll be on the news," she said.

"Seriously? Big Ben lives in Albuquerque, New Mexico. These women in West Texas won't make headlines out of Arroyo County."

"Okay," Josie said. "I think we're done here."

She stood and he looked up at her. "I don't want to go back into that jail cell."

"You should have thought of that a long time ago."

"You said you'd get me my own cell! Since I helped you here?" he asked, suddenly sounding desperate.

"I'll see what I can do."

Josie walked out into the hallway and found Roy standing just outside the door.

"You get what you needed?" he asked.

"I did. I seriously appreciate this."

Roy waved it off. "Nail that woman and we're even."

"Deal." Josie started off and turned back. "Also. Josh would like a private cell, since he's been such a good prisoner."

He rolled his eyes. "That's my top priority."

———

Josie was glad to see the parking lot as empty as when she'd arrived. As she pulled out of the lot she called Dell. "What do you think about driving to Albuquerque in the morning? Leave about five o'clock?"

"You bet. You driving that little pickup?"

She smiled. Dell was cheap about everything except his truck. "How about you drive and we take your limo?"

"Deal. I'll pick you up at five sharp."

Josie stopped in front of Manny's Motel and saw the light on in the room where her mom was staying. She felt a wave of guilt at the lack of time she'd spent with her since she'd arrived. Josie knocked on the door, and her mom opened it wearing a bathrobe, reading glasses perched halfway down her nose and a paperback book in hand.

"Well, look what the cat dragged in!"

"Are you headed for bed?" Josie asked.

"Already there. But I can still visit. Come on in."

Josie shut the door behind her and sat in a wicker chair beside the bed. The covers were rumpled up on the side next to the lamp where her mom had been reading. The homey sight made her ache for something more than they had.

She wanted to call her mom when she had a lousy day, and feel better when she hung up. She wanted her mom to be able to call when something good happened in her life. And she wanted her mom to know that she loved her, but she had no idea how.

"I've been listening to the radio. Sounds like you got a heap of trouble," she said.

Josie sighed. "It's a mess."

"What's it all about?"

"The mayor thinks I accused someone of something that isn't true."

"Isn't that what police do? You arrest people. Then you let the judge and jury decide if they're innocent or guilty?"

Josie made a face. "Sort of. But you can't arrest someone without probable cause. You need solid evidence that'll convince the prosecutor that the person committed a crime."

"Did you have solid evidence?"

Her mom had settled back down under the quilt and was leaning against the headboard, seeming keenly interested. Josie could imagine her mom having a similar conversation with her dad when he was a young cop, still imagining he could make a difference in the world.

"I think it's solid. But some of the information is coming from pretty sketchy people. That's the problem. And I'm accusing someone who is considered to be an upstanding community member."

Her mom hummed. "That's a tough one. A reliable witness thing."

Josie smiled. "Exactly."

"You just need more evidence."

"That's partly why I'm here. I'm going out of town tomorrow. I'm trying to track down some evidence that might clear this mess up."

"So you're telling me you won't be around tomorrow," she said.

"That's pretty much it," Josie said.

"You know, I was a cop's wife. I get all this. I remember what it was like when your dad missed suppers and birthdays. It wasn't like he wanted to. It's just what had to be done."

"I appreciate that," Josie said.

Her mom held up her book, suddenly looking uncomfortable with the personal nature of the conversation. "Anyway, I got a good book to finish tomorrow."

Josie stood, briefly contemplated giving her mom a hug, but just as quickly decided it would be too awkward and walked to the door. "I'll be on the road about sixteen hours tomorrow, up and back. I'll call you along the way."

Her mom waved her book in the air. "Good enough. Go catch those bad guys."

———————

Because the police department was off-limits, Josie drove home and set up shop with her laptop at the kitchen table, where she searched the Internet and found phone numbers for the Albuquerque Police Department. She finally connected with an officer in the Criminal Investigations Bureau, who then put her in touch with an officer named Townie Davison, who was very interested in the information she had to share. He said that he'd been investigating the Maid's Quarters for several months and would gladly trade information.

"Based on our intel, it's a growing organization. Most of the trafficking crimes in Albuquerque are small-scale. Some guy who decides he can make more money selling his girlfriend than he can selling drugs and guns."

"Jeez," she said, resting her forehead in her hand.

"No joke. They feed on the most vulnerable. They get girls, and some guys too, down on their luck, needing help, and they exploit them."

"The sex trade?" she said.

"Sure. Some sleezy guy connects with a runaway girl. He gets her hooked on cheap heroin. After that, she'll work for dope, food, and a place to sleep."

Josie imagined Isabella and the other three women, and wondered if that might have been their fate.

"Easy money," he said.

Josie explained the case she'd been working. She gave Townie the address and the name, Big Ben, and he laughed and yelled at someone in the background.

"Chief Gray, you just made my day. New Mexico thanks you and the great state of Texas."

They spent the next several hours planning Josie's venture into the Maid's Quarters in downtown Albuquerque.

———

When Dell picked Josie up the next morning at five, she'd only had two hours of sleep. She dressed for her role that day, wearing ripped jeans and a faded red IU sweatshirt. She ate a granola bar once they were on the road, then told Dell roughly what they'd be doing that day. Outside of El Paso, she finally gave in and fell asleep for the next four hours until they reached the outskirts of Albuquerque. She felt a tap on her arm and pulled herself up from the corner of the window where she'd been sound asleep, struggling past the bizarre dreams that had pursued her during the long drive north.

She tried to focus on Dell's voice. "Wake up. Let's get you some caffeine."

She shook her head, trying to clear the fog. Dell pulled off the interstate and filled his gas tank, buying them both a Coke and a bag of pretzels, while she walked around the truck and mentally woke herself up.

Back in the truck, she gave him directions to downtown Albuquerque, and they spent the next twenty minutes navigating through narrower and narrower streets, down one-ways and around construction barrels, until they found the address that Townie had provided. Josie and Dell took the steps to a brownstone apartment building and knocked on apartment number nine.

A man with red hair, freckles, and bright green eyes answered the door. He motioned them inside and smiled at Josie as if he already knew her. Without asking her name he said, "You have any trouble getting here?"

"Nope. Directions were good."

"Okay. I got four women ready to ride with you. Let's get you set up."

"You're Townie?" she said.

"Yeah, yeah. Sorry. I've already seen pictures of you. Googled you. Saw the press about you and the Medrano Cartel. It's a wonder you're still breathing."

Josie smiled but didn't respond, hoping to keep the conversation focused on the current drama. She introduced Dell as a department consultant and driver.

"Dell will be in the parking lot, waiting in his truck, until we're done today."

"Works for me. You said Big Ben doesn't expect a certain person?"

"According to my source, all we do is send the text that says, *ready?* Then we send the time we'll be there."

"Let's do it. You've got the number, right?"

Josie nodded and pulled the piece of paper out of her jeans pocket. She texted the number and a few minutes later her phone buzzed.

The message read, *Date and time.*

She gave Townie a thumbs-up and asked what time.

He glanced at his watch. "Tell him today at three."

Josie texted back and less than a minute later she received the okay response that Josh had told her to expect.

Townie laughed and gave her a high-five. "That gives us about an hour and a half. Let's get you set up."

She looked around the apartment and was surprised by how normal it appeared.

"I'd expected a flophouse," she said.

He laughed, a short choppy sound that made her smile back. "A friend of mine lives here. She's also a cop. I didn't want to chance taking you into the station. And we had to get you wired up somewhere."

They had agreed on the phone that, since Josie was more familiar with the trip from Guatemala and the arrangements that had been made by locals from Texas, it would make more sense for her to actually deliver the undercover females to the drop-off point. Given the distance between Artemis and Albuquerque, there was no worry about small-town news coverage of the human trafficking case reaching Albuquerque and blowing her cover. However, she hadn't gone into the mayor's backstory with Townie, nor the fact that she'd been stripped of her gun and badge. She'd deemed that information irrelevant, and hoped like hell she hadn't made a terrible decision.

A female walked out of a doorway wiping her hands on a towel and smiled at Josie. "I'm Officer Tammy White. I work homicide for the city." She put a hand up to her mouth like she was shielding the words from Townie. "And I date him on the side."

"Ah," Josie said, not sure yet what to make of them.

"I'm here to help you get the wire on. Townie's an old-fashioned guy. He figured you'd prefer having a female help you get your wire set up. Come on in the kitchen. I have it laid out."

Josie followed her into the kitchen, where a black device that looked similar to a pen cap lid with a clip on it sat on the counter.

"Obviously there's no wire anymore. We still call it setting up a wire because it's easier than telling you we're connecting a digital voice recorder." Tammy smiled and turned to look at Josie. "You ever work undercover before?"

"No. Not like this."

"Nothing to worry about. This is just a voice recorder. It works best if you slip it right inside your bra and clip it. It's flat enough you can't see it through your clothes. And it's less obvious than some of the sunglasses or jewelry recorders people wear."

Josie lifted her sweatshirt up and the woman helped her clip the voice recorder to the edge of her bra.

"No one will have any idea you're mic'd. And here's the other thing. These guys have a successful business set up at this point. They're no longer looking for cops around every corner. They think they beat the system. When that happens they get lazy. And that's when we pop in." Tammy winked and then turned serious. "You okay with this?"

"I'm good. I want to nail these bastards."

"Excellent. That's the plan."

Back in the living room they found Townie on his cell phone, talking animatedly, with his hand gesturing and chopping through the air. Dell stood by the window with his hands shoved in his jeans pockets, looking like he was trying to stay out of the way.

Tammy pointed at Townie. "That's how he is. All the time. He's the only man I know who gestures in his sleep."

Josie laughed at the visual.

"I am not even kidding."

He finally hung up and slid his phone into his back pocket. "We're ready. We've got four undercover females wired up in the back of a van. The van is sitting outside. A woman named Sheila will get you to the apartment address. She's undercover narcotics and she's a pro. Once you sign the ladies over to Big Ben, you come back out, get in the van, and drive off. Take the van directly to the police station, where I'll be waiting for you. We've got another undercover minivan parked in the back of the apartment lot as backup."

He paused and Josie nodded to indicate she was following along.

"The females get two hours inside, long enough to get the basic logistics for what happens when new females arrive. Then we'll bust as many people as we can get. We'll send a message with this one."

Josie nodded. "They're all wearing recorders?"

"Three of them are. Sheila's wearing a ratty shirt with ugly buttons on it. One of the buttons has a tiny camera on it. That'll give the team a visual of what they're walking into."

Townie handed her a manila envelope filled with fake driver's licenses and passports. "You said the guy you referred to as Big Ben will ask for the girls' documentation. Here you go. He'll actually expect fake documents. That's part of the deal—the girls get delivered with U.S. documents ready to use."

"You move quick."

"Like I said, we've been working this for a while. Your phone call? It killed me." There were crinkles around his green eyes when he grinned. "We knew there was a labor trafficking group for some local fleabag hotels. We had the players, but not the logistics."

"Well, I need the players. I need the name of the female who's organizing the transportation from Guatemala," Josie said.

"We'll work on it for sure. We'll make the bust this afternoon. Depending on what the undercover officers find, we'll shut it down today. If things get touchy we'll go in early. The code word is *stop*. We've got a SWAT team on standby. The plan is, exactly two hours from when they enter that building, we go in with the SWAT team and pull them out." He paused and eyed Josie carefully. "You ready for this?"

"Absolutely. Let's roll."

He eyed Dell. "You want to hang out with me in the control van? I'll just be monitoring radio traffic. I won't be entering the crime scene. Hell of a lot better than sitting in your truck all day."

"That'd be great." Dell grinned like a kid. He was a loner who loved the isolation of the West Texas backcountry, but there was also a part of his character that thrived on adventure.

Townie explained where the undercover van was located in the parking lot of the brownstone and that Sheila had directions to the address Josh had provided Josie. The van was a dark blue beater that could hold twelve passengers. Josie got into the driver's seat and turned to see the women sitting in the back. They all smiled and waved, calling hello. It was a surreal sight. They were dressed in shabby clothes, with messy hair. Josie guessed most of them hadn't showered that day, to get ready for the undercover assignment. But their expressions were clear and bright. They all had the confident bearing of cops ready for action.

Josie introduced herself, and the women each did the same. She took the documents out of the package and matched them up with the women to get a sense of who she was working with. She asked each of the women questions about their fictional background, memorizing each woman's name before proceeding. If Josh's story was accurate, it would be a simple exchange, but if she was questioned she needed basic information on each of the women who had supposedly been in her care.

Josie finally said, "I think we're ready."

She got a thumbs-up from the other women and Sheila said, "Take a right out of the parking lot and turn left at the stoplight."

Josie followed Sheila's directions and listened to the cops' banter in the backseat as they discussed the players they would most likely encounter once they were inside the apartment building. One of the women worked vice, and they were still catching her up to speed on the investigation.

After a ten-minute drive, Sheila directed Josie into the parking lot of a building that looked like public assistance housing gone wrong. Three dumpsters were backed up against the side of the five-story building, each one with trash overflowing onto the ground. Windows were broken and duct-taped together, and a general sense of misery pervaded the block of tenement buildings.

Josie pulled the van into a space and scouted out the parking lot. There were about ten vehicles in various states of disrepair, but all of them appeared empty. She noticed an old minivan parked in the rear of the parking lot and asked if it was the backup under-cover vehicle.

Sheila laughed. "That's our backup. Sad old piece of junk smells like mold and cat pee. The SWAT team is also ready to go on our call. We need to communicate space and size and the number of people for them to expect when they get inside."

Josie called Townie, the project lead, who was communicating with the backup van, and asked, "Is the backup picking up my mic?"

"You're good to go."

"Okay." Josie turned and faced the women in the back of the van. "Good luck."

She received a similar chorus of voices telling her to be careful, and she left the van.

SEVENTEEN

Vie Blessings called Otto at noon. "We're ready to release the women, but I'm not sure what to do with them. Have you heard from victims' assistance? I've called and left two messages but can't get anyone to respond. We've got two rooms tied up, Otto. As much as I want to help, we can't use the trauma center for long-term care when there's no medical issue. And, sorry to say it, no money to pay for it."

The frustration in Vie's voice was obvious. Aside from Isabella, the other three women weren't suspects. They were victims. With no money. And no identification. When the van that Josh Mooney was driving was confiscated for evidence, the police found useless fake IDs and passports. Meanwhile, Otto had no idea what to do with the women, and now one of them was a prime murder suspect with no known motivation.

Josie had wanted to wait to interview Isabella Dagati, but Otto was the lead on the case, and he couldn't afford to sit on his haunches and wait. He drove to the trauma center and convinced Vie Blessings to give up the staff lounge again so that he could speak with Isabella. Next, he called Selena Rocha and asked if she would come to the hospital for an hour to translate if language became a barrier. She had agreed to meet him there in thirty minutes. Police work was about problem-solving and often making split-second decisions that could make or break a case. But when immigration issues and cross-border crimes were at play, it complicated things immensely. There were no rule books, only best guesses.

Otto and Selena sat at the staff lunch table and waited for the nurse to escort Isabella into the lounge. She entered wearing black pants and a woman's button-down shirt. Obviously someone in the community had provided clothing for the women. He wondered if Caroline Moss's group was trying to find the women transportation home to Guatemala. He thought how bizarre the entire situation had become.

"How are you feeling today?" he asked.

She nodded and smiled shyly. Her hair was pulled back in a long braid behind her head and she looked rested but nervous, frequently glancing away from Otto as if not wanting to make eye contact.

"It's time to talk about what happened the night that Renata was shot," Otto said.

Her face clouded over and she shook her head.

"Not talking about it is no longer an option." He paused to let his words sink in. "We found a gun in the pasture where Renata's body was found. Your fingerprints are on that gun."

She closed her eyes and her body slumped into the chair.

"I need the truth, Isabella."

Otto's phone vibrated in his pocket and he saw that it was Ernie Mays. He stood and excused himself into the hallway. What timing, he thought.

Ernie apologized for not getting to him sooner and began explaining another case he'd been working on that took precedence.

Otto listened patiently, wanting to hurry him along. Ernie finally said, "I've got your information."

"That's great news. What did you find?"

"I test-fired the gun and fed it into the ATF's database. The gun didn't match with any other crimes. But when I checked the bullet casing against the gun, there was no match there either."

Otto frowned. "So, you're telling me that the bullet found inside the victim's body did not come from the gun we found at the crime scene?"

"That's what I'm telling you. The bullet and casing associated with the murder are .380-caliber. The gun you gave me is a nine-millimeter Luger. To the naked eye the rounds look almost identical. Under the microscope, the rounds are clearly different."

"I'll be damned. Ernie, get your appetite ready. I'll be up to deliver on that steak dinner soon."

Ernie laughed. "If everybody had delivered on all their steak dinners through the years, I'd be a well-fed man."

Otto entered the lounge again and found Isabella crying. Investigations with the roller-coaster effect irritated him: up and down; one minute things were coming together, the next falling apart.

He sat down across from the young woman and hoped to get her side of the story without first telling her the information about the casing and the gun. He lightened his tone. "Just tell me what happened," he said. "Help us understand so that we can help you."

After several false starts and more tears and hand-wringing, she finally gave in and told Otto the story.

Isabella and Renata escaped from the motel in Piedra Labrada, just like Isabella had told Marta. But as they left the motel, Isabella took the gun that she knew Josh hid in his shoe each night when he went to bed. She hid it under her sweatshirt, tucked into the back waistband of her jeans. They found a Catholic church a few blocks away and learned about Señora Molina. They hiked out to the river to find her, and after staying with her for a night, they crossed the Rio Grande in search of Josie's house. They found it one afternoon while Josie was at work. They made a place to sleep in her toolshed, gathering courage to approach Josie one evening after she came home from work.

Meanwhile, they heard a vehicle driving slowly by the house their second night there and feared the people in the vehicle were searching for them. On the third night, Josie wasn't home yet and a car pulled into the driveway with its headlights on and stopped. Isabella figured it was somewhere between nine and eleven o'clock. It was much earlier than the other nights the car drove by. They heard someone get out of the car. They could see through knotholes in the toolshed that someone was prowling around outside. Isabella grabbed the gun and they snuck out of the toolshed without being heard. They had reached the back of the house, ready to run down the lane toward Dell's house, when Renata tripped over something and a man shouted both their names. Isabella couldn't be sure, but she didn't think it was Josh or Ryan's voice.

The women took off running into the pasture, parallel with the road. A man followed them, yelling their names. There was enough starlight to see to walk carefully, but they were terrified and confused and desperate to get away. Then they noticed headlights moving slowly down the road from behind them. They changed course and turned to run toward the mountain range, directly behind Josie's house.

A short time later, Isabella said she heard a gunshot from behind her and she flung her arm around and pulled the trigger on the gun, not having any idea if she was going to hit the person, but wanting to scare him. She heard two more gunshots and turned to look behind her and saw Renata stumble and drop into the dirt.

Isabella's voice turned to a whisper. "I thought Renata was

running next to me. I don't know if it was me that shot her. I don't know. I thought she was right beside me, and then I turned to see where the shooter was, and there was Renata, stumbling forward, and then she hit the ground, and I turned and moved as fast as I could, tripping over rocks and cactus. It all happened so fast I couldn't make sense of any of it." She took a deep breath, obviously forcing herself to continue. "I hid behind rocks at the bottom of the mountain until I was sure they were gone and I went to check on her but she was dead. I threw the gun into the pasture and went back to hide in the toolshed until I could figure out what to do next."

"It wasn't you that killed her," Otto said, feeling a rush of compassion for this young woman. "Renata was shot in the back. If you turned and fired behind you, the bullet would have entered her chest. And we have the bullet that killed Renata. It didn't come from your gun."

Her mouth opened and she looked stunned.

"The phone call I just took was from the police lab. Someone else shot Renata. It wasn't you."

───◆───

A bullet had pierced the shatterproof glass of the entrance door to the apartment building, leaving a spiderweb of chipped glass. Josie pushed the door open and the smell of backed-up sewage made her wince. Flickering fluorescent lights cast a yellow glow across the stained carpet. The lobby was no more than a hallway that led to an elevator that clearly hadn't worked in years, a bank of mailboxes that appeared as if someone had taken a baseball bat to them, a stairwell leading both upstairs and down, and at the end of the hallway, a door with the word OFFICE painted in black.

She took a deep breath and wished she knew how to pray. She would have said a prayer. As the chief of police in a small-town city department, working undercover was not her specialty.

She knocked on the door and a man with a gruff voice yelled, "What?"

Josie put her hand on the sticky doorknob and turned. The space was the size of a bathroom and seemed to serve as both a custodian's supply closet and an office with a small wooden desk. The bald gaunt man with a goatee in a three-piece suit did not fit the voice that had bellowed out at Josie.

"What?" he repeated.

"I need to see Big Ben."

"Why?"

"I got a delivery."

"Of what?"

"Women."

"Who are you?"

"Who are *you*?" she asked back.

The corner of his mouth lifted and he rolled his chair away from his desk a bit, finally seeming to take her seriously.

"I'm Big Ben."

"Well, then I'm Deirdre."

"Bullshit."

She let the corner of her mouth lift but said nothing.

"Where are they?" he asked.

"In my van. In the lot."

"How many?"

"Four."

"I'm waiting on five."

She smiled, cocking her head slightly. "Well, now you get four."

"Deirdre makes five," he said.

"Deirdre's getting the hell out of here."

Josie pitched the manila envelope onto his desk, and Big Ben dumped the contents onto the pile of papers in front of him. He flicked through the documents to find the driver's licenses, study-ing each one, mumbling the girls' names and their weight and eye color, commenting on their appearance. He spoke with a light Mexican accent, drawing out some words, clipping others. He held up one of the licenses and read off the name. "Susita. What's she like?"

Josie shrugged. "She's all right. A little attitude."

A gold tooth glinted when he laughed, giving him the appearance of a cartoon character. "I knew it. I know these mamas before they ever walk into my life, just by their picture." He tapped the photo on the license. "This little mamacita needs to be trained."

Josie smiled and nodded. He was referring to Sheila. Trained? "She's a tough one."

He stroked his goatee and eyed Josie. "Tough, huh? She won't be tough for too long. I guarantee you that, my friend." He laughed and stood from his desk. "Let's go."

He brushed past Josie and into the hallway. She followed him outside, where he peered into the parking lot and spotted her van. "Pull it around behind the building."

He started to walk away and she said, "Hey! What about my check?"

"Don't be rude, mama. Meet me in back."

Josie climbed into the van and was peppered with questions. The undercover officers were wired, but they had no audio of Josie's communication, nor could they communicate with each other once they entered the building. Josie's transmission was only connected to Townie.

"I spoke with one man who identified himself as Big Ben. Tall, middle-aged with a goatee and a cheesy three-piece suit." Josie turned in her seat to look at Sheila before driving the van around back. "He singled your driver's license out and asked about you. I said you had an attitude. I think he's looking forward to messing with you."

One of the others, a Hispanic woman with big hair and a loud laugh, gave her grief. "Oh, girlfriend. He picked the wrong UC to mess with. Sheila will rip his ass good."

The mood in the van would have seemed lighthearted to someone outside of law enforcement. But Josie knew it was nervous energy. Any situation with criminals involving innocent people, money, guns, and drugs could end in disaster in seconds flat. Everyone in the van knew that one wrong move could put their lives in jeopardy.

The back of the apartment building was down a sloped drive that ended in what looked like a loading dock and the building's basement. Josie stopped the van where Big Ben was standing beside the basement door stroking his goatee. She opened the van's side door and four women stared out at her, eyes wide, looking terrified, playing their parts well.

"Ladies. Welcome to the beautiful United States of America. My name is Big Ben and I'll be your tour guide. We'll get you set up in your lovely room and then I'll introduce you to your trainer. For now, let's see which one of you lovely ladies will rise to the top." He held up one of the driver's licenses. "Contestant number one. Juanita! Come out here and let me see you."

The woman with the loud laugh climbed out of the van looking timid and scared. Big Ben pointed to the wall next to the entrance door and had her stand there. "Arms to your side," he said. They all stared at the woman, who looked away, possibly searching the parking lot for the backup undercover minivan, but more likely humiliated at being treated like a piece of property.

"Not bad. Drop a few pounds, fix that mess of hair," he said. "Now turn around, slowly."

She did as instructed. Josie knew the women would thoroughly enjoy watching the handcuffs click tight around the man's wrists.

This went on for at least fifteen minutes as Big Ben took each girl out of the van and assessed her physical qualities in front of the others, making it clear that he was in charge.

"Okay, ladies. You're all mine now. Let's set you up in your room, where you can pick out some clothes. Then you get your first lesson on cleaning toilets and keeping your mouths shut." He turned to Josie and pulled an envelope out of the inner pocket of his suit coat and handed it to her.

Josie held the envelope in the air. "I bet I can make you a better deal," she said.

He raised his eyebrows. "I don't make deals with the drivers."

"I'm not your typical driver."

He considered her for a moment. She was off-script. They hadn't planned for her to talk business with him, and she hoped she wouldn't blow what was so far moving along as planned.

"I can see you aren't a typical driver, Miss Deirdre. What's your cost?"

"I'll do you ten percent better than what she was charging you."

He frowned as if contemplating the offer, but didn't seem surprised that she'd referred to the person arranging the current deal as female. He took out his wallet and handed Josie one of his business cards. "Be in touch," he said, and turned away from her.

Josie got into the van and took one quick look back as he led the women into the basement.

EIGHTEEN

Four hours after leaving a cocky Big Ben lording his power over four seemingly frightened women in the Maid's Quarters, Josie walked into an interrogation room to find Benjamin Dominguez sitting in a chair, bent over at the waist.

He braced his hands on the side of the chair and leaned up slightly to speak. "I have anxiety attacks. It's a medically diagnosed condition. I need to get to the hospital immediately. I will pass out without medical care."

"We're not taking you anywhere," Townie said. He rolled his eyes at the theatrics and pointed to an empty chair for Josie.

The interrogation room was in the basement of one of the police department substations. She was certain more accommodating rooms were available, but the setting fit the occasion. The room was barely large enough to hold Big Ben, Townie, and two other officers that she'd not seen before sitting in chairs, and another officer who was running a video camera behind a tripod in one corner of the room.

Josie liked that Big Ben had no table to hide behind. When he finally sat up in the chair, Josie looked in disgust at the tears that ran down his splotchy face. His cheap suit hung off his shoulders in a wrinkled mess as he dangled his hands between his legs and scanned the room, noticing Josie for the first time. His anxiety symptoms gave way to a momentary expression of recognition that gave way to fury, before he could resume his pale-faced misery and look away. Josie smiled.

"I'll remind you again that you have been read your Miranda rights. Do you still wish to waive your right to counsel at this time?"

Ben seemed conflicted. Common sense would indicate an attorney would be the best option, but Townie must have already convinced him that cooperating with the cops would be very advantageous to his situation.

"I don't want an attorney. But I want the cuffs off," Ben said. "I'm obviously not going anywhere, with a room full of police officers packed in around me like sardines."

Townie stood to remove the handcuffs. "You were having such convulsive fits I was afraid you'd harm yourself from all that anxiety. Since you've calmed down, I think we're safe to remove the cuffs. Lift 'em up here, Ben."

Once the cuffs were removed, Townie and the other two cops who'd also been working the Maid's Quarters investigation spent the next ninety minutes interrogating him about the operation.

Initially Ben was reluctant to offer anything, but once he gave up the first real morsel, Townie was unrelenting. Josie was impressed with the way Townie would ask the same question again and again with only subtle differences, until Ben would forget he'd denied something and offer up a new detail. Then Townie would take the new piece of information, combine it with something else, and re-form it into a new question. It was like watching a stone sculptor chip away at rock, and then backing away to see the complete picture from a distance. Townie was one of the best interrogators she had seen in action.

Josie sat patiently, listening to the exchange, knowing eventually he'd bring it around to what Ben had referred to as the "suppliers." She'd talked extensively with Townie on the phone the night before, explaining the transport from Guatemala, Caroline Moss's involvement, and the two drivers.

Townie finally asked, "How many suppliers do you work with?"

Ben shrugged and then said, "Four or five."

"So you work with five suppliers?"

"Yeah."

"What countries do they ship from?" Townie asked.

"Guatemala and Honduras. And all you have to do is get on the Internet and look at where these ladies come from. Then tell me what I give them isn't better than what they had. Tell me I'm not providing a—"

"Spare me the goodwill lecture," Townie said. "Ain't gonna fly here. Start with your suppliers from Guatemala. How many?"

"Just one. The rest are Honduras."

"What's her name?" Townie asked.

Once again Ben didn't seem surprised at the use of the female pronoun. "Lilith."

Josie jotted the name down on the notepad in her lap.

"How many deliveries do you get from her each month?"

"From Lilith, maybe four or five times since last fall. She's only been sending me girls for about a year."

"Did she negotiate the deal for the girls you received today?"

"Yes."

"How much did you pay her for the four girls?" Townie asked.

Ben turned in his seat and pointed at Josie. "Ask her. She took the envelope."

Townie had opened the envelope when Josie and Dell had arrived at the police station, and they'd found four one-thousand-dollar bills.

"I'd like to hear it from you," Townie said.

"A thousand per head."

"How does she contact you when she has a load ready?"

"She calls me."

Josie felt the skin prickle on her arms. She hadn't expected a phone connection. It would be easier to trace.

"On what phone?"

Ben gave Townie a scathing look. "The phone you took from me."

"This one?"

"That's it."

Townie passed it over to him. "Go ahead and pull up Lilith's contact information. Let me see it."

Ben scrolled through, found what he was looking for, started to hand the phone back to Townie, and stopped. "Not until I get some guarantees. How do I know you won't take everything I've given you, and then you'll arrest me anyway?"

Townie laughed and grabbed the phone from him. "Ben. You're already under arrest. You're going to jail, pal. We were just providing you an opportunity to come clean before we put you away."

Ben's face turned an angry red color. "You told me I'd help my case if I talked to you without an attorney."

"And you did. We appreciate the information greatly. And so will the prosecutor."

Big Ben came unhinged, yelling and swearing and demanding his attorney. Josie left the room feeling flattened. They'd finally gotten around to the information she needed and Townie had let the interrogation die out.

Josie stood in the lobby and talked to Dell on the phone while she waited to debrief with Townie. Dell was sitting in his pickup truck outside in the parking lot waiting for her to finish.

Townie finally came out of the booking area holding the phone in the air.

"I know you're disappointed with the end of that interview, but this'll make up for it." Townie powered up the phone. "This is Big Ben's. Entered as evidence. Guess whose number is in his contacts."

"Tell me it's Lilith," Josie said.

He grinned and handed her the phone. Not only was the name Lilith in his contacts, but she saw that the phone number utilized the area code for Arroyo County. Josie opened her phone and took a photo of the contact information on Big Ben's phone.

"That what you needed?" Townie asked, smiling, knowing it was.

"The trick will be tying the so-called Lilith to an actual person." Josie handed him the phone back and shook his hand. "I appreciate you letting me sit in on the interview. It was impressive, the way you worked him over."

"Slow and steady. Best advice I ever got as a new investigator."

———————

Dell drove the first four-hour stretch to Artemis while Josie spent the time making calls to every law enforcement contact she could think of who might have information that could tie a phone associated to a Lilith to a human trafficking scam associated with Caroline Moss. She realized the name was most likely a fake, but it was a connection she would pursue until it dried up.

After several futile hours Josie opened a search engine on her phone and typed in *Lilith* + *"Caroline Moss."* Surprisingly, several links appeared, and Josie clicked on one that took her to an obituary for Lilith Ann Rockwell, who had lived in Philadelphia, Pennsylvania. She scrolled down and read that the woman passed away ten years ago, and was survived by her daughter, Caroline Ann Moss, of Artemis, Texas.

———•———

After arriving home at three in the morning, Josie fell into a deep sleep that she'd not experienced in days. She woke at ten the next day feeling refreshed and confident. She started her day with a cup of coffee and a phone call to Otto, briefing him on the day's events.

"So what's her mom have to do with this?" Otto asked.

"What do you use when you need a security code, or a password, or you want to disguise some piece of information? You use your mom's name, or your sister's, or some relative that makes it easy to remember and, you assume, unlikely for anyone else to trace back to you."

"You think she used her mom's name as her contact name for when she talked to Big Ben?"

"Exactly. It was easy for her to remember and probably not many people around here know her mom's name. She lived in Pennsylvania when she died." Otto was quiet and she added, "How many Liliths do you know? What are the odds this could be anyone other than Caroline?"

"It's not conclusive, but it's a hell of a good connection."

"We've got her. I can feel it."

"What now?" he asked.

"I have a plan," she said.

"Let's hear it."

"Don't worry about it."

"Josie. You know I hate that phrase."

"As the lead investigator on the case, I don't think you really want to know my plan."

"What does that mean?" His voice had turned guarded.

"It means you don't want to know what my plan is."

"You don't want me to know, because I won't agree with you. The last time you didn't listen to me you ended up suspended. Sometimes I know what I'm talking about. Give me some credit."

"I'll check in later."

Josie ended the call, feeling a twinge of guilt for leaving him hanging, but he'd been correct. Otto would no doubt disagree with her plan, but she didn't care. She needed to take care of business.

———————

Josie showered and dressed in khaki pants and a short-sleeved top and sandals. She'd have been more comfortable wearing her gun and badge, but the lack of a uniform wouldn't stop her.

She drove about five miles out of town north of the Mud Flats, to a small subdivision that held four homes situated around a cul-de-sac. With no other houses around for miles, the small cluster of homes had always made Josie think of a group of elite homesteaders.

The homes were a variety of styles, from modern minimalist steel and glass, to a rustic stone and wood cabin. Her destination was a two-story that looked like it belonged in the Texas hill country, built with blocks of limestone so light in color they were almost white. Josie pulled into the paved driveway of Steve and Caroline Moss and didn't stop to reconsider before she exited the jeep.

She followed a stone pathway to a massive wooden door fit for a castle. No doubt Caroline's parents had paid for the lavish home. As mayor of Artemis, Moss's salary was paltry, and his side consulting job could not support this kind of home. As far as Josie knew, Caroline had never worked for a salary outside the home, at least legally. For years, her focus had been setting up political functions for her husband in an attempt to get him into the limelight; her goal was national recognition. Josie had no idea if the Republican Party ever considered Steve Moss as a contender for anything, but she'd not seen anything to support that idea.

She rang the bell and was surprised when Caroline Moss answered. She wore dress slacks and a cream-colored blouse. Her blond shoulder-length hair hung loosely around her face and gave her a polished look, although Josie noticed fine lines around her eyes and a tired sag around her mouth. Josie wondered if her appearance at Caroline's door had caused the weariness.

"Good morning, Josie. Are you looking for the mayor?"

Caroline typically referred to her husband as the mayor, rather than as her husband. Josie figured the term put the emphasis on Caroline's priority.

"Actually, I'd like to have a word with you. Do you mind if I come in?"

"No, of course not. Come on in. Let's have a glass of iced tea out back. The patio is in the shade this time of day. It's a nice time to sit outside."

"That would be great. Thank you."

Caroline led Josie down a hallway past a cream-colored formal living room, then past a dining room filled with colorful artwork and a massive dining room table where Josie figured much politicking took place.

In the back, a covered patio ran the length of the house and connected to a pool and a tiered garden area. Caroline gestured to two comfy chairs situated around a coffee table, but Josie opted for the chairs arranged around a dining table. She wasn't there for comfort.

Several minutes later Caroline carried out a tray with a pitcher and glasses and set them on the table. She poured them each a glass of iced tea and Josie suffered through small talk about the drop in temperature that morning and the enjoyable eighty-degree weather.

At the first lull in the conversation Josie said, "I suppose you've heard that the mayor placed me on administrative leave."

Caroline tilted her head and gave Josie what appeared to be a sympathetic look. "I hope you aren't here to discuss that with me. You know that I support you, but I'm afraid he's been tight-lipped about your suspension. With everyone, including me."

"You're saying that you don't know why I was suspended?"

"No. I have no idea."

"It involves you," Josie said.

Caroline placed a hand over her heart and looked incredulous. "What an earth would I have to do with your suspension?"

"I told the mayor I had evidence that connects you to a human trafficking organization."

Her mouth dropped and she laughed like it was an outrageous statement. "What are you talking about?"

"I'm referring to the five women that paid you to transport them from Guatemala to the United States." Josie paused and watched Caroline's shocked smile turn into a frown. "More specifically, to New Mexico to work as maids."

"I'd hardly call the humanitarian work I do human trafficking. If you're spreading rumors like that, then it's no wonder you were suspended."

The French doors that led from the kitchen to the veranda opened and Mayor Moss stepped outside. His face was bright red and his eyes were bulging before he'd even seen Josie. Her jeep was likely enough to cause the reaction. It had been about ten minutes since she'd arrived at the house, and she assumed Caroline had called the mayor for help as soon as she pulled into the driveway. Josie figured the iced tea and friendly small talk had been a stalling technique until her husband could get here. Josie also assumed that Caroline knew exactly why she had been suspended.

"Not only will I have your badge and your gun, but I'll also have your ass in a jail cell by the end of the day for harassing a public official," he yelled. He walked directly up to her and stood beside her chair, pointing directly into her face. "Now get the hell away from my wife."

"I went to New Mexico. I sat in on a sting operation where we delivered four undercover police officers to a man named Big Ben. He was expecting five women, but since one woman was murdered—"

"Get the hell out of my house! I won't tell you again," he yelled.

Josie glanced at Caroline, who was looking down, unblinking, staring at the iced tea sitting in front of her, watching the sweat drip down the glass.

Josie continued. "We delivered the four agents to a place in New Mexico called the Maid's Quarters. It's where young women from Guatemala pay twelve thousand dollars to endure a trip from hell to be delivered to a man who treats them like property and makes them sleep together in a room that looks like third world squalor."

The mayor grabbed Josie's arm. "I'm calling the sheriff to remove you."

Josie jerked her arm out of his grasp. Her face was heated and she could feel her temper flaring. She would finish what she came for. "After Caroline collected sixty thousand dollars from the women's families, she was also set to receive another four thousand for delivery of the girls to Albuquerque." She paused and stared down Caroline until the woman looked up at Josie. Josie repeated her earlier statement. "It would have been five thousand, but one of the women was murdered."

Josie heard the click of numbers being pressed on a cell phone behind her. No doubt the mayor was calling the sheriff, and she hoped he would. She'd enjoy listening to him try to explain his way out of this one.

"But here's the killer," she said. "When Caroline has a delivery ready, she calls Big Ben to let him know she has a load. That's what they call the girls. A load. Caroline? She's called the supplier."

"Stop it," Caroline said, but her voice was quiet, and her eyes had the unfocused look of someone whose brain was on overload, no longer able to process information.

"After Big Ben was arrested and his phone seized, he told me that his supplier for Guatemala was named Lilith."

Mayor Moss made a noise behind her, almost a whimper, the noise he might make while having a nightmare.

Josie pressed a button on her cell phone and held it up toward Moss. He knocked her hand away but said nothing. "I've since learned that Caroline's mom's name is Lilith. I might not have made that connection, but when I looked at the phone number and recognized the West Texas area code, I found the obituary online for Caroline's mother."

Caroline again called out for Josie to stop. Josie turned in her chair to face the mayor. "This is over. There's too much evidence for you to pretend this isn't happening."

Moss had grown quiet behind her, no longer yelling for Josie to leave. She scooted her chair back, bumping against him as she stood from the table. "I want my badge and my gun delivered to the police department by three o'clock today."

Josie opened the French doors and walked through the house the way she had entered, leaving the Mosses to sort through the shrapnel from the bomb she had just exploded on their patio. But she damn sure knew the first step he had better make was to revoke her suspension.

———•———

Driving home with the windows down, she did not feel pleased or vindicated by the altercation at the mayor's house. It was unsettling to think that someone in a position of power, a woman she knew well as a community leader, could turn such a blind eye to others' suffering. Josie wondered if it had all started out as something positive but had somehow gone terribly wrong. But hard as she tried, she couldn't escape the fact that Caroline Moss was making money off the plight of people who believed she was going to take care of them. And they had been brutalized while Caroline looked the other way.

Josie didn't call Otto on her way home. She showered, dressed in her uniform, and drove to the police department. Lou smiled when she walked in.

"Welcome back," Lou said.

Josie shook her head in amazement. "The news has already spread?"

Lou held up Josie's gun in one hand and her badge in the other. "Helen brought these over about two minutes ago. She carried them in a paper bag and dropped them on the counter. She said the mayor asked her to make a delivery. That's all she said. What did you do to piss Helen off so bad?"

"I made her boss mad."

"So the drama's over?" Lou asked.

"It hasn't even started. But at least I'm back on the job. Let me know if you hear anything on the radio about it. Hopefully the mayor will make some sort of announcement."

"Don't hold your breath," Lou said. "Otto doesn't know yet. He'll be glad to see you. He's been a grouch ever since this happened."

"Is he upstairs?"

"Yes, ma'am." She smiled and handed Josie her badge and gun. "Good to have you back, Chief."

Josie walked upstairs and held up her equipment as she entered the office. Otto turned away from his desk looking shocked. "How did that happen?"

They sat together at the conference table and Josie explained her visit with Caroline and the mayor.

"You were right not to tell me. I'd have told you to quit being foolish." He gestured to her gun lying on the table. "And now this. Good for you."

"I have to talk to Holder. I have no idea what kind of charges he might bring against her."

"Maybe none, since this is still circumstantial. The only physical evidence that ties her to trafficking, other than Ryan's admission, is the Visa payment to set up the Web site four years ago. The name Lilith doesn't exactly make the case."

"Understood. But a jury will love it."

"You know she won't do jail time," he said. "She'll get a high-dollar attorney who'll claim she was framed."

"We also have an unsolved murder. Who says she's not involved?"

"Speaking of the murder, Cowan called this morning. The lab ran the mouth swab from Josh Mooney. They were able to collect DNA off Renata's underwear that was still intact. It matched the DNA collected from Mooney."

Josie put a fist in the air. "Excellent. I hope that bastard pays like hell for what he did."

Otto studied her for a moment. "Let's go back to Caroline. To our former Citizen of the Year. What's your opinion?"

Josie raised a hand to dismiss his question. "That's why we have judges and juries. I just arrest them. I don't have to decide guilt."

"Come on. Don't be such a cop. I'm asking your personal opinion about what Caroline did."

Josie had thought about little else for days. "Okay, then. She used her humanitarian work to cover up something illegal. To me, that makes what she did even worse." Josie walked to the back of the office to look out the window. She finally turned back to Otto. "But this goes deeper than that. It reminds me of one of those companies that make their money on the backs of the little people, with no regard for their safety. As long as they make their money, and they get away with their crimes, they can look the other way and get rich. Pretend what they're doing is helping society. Until someone catches them. That's what I think Caroline did. She didn't care what was happening to those women. She didn't bother to check on their safety because she didn't want to know. That's not just irresponsible, it's criminal."

Otto's lips were pursed and he was nodding as she talked. "I doubt Holder can use any of that, but it sure as hell makes sense to me. Let's get her."

———————

At four-thirty, Josie and Otto sat down with Holder and spent the next several hours discussing Josie's trip to Albuquerque and her involvement in the investigation while officially suspended. She and Holder had a good relationship, and she hadn't wanted him to find out about her involvement when he was in the middle of presenting his latest case to a jury. At one point, Holder called Smokey Blessings, who said that the counsel never officially recognized Josie's suspension because the mayor had not followed proper protocol. Holder asked Blessings to write up his explanation and deliver it to the prosecutor's office.

"I'll be honest, Josie. I don't like any of this. I understand why you went, and I get that you had to go when you did, but you put me in a hell of a bind. This is one of those jury minefields. They could either turn on the mayor for suspending you, or they could sympathize with him because he supported his wife. In that case, they could turn on you for investigating a case without your badge."

"But Smokey just said—"

"I know what he said. But Caroline Moss will have a first-rate attorney who will take anything outside of the investigative norm and paint it as questionable. It comes down to perception and the makeup of the jury. I hate cases like this. I want to take a case to trial that revolves around evidence, not bad decisions."

"What will you charge Caroline with?" Otto asked.

"That depends on what you bring me. I'm not ready to file yet." Josie started to protest and he cut her off. "Under Texas criminal code, I can charge her with the first-degree felony called 'continuous trafficking of persons.' But it only applies to people who commit two or more acts of trafficking. As a first-time offender, she could get twenty-five to ninety-nine years. You get me the timeline. I want to know how many women she delivered, and the dates they were delivered."

"We've got Josh Mooney and this Big Ben fella in Albuquerque to work for information," Otto said.

"Hell, no," Josie said. "I don't want to give Josh Mooney a break. That piece of scum needs to spend every second in jail that we can get."

"Talk with him. See what you can get without making any deals," Holder said. "And see what your buddies in New Mexico come up with. If Big Ben can provide us a list of dates and women's names, and we can link them to the Web site and their families? I'll feel better. I want the connections between Caroline Moss and the various players to be crystal clear."

"What do we do about the mayor?" Otto asked.

Holder pursed his lips and shrugged. "We do nothing. Do

you have any indication he's involved with the trafficking operation?"

"No."

"Then we do nothing. Josie tried the professional courtesy route. We won't do that again," Holder said.

NINETEEN

Josie drove home that night feeling like she was back on top of the world. She and Otto had left the prosecutor's office and called Townie in New Mexico, who had already made headway with Big Ben. Turned out he was a midlevel player in an organization that had spread northeast to Oklahoma City. And he kept impeccable records of the girls entering and exiting the Maid's Quarters. Bottom line, Big Ben was selling out everyone he could think of in order to strike a deal with the prosecutor. Big attorney or not, Caroline was in trouble.

Earlier that day Nick had called to get the story behind the cancellation of Josie's suspension, and he'd asked her to meet him at Dell's house when she got home. Dell had offered to make barbecue brisket for Nick, Beverly, and Josie. When she arrived home at eight o'clock, the lights were off at her house, but she could see a bonfire in front of Dell's. She changed into jeans and a sweatshirt, and found the three of them sitting in lawn chairs around the bonfire, talking and laughing.

The sight of the people she cared most about in the world sitting together and enjoying each other's company made her chest swell up with happiness. She thought it was the kind of simple moment that comes out of nowhere and knocks you to your knees: the kind of happiness that has nothing to do with money or success or material things. She realized in that moment how fortunate she was, and she was glad that her mom was a part of it.

"We got a plate full of brisket waiting for you over here. Come sit down and take a load off," Dell said.

Nick held a beer in the air. "Fresh out of the cooler. Ice cold." He scooted the empty chair closer to his own and Josie sat down, accepting the beer with a wide smile.

"This is nice," she said, looking around the fire.

"We're celebrating that you're back on the job," her mom said, raising her own beer and tilting it in Josie's direction.

"Smokey Blessings made a statement on the public radio station about an hour ago. He said that the information about your suspension was shared in error, and that you were never suspended. He said Chief Gray has the full support of the council and that you were, and still are, actively serving the community."

Josie tipped her head back against the seat and exhaled a long slow breath of relief. "That's more than I expected. I figured they'd just pretend it never happened."

"Smokey's got your back," Dell said.

And that was all that was said. The conversation turned away from the mess the town was now facing. The drama could wait until morning. They enjoyed the cool evening and the warmth of the fire and the easy conversation of friends and family. At midnight, Nick and Josie drove Beverly back to Manny's Motel. Josie walked her mom to her room and asked if she'd thought any more about her plans.

"I won't lie to you," Beverly said. "I like it here. I like being near you. I like your friends and this little town. But there's a part of me that knows this isn't mine to like. It's yours." She leaned against the motel door and looked down the quiet street. "I know I'm pushy. But this time I want to do it right. So I've been thinking. I'm going to head on back to Indiana. I'll give you and Nick some time to think about this. And if you want to invite me to your town to get an apartment and set up a new place here, then we can talk about it. But I'm going to wait to hear from you first."

The lump in Josie's throat kept her from speaking, but she smiled and reached out to her mom, and the two women hugged without hesitation for the first time in many years.

"I'm going to leave in the morning. First light. You give me a call when you're ready."

Josie's throat was so tight she barely got the words out. "I love you."

Beverly smiled. "I love you too, Josie. Always have, always will, no matter what."

Marta had worked a swing shift the night before so that the three officers could meet together at ten to debrief and plan next steps. Once they were seated around the conference table, Josie began.

"We've got two focus areas," she said. "Solving Renata's murder, and breaking down the trafficking organization." She went to the whiteboard hanging on the wall and drew a line down the middle, with Renata's name on one side and Caroline's name on the other.

"Let's start with Caroline. That's the easy target," Otto said.

They listed a dozen calls to be made, including to Townie, to follow up on his investigation; to the prosecutor working the case in Albuquerque, checking the warrant for Caroline's, Josh's, and Macey's phone records; to check on the warrant for the online site Jobs Without Borders; and to review information with the state's cybercrimes unit. The three officers worked up a to-do list for the day and moved on to Renata.

"The search warrant for Josh and Macey Mooney's apartment should come through this morning," Josie said. "Josh Mooney is our number one suspect."

"Even though Isabella didn't think she heard Josh's voice?" Otto said.

"Consider the situation," Josie said. "They're stumbling through the pasture at night with unknown men chasing them. At some point, there's gunfire. Do we really trust her auditory memory?"

Otto tipped his head to acknowledge her point.

"Talk me through what you have," Marta said.

"Isabella and Renata escaped from Josh and Ryan when they were in Piedra Labrada. They made it to a woman's home along the Rio, named Señora Molina, who told them to cross into the U.S. and find me for help. The two women made it to my house and were hiding in the toolshed when a car appeared several nights in a row. The car stopped the second night and a passenger exited the car. The women assumed the person was searching for them. They took off for the pasture. We know that Renata was shot in the back while fleeing from at least two individuals at about ten o'clock in the evening."

"How do you know it was two?" Marta asked.

"Isabella said that as they were being chased, the car continued to move down the road," Josie said.

"Time of death was ten o'clock. It most likely happened while Josie and Dell were at the water meeting in town," Otto said.

"And he's admitted to driving by my house several times to look for Isabella and Renata. He just seems an unlikely suspect for the murder," Josie said, holding her hands up like a shield against

Otto's incredulous look. "Drug fiend, yes. Rapist even, yes. But hunting down a woman to murder her seems a stretch to me."

"But why are you only referring to Josh and not Ryan? Weren't they a team? They were both driving the girls from Guatemala to the U.S., so why's Ryan off the hook?" Marta said.

"Ryan claims he was home the entire night of the murder. I'll check his alibi with his parents," Otto said.

"According to Ryan, when Isabella and Renata ran from the hotel room, he left too. He claimed he couldn't take one more day with Josh. And Josh confirmed that Ryan left. He said he got Ryan to look for the women around my house one night, but that they couldn't find them, and Ryan refused to come back," Josie said.

"So, Josh is saying that he was searching for the two women beside your house for several nights, except for the night that Renata was killed. And it just so happens that someone else showed up that night and killed her?" Marta said with a sneer. "He's lying."

"According to the timeline we've established, two people drove by my house at about ten o'clock and murdered Renata while I was at the water meeting. I think they got spooked about me arriving home from the meeting and finding them, so they left. But they came back to finish the job. That's when I heard the car drive by, at approximately two in the morning."

"So the murderer came back to finish the job, but couldn't find Isabella," Marta said.

Josie nodded. "Exactly. I'm assuming Josh was one of the two, but we have nothing to tie the murder to him," Josie said. "We have a bullet and bullet case that don't match the gun I found at the murder scene. The gun that Isabella threw into the pasture was Josh's. She stole it when she and Renata took off. But the prints belong to Isabella, not Josh."

"What a mess," Marta said. She shook her head and looked at Otto. "Remind me where we are with the search warrant for Josh's apartment?"

"I expect we'll have that today. The judge was out of the county yesterday, but should be back this morning."

"Okay. Marta, why don't you start working the case against Caroline. Otto, you want Josh or Macey?"

"I'll take Josh in jail. At least I don't have to go back to that apartment."

"Tell him we're about to serve a search warrant on his apartment and see if you shake anything out of him. I'll get a jump on the warrant and go talk to Macey Mooney."

Marta rolled her eyes. "Better take your BS detector. That woman wouldn't know the truth if she lived it."

———

It was eleven-thirty when Otto left the office for the jail, so he slid home first for a quick lunch with Delores. He found her behind the house in a lawn chair, petting the cat she was now calling Fergie. The cat's purr was so loud he couldn't hear the words Delores was speaking to the animal. As much as Otto hated cats, Delores seemed to love them to an equal measure.

He startled her when he walked up the stairs to the back porch.

"What on earth are you doing home?" she asked.

He laughed at her response. "You don't sound very excited to see me."

"Well, you always call. Why didn't you tell me you were coming? I'd have had lunch ready for you."

"It's fine. I'll just grab a bologna sandwich and some tea."

Delores shooed the cat off her lap and followed him inside, chatting about her day and the trip to Odessa she was planning to visit their daughter.

Once their sandwiches were fixed they sat and ate while Otto filled Delores in on the growing case against the mayor's wife.

"I just can't picture Caroline in a jail uniform. Do you suppose she'll spend time in jail for this?" she asked.

"It could happen. Look at Martha Stewart."

"True," she said, but her look was skeptical. "Do you think she's a bad person?"

Otto looked up from his plate, surprised at the question. "That's not really what police work is about. We don't necessarily arrest bad people, we arrest people who break the law."

"Makes it easier, though, doesn't it? When you're arresting someone who's a bad person over someone who just made bad decisions?"

Otto took a long drink of his iced tea. He scooted away from the table and carried his dishes to the sink. "I'm afraid I can't answer that question because I'm headed to the jail for an interview." He kissed her on the head and walked toward the front door.

"You can't answer that question because you don't want to," she said, following after him.

"True enough."

"Well, I don't think she's a bad person."

"And what would you like for me to do with that tidbit of information?" he asked, noticing the worry lines around her eyes.

"I don't know. Just take it into account when you arrest her. Be nice about it. And for heaven's sake, don't use handcuffs."

Otto drove back into town to the Arroyo County Jail, where Josh's attorney had agreed to meet at one o'clock. Josh had finally wised up and decided representation would be a good idea.

Otto's mind wandered as the flat sandy desert rolled by, and he thought about Delores's take on the world. She was a good woman who saw the world in shades of gray. But she didn't have conversations with the likes of Josh Mooney. She had the luxury of continuing to see the best in people. Otto thought those years were long gone for him.

Otto waved at Oliver Greene as he parked his Mercedes beside Otto's old jeep. The men walked into the jail together, chatting good-naturedly, and sat together in the conference room, where ten minutes later the jailer delivered Josh. He sat down next to Oliver, who winced at the smell that wafted over them.

Otto was fairly certain that daily showers were required at the jail, but Josh looked greasier and smelled nastier than the last visit. His hands shook and a sheen of sweat covered his forehead. Otto assumed he was suffering from withdrawal symptoms, but their understaffed jail had little in terms of medical help. Tough it out was about as good as they got in terms of detoxing an inmate.

Josh crossed his arms over his chest, shivering underneath a layer of sweat, as Otto set up the meeting and got the preliminaries on tape.

"I just discovered that the judge has granted a search warrant for your apartment. What do you think about that?" Otto asked.

Josh shrugged.

"The police will be headed over there this afternoon to pull all that junk off your shelves, searching through all your treasures for the murder weapon."

Josh rolled his eyes and tipped his head back so far that Otto thought he was passing out. He finally snapped his head forward and said, "All that crap is Macey Jane's. She's the one that drags all that crap home. I just have to find a place to put it."

"Are the police going to find the murder weapon when they search?"

He frowned. "No. Because I didn't kill anyone. I don't know where the gun is, but it's not in our apartment. All you're going to do is freak out Macey for no reason."

"So clear this up for me. Who shot Renata?"

"No clue."

"To my knowledge the only two people who drove out to search for her were you and your driving buddy, Ryan. Is that true?"

"Obviously not! The night I didn't drive out there somebody else did. And somebody else shot her."

"But who? Nobody else has the motivation. You're the only person who gains by killing her."

"Uh, no. Not so." He rubbed his hands up and down his arms to warm up. "Can you get me a cigarette?"

"I'll make a deal with you. Tell me who killed Renata, and I'll personally go buy you a carton."

Josh shuddered all over. "Look. I'm not stupid. I didn't kill her. I don't have the weapon because I didn't do it. So you got nothing to tie me to the murder. I keep my mouth shut and I get out of here. That's how it works."

"What about your boss? Caroline Moss? Does she know anything about the murder? Maybe she asked you to get rid of Renata before things spun even more out of control. You owed her something, right? You screwed up the operation. You raped five women you were transporting."

Oliver interrupted, for the sake of the recording. "Officer Podowski, that's conjecture. There's nothing tangible that links Josh to the rape of those women."

"Actually, there is now. We have DNA from Josh that matches DNA found on one of the women's underwear."

Josh looked offended. "That doesn't mean I raped her!"

Otto felt the questions going off track and tried to redirect to his point. "The fact is that Caroline Moss had all kinds of reasons for wanting you to murder those women. Both of them were hiding out at Chief Gray's house, and you weren't able to capture them. If she asked you to kill those women? To solve the problem for her? Then that takes some of the burden off you. Puts it on her. You get what I mean?"

Josh pointed his finger at Oliver and jabbed it into his arm, causing him to flinch. "My attorney told me, keep your mouth shut, and I'll get you out of here. So that's what I'm doing."

"Even though fingering someone else could get you off the hook?"

"My attorney told me, keep your mouth shut, and I'll get you out of here."

When Macey Mooney opened her apartment door, she had the same sweaty, winded appearance that she'd had the last time Josie visited. Macey was wearing black jeans and a black hoodie that looked completely at odds with her bleach-blond pigtails and big innocent-looking eyes. She stepped back about a foot and allowed Josie to move just inside the doorway.

Josie sensed things were different in the apartment—not cleaner, just different. She noticed the collection of snow globes and ash-trays that had been on the bookshelf to the right of the entrance was gone. The shelves were still there, but the ashtrays and snow globes had been replaced with four shelves of empty jars. Not useful canning jars, just a collection of empty pickle and jelly jars. She glanced around the apartment and thought more shelves had been added since the last visit, and then she noticed a box of ashtrays on the floor by the kitchen table. The organized chaos put Josie on edge.

"I been cleaning since last time you were here," Macey said. "I've seen those shows where the police come in and make a person leave because of their stuff."

"You mean the hoarding shows?" Josie asked.

"Call it what you want. But I been cleaning. Getting things systematized. When Josh gets back we're gonna get a new place in the country. This place ain't big enough for our stuff." Macey gave Josie a quick sideways glance, as if gauging her reaction. She could imagine Macey maniacally moving junk from one location in the house to another while her brother was in county lockup facing murder charges.

"Josh has his eye on a place out by the river. It's a trailer with a shed and a carport."

"I'm not here to talk about your apartment. I want to talk about Josh and what's going on with him."

Macey flinched as if Josie had lifted a hand toward her.

"Let's sit down and have a talk. Your brother's in a lot of trouble. He probably won't be coming home from jail for quite a while."

"Leave Josh alone. I got cleaning to do."

"Macey, your brother is in jail for rape. Doesn't that bother you?"

"Yeah, it does. Because it's not true!"

"How do you know?"

"'Cause he's the sweetest person I know. And he would not do that to me or to anybody else."

Josie thought about Ryan's description of Macey being the more intelligent of the brother-and-sister team, but Josie wasn't seeing it. The woman had the mannerisms and verbal skills of a preteen. But she also seemed more immature since the last time Josie had spoken with her. Josie figured it was either an act to keep out of trouble, or she was doped up.

Josie motioned toward the kitchen table. "Let's sit and talk for a few minutes."

She felt her phone vibrate in her pocket and checked a text from Marta. The warrant for Josh and Macey's apartment had come through. She texted Marta. *Bring it now.*

Macey pouted and led the way through a maze of boxes and piles and stacks of flea-market finds over to the table. She sat down and Josie sat in the chair next to her. She was hoping to get everything she could out of Macey before Marta arrived with the search warrant. Macey would be furious and all conversation would certainly stop at that point.

"Tell me about how Josh got involved transporting the girls."

Macey shrugged.

"Come on, Macey. He's admitted to all of it. I just want to hear your side of what happened."

"Why?"

"I'm trying to understand how you and Josh ended up working for Caroline Moss."

Her eyes shot open. "He told you that?"

Josie nodded. "We know all about it. He told us about the money, about Caroline setting you guys up with Ryan. All of it. I'm just wondering why Caroline Moss picked you and Josh to begin with."

Macey grinned and slid her hands under her thighs so that she was sitting on them. "He was delivering salt. That's how he met her."

Josie sighed and tried not to let her growing impatience show. "What do you mean, 'delivering salt'?"

Macey squinted at Josie like she'd asked a stupid question. "Working for the co-op. Delivering salt for water softeners."

"So he was delivering bags of water softener salt to Caroline's home, and he got to know her that way?"

"Yep. She saw he was a good driver. She said he was dependable and always showed up on time, not like a bunch of the others. So she asked Josh if he wanted to make big money driving all the way to Guatemala."

"How long has he been driving for her?"

"A long time. The first time was last September, because he was gone on my birthday."

"Do you know how many times he's driven for Caroline?"

She turned in her chair and pointed to a wall calendar hanging above the kitchen sink. "I mark it on there. That's where I mark all his trips."

Josie felt a surge of relief. This was the information that Holder specifically requested. And she would be able to confirm it against Big Ben's records for deliveries.

"Can you show me what you mean?"

She lifted a shoulder and looked uncertain, but retrieved the calendar. "These *x*'s that are in red are the Guatemala trips. I thought Guatemala seemed like a red color."

Josie asked Macey to flip through the calendar and she identified seven different trips. "Can you tell me how many girls Josh picked up on these trips?"

She frowned and shook her head.

"Do you have any other information on the trips Josh took?"

She pointed to the calendar. "Just that. Why?"

Josie wasn't sure how to answer, and took a moment to respond. "I'm trying to understand how Caroline's business works. If you and Josh can help us understand how the transporting of the women worked, it'll help Josh's case. The judge will like that Josh helped us."

Her phone buzzed again and she read Marta's text back to her. *Be there in five.*

Macey looked at Josie's phone, and then at her face, her expression changing from a childish curiosity to suspicion.

"Are you talking about me?" Macey asked, looking at the pocket where Josie had replaced her phone.

"Sorry about that. Just keeping up with police business." Josie shifted in her seat. With Marta on her way, it was time to hit Macey with the tough questions.

"Did you ever ride with Josh when he was transporting the women?"

Macey narrowed her eyes at Josie. "Are you here to arrest me too?"

"That depends on several things."

"Like what?"

"Did you meet any of the women that Josh transported this last time?"

Macey said nothing.

"Come on, Macey. Don't play dumb. I know you did. Because you were with Josh when the police picked you guys up outside of Van Horn. When you made that last attempt to deliver the girls to Albuquerque."

She sat up straighter in her chair, but remained sitting on her hands. Josie wondered if Macey was stilling the shakes. "The police let me go 'cause I was just riding along with Josh. He just wanted somebody to ride in the van with him for that long drive. So I did."

"So you convinced the police that you were helping Josh deliver those women legally. They didn't charge you with anything because Josh took the fall. But I don't think that's really true, is it? I think you like to play dumb. You think it keeps you out of trouble."

Macey reached up and slowly pulled the hood up from her sweatshirt and pulled it down as low as she could over her forehead. She stared into Josie's eyes in an apparent attempt to intimidate that came across as more bizarre than threatening. Too many fried brain cells.

"Here's the deal," Josie said. "The judge has signed a warrant to search your apartment for the weapon used to murder Renata."

Macey straightened her back again, freeing her hands and forgetting her death stare. "You can't just come in here and search my things. I'm not in jail, Josh is!"

"We have a search warrant that gives us full access to the contents of this apartment as they relate to the crime."

Her mouth dropped open and she stared, unblinking. "But it's my apartment too! They told me you couldn't search the apartment because it's half mine!"

"Who's they?"

"Just somebody I know."

"Somebody gave you bad information."

"There's nothing here you'd want anyway."

"You can save yourself a lot of time and a lot of mess by getting the gun now and handing it over."

"Why are you doing this? You really think Josh killed that woman?"

"I do. And I think you were in the car with him that night. I think you drove and Josh got out of the car to find the two missing women. When he couldn't catch them, he shot one of them, and the other escaped. That makes you an accessory to murder."

"No! That's not what happened!"

"Then tell me what did happen."

"I don't know. Josh wasn't there that night. He didn't have anything to do with it. Go ahead and search this stupid place for the gun. You won't find it."

They both turned toward the door when they heard a knock. Josie stood and Macey continued talking behind her.

"He didn't kill that woman. I swear to you on a stack of Bibles that he didn't kill her."

Josie opened the door for Marta to enter and she turned back to Macey. "Did you kill her?"

"No! And I don't know who did it either. I just know it wasn't Josh."

"It's going to be a long day, Macey. We're going to have to look through all of your collections. We'll have to move everything until we find the gun. Unless you give it to me now."

"I don't have any gun!" she yelled.

Josie turned to Marta, who was glancing around the apartment looking overwhelmed. "This will take days," she whispered.

When Otto finished at the jail, he joined Marta and Josie to carry out the search warrant. They spent three hours searching the apartment and came away with only one find. The women's IDs and documentation from Guatemala that were not found in the van the night the police pulled them over on their way to Albuquerque. One more nail in Josh's case, but nothing to tie it back to Caroline, and no closer to finding the murderer.

———

Back at the office, Marta was called for a burglary while Josie and Otto settled into an afternoon of paperwork. Using the women's identities on the fake IDs, Josie theorized Renata's last name was Carrillo and she asked Lou to begin tracking down her family.

Ten minutes later Lou called her.

"Good news. Phone records just arrived. I've got the document in my email. You and I were both copied."

"Thanks, Lou."

Josie opened the documents on her computer and sighed. "This is huge, Otto. This could take days."

Otto looked over her shoulder as she scrolled through page after page of phone numbers, sent and received, for each person's records.

"Break it down. Print off the records for the past month and we'll start there."

Josie printed the past four weeks of phone calls and laid the piles on the conference table. Josh and Big Ben had used throw-away phones to conduct their illegal business, but both men's phones had been seized during their arrests. Josie had found that the foolproof methods criminals used to cover their tracks often sealed the cases against them.

"Okay. We've got six sets of records for the past four weeks, leading up to the murder of Renata. We've got Caroline Moss's home phone. And we have the records for the contact in Big Ben's phone named Lilith, which we assume is Caroline too."

"Is the number from the Lilith contact registered to a specific person?" Otto asked.

"It's a throwaway phone, so all we have is the call log, not who it's registered to. We also have Josh and Macey Mooney's cell phone records, as well as Ryan's." Josie held up another piece of paper she pulled off her desk. "And more good news. Townie faxed this to me today. It's phone records for the past year for Big Ben. We can start with the past month for him too."

"Do we actually have proof each of these phones is linked to each person?" he said.

"We seized Josh and Macey's throwaway phones, so their numbers are confirmed. Ryan's cell phone was registered in his name because his parents pay for the bill. And Big Ben's phone was seized. The only phone there's any question about is Lilith's, who we think is Caroline." Josie groaned and reached back to rub her neck. "Basically, it's a big tangled mess of numbers, but it's a start."

Otto pitched a pad of paper on the conference table and used a marker to begin writing down key phone numbers they were looking for. They made a list of known phone numbers for the following people:

Caroline Moss (home phone and cell—registered)
Lilith (cell—throwaway)
Josh Mooney (cell—throwaway)
Macey Mooney (cell—throwaway)
Ryan Needleman (cell—throwaway)
Benjamin Dominguez (Big Ben) (cell—throwaway)

"I'll export the phone numbers into Excel and search and find the phone numbers over the past year. I'll highlight the numbers and we'll get a quick look at who's calling who. We'll see if we can connect Lilith to Big Ben for each of the seven trips," Josie said.

"Then we'll piece them together with a timeline to figure out who was communicating with who."

It took several hours to search the documents and narrow down the list of numbers. Next, they laid out a piece of butcher-block paper on the table to draw a four-week timeline and a diagram with lines connecting the six numbers of interest. They discovered Macey had only communicated with Josh and Ryan, so they eliminated her from the diagram.

They found that four weeks ago, two days before Josh and Ryan departed for Guatemala, the two of them had communicated frequently by cell phone. They also found one phone call from Lilith to Josh, and two from Lilith to Ryan. There was no more communication from Lilith to Josh or Ryan until two days before the murder, but none after that. Josie placed red stars by Lilith's calls.

They also discovered two calls that Lilith received the week that Josh and Ryan set off for Guatemala. The calls were from Big Ben's cell phone. It was the direct link to the transportation ring that they needed.

Josie used the calendar she had taken from Macey Mooney and typed up the list of days that Josh had allegedly driven for Caroline and printed it. They found cell phone communication between Lilith and Big Ben on all seven occasions. Holder had what he needed.

TWENTY

As requested, Tyler Holder walked into the police department office at eight-thirty the next morning. He was wearing khaki pants and a white shirt, unbuttoned at the neck, and was looking much more at ease than the night Josie had slammed him with her theory on Caroline Moss running a human trafficking ring.

"No suit today?" Josie asked.

He smiled. "Closing arguments were yesterday. My wife was ready to throw me out of the house if that trial hadn't ended soon."

"You won't like this any better," she said.

"Lay it on me."

Josie and Otto spent the next thirty minutes presenting their case, with dates, times, and a phone chart that detailed all of the known players in the trafficking organization, including those that Townie had confirmed from Albuquerque.

He studied the diagram for some time and finally said, "This is excellent work. I'm really impressed."

Josie glanced at Otto, who acknowledged the compliment with a nod. It was a huge relief.

"How did you get the dates for the trips?" he asked.

Josie showed him Macey's calendar with the red *x*'s, and the matching dates from Big Ben's office records.

"You don't have anything else to confirm travel dates? Credit card slips for gas, hotel bills, anything?"

"Not at this point. But we do have the cell phone records to and from Lilith, who we assume is Caroline, to Big Ben in Albuquerque that match those dates."

"What about a murder charge?" he asked.

"I'm confident the murder is tied to the four people from Artemis we just discussed, but we have no murder weapon, and nothing to tie any of them to the murder site that night," she said.

"I'm going to place a few phone calls about this one. We'll end up with national media attention before it's over with. I want to make sure I have my business in order before I file a warrant for her arrest. Until you hear from me, keep this under wraps. Are we clear?"

"Understood," she said.

They gave copies of their documentation to Holder, and Josie and Otto sat down at the conference table, exhausted from the late night and early morning.

"What do you think?" Josie asked, rubbing her burning eyes and yawning.

"Personally, I think we did a hell of a job. I'm guessing Holder may take a day or two to sort this all out. He won't hang his neck out there for a senator's daughter-slash-mayor's wife without knowing he's got a good case to back him up."

"You realize Moss is my supervisor," she said.

"That's crossed my mind many times over the past week."

"If she isn't arrested? Or if the charges are dismissed?"

"You'll lose your job," he said, finishing her train of thought.

Josie took a gulp of cold coffee and slumped back in her chair, worn out with discussing the case. "My mom is headed back to Indiana today."

Otto winced. "She get tired of waiting around for you to visit?"

"No, it wasn't like that. She said she wanted to give me some space to think about her moving here. She's ready to make the move if I give her the okay."

"Really?" Otto's bushy eyebrows rose at the notion. "She's waiting on an okay?"

Josie grinned. "I know. She's so much mellower than her last visit. To tell you the truth, I'm a little freaked out by all of it."

Otto leaned back in his chair as well and crossed his legs out in front him. "You aren't going to get all philosophical on me, are you?"

"I don't even know what you mean by that."

"We don't have to talk about people changing, or becoming a better person, or any of that, do we? Delores wears me out with that kind of thinking."

Josie laughed. "I don't guess I have much control over any of it anyway. Not much point in discussing it."

"Exactly. Live your life and the rest will fall into place."

"Or not."

He grinned. "Or not."

"Let's go home and get some sleep."

———

At five o'clock the next evening Holder reached Josie on her cell phone as she was driving back to the police department from a child welfare call. A mother had scalded her little girl's hands as punishment for eating candy when she'd been told not to. Josie was angry and she had a headache.

"Yes, sir?" she answered when his number showed on her cell phone.

"I've got an update on Caroline Moss."

"I hope it's good news," she said. "I could use some."

"It depends on how you look at it."

"Hmm. Go ahead," Josie said, knowing already that it wouldn't be good news.

"I'm turning the case over to the FBI."

"Now?"

"Josie. Think about the case. This isn't just a human trafficking case taking place in Artemis. Not only does it cross an international border, but it now crosses into New Mexico and Oklahoma. This is a federal crime. They can help us track down the phone connection between Caroline and Lilith. This isn't something for local law enforcement to handle."

She bristled at the comment but said nothing.

"Obviously it's not that you haven't done an excellent job with the investigation, but we've got three different states involved, as well as Mexico and Guatemala. I don't need to tell you what kind of hell goes into working with two foreign countries during a criminal investigation. This goes beyond me. We need help. And I don't want to screw this up. Agreed?"

Josie unclenched her jaw and forced a reply. "That's fine. Just let me know what I need to do on my end."

"Good enough. I appreciate it. I'll be in touch."

Josie hung up and banged the steering wheel. She called Otto.

"We lost the case," she said.

"FBI?"

"Holder passed it off."

"Damn, Josie. I know we saw this coming, but it doesn't make it any easier to stomach."

"Yeah, well. I didn't think we'd lose it this fast. And I'm pissed off. I was suspended from duty over this case, and I don't even have the satisfaction of bringing it to a close."

"We're not done. We have an unsolved murder."

Josie blew out a rush of air. "I know that, Otto."

"Okay. Well. It's after five. I'm tired and you're grumpy. So I'm going home before Delores threatens mandatory retirement again. Okay?"

"All right. See you in the morning."

Josie hung up and continued her drive back to the department. Her anger fired her adrenaline, so she maintained her course to the PD. She pulled in front of the department and texted Nick. She'd lost track of his schedule and couldn't remember if he was going to be at her house that night.

Working late. Where are you? She paused before she clicked send. It seemed like a pathetic question to ask someone you cared about, but one of the positives with Nick was that he took her for the mess that she was.

Ten seconds later he texted back. *In Mexico. Surveillance tonight. Remember?*

Now I do. Love you.

Love you too. Enjoy that warm bed. I'll be sitting by a trash can in an alley.

She smiled, imagining him crouched down in an alleyway, wearing his black Kevlar and ski mask for disguise and warmth. He could be scary as hell when he wanted to be, and she had to admit, she liked that about him.

Josie waved hello to the night dispatcher, Brian Moore.

He was on the phone, so he passed a stack of mail to Josie as she walked by and mouthed a silent hello. When she got to the office she found Marta working on a case report at her desk.

Josie opened a pull-top can of fruit cocktail and poured it into a bowl. She drank the juice and ate the fruit for her dinner as she filled Marta in on the latest from Holder.

"Sorry to hear that," Marta said. "Why don't you go home and give your brain a rest. Get a good night's sleep and start fresh tomorrow."

"I can't. I'm too pissed."

Josie finished off a package of cheese and peanut butter crackers and spread the phone documents out across the conference table, on top of the phone diagram, and stared at the numbers and the timeline of phone calls for a long time.

She went back to the night of the murder and examined Josh's calls. He had not placed a call to Lilith that night. And Lilith had not called anyone after three that afternoon. She hadn't talked to any of the other suspects that day, or since then.

Josh had placed several local calls the day of the murder, and received several from Macey earlier in the day. The last call he received that day had been at 6:37 p.m., from a local number Josie didn't recognize. Josie typed the number into a search engine but got nothing in return.

Next, she pulled out Big Ben's phone records and studied them again. He had placed and received hundreds of calls on his cell phone over the past month, most of them with the area code for Albuquerque, New Mexico. Josie ran her finger down the list of area codes and stopped at 432, a West Texas number. She checked the number against Josh's, Macey's, Ryan's, and Caroline's numbers, but it didn't match up. That meant Ben had been called by another person in West Texas.

Josie compared that number to the number that had called Josh Mooney at 6:37 p.m. the evening of the murder. The numbers matched.

"Damn. Marta. Come here."

Josie ran through what she had just discovered and Marta clamped a hand on Josie's shoulder. "How do we trace that number down?" she asked.

On a whim, Josie pulled her cell phone out and typed the number in to see if it registered as one of her contacts. The contact Mayor Moss appeared.

"Son of a bitch," she whispered, and held her phone up for Marta to see.

Marta sat down heavily in the chair beside Josie. Her forehead was bunched into worry lines. "The mayor called Big Ben one day before Renata was killed."

"And that was several days before I went to his office to tell him about Caroline being involved. So he obviously knew about this before I showed up. It's probably why he took my gun and badge away. He wanted to block the investigation."

"I just can't believe this," Marta said.

Josie went to her daily notes logbook on her desk and flipped through it. "Did I mention to you that Mayor Moss stopped by here before all this broke loose to say the mayor's office had received a weird voice message?"

Marta frowned and shook her head. "Doesn't sound familiar."

"It wasn't a big deal at the time. He said the message was about something bad going on in town. He said Helen accidentally deleted it." Josie found the note in her logbook and looked up at Marta. "He stopped by the office the morning of the day we found the body in the pasture."

"Why would he say that to you, knowing Caroline was mixed up in this?" Marta said.

"Maybe Moss has been a part of the organization all along. Maybe he was trying to deflect attention."

She and Marta sat down at the table and stared at the phone records from Big Ben until the numbers blurred. Examining the calls over the past year, they weren't able to find any other from Mayor Moss, nor did they find any additional calls from Big Ben to the 432 area code.

"Mayor Moss?" Marta said. Her voice was breathy, unbelieving. "Caroline was shock enough."

"It's not that he has a high regard for women; he obviously

doesn't. But he defends the law. That's the part of his personality that always felt genuine to me," Josie said. "It was the part of his personality that I respected. This is the kind of news that makes you question everyone."

"What do we do now?" Marta said.

Josie looked at her watch. It was almost eight p.m. She wanted to call Otto, but refrained. "Holder told me to stand down while he turns the investigation over to the FBI. I want to go home and think on this tonight. I'll wait until morning to turn Holder's world upside down."

TWENTY-ONE

Josie drove home, fed the dog but skipped her own supper, and then climbed into bed at nine o'clock, where she lay on her back staring at the ceiling. Her mind flitted from Nick sleeping in Mexico, to her mom driving back to Indiana, to five women traveling from Guatemala, to Josh Mooney in lockup, until she finally got out of bed and dressed in jeans and a sweatshirt to take Chester outside for a walk.

Behind the house, Chester hit on a scent and zigzagged around the backyard sniffing out a jackrabbit or some other little animal. Josie decided she didn't have the energy for a walk, so she took advantage of the bright moonlight and sat on the ground with her back against a large rock to watch Chester scout out the yard.

She allowed her gaze to travel out across Dell's pasture and wondered how long it would take her to view the field with the same sense of serenity she'd once had. A day spent working with twisted dopers like Josh and Macey Mooney slipped out of her mind when she and Chester took off into the desert, looking for nothing but interesting rocks and glimpses of wildlife or a bright blooming flower thriving in the midst of sand and dust. Now she looked into the pasture and the vivid image of two young women fleeing for their lives from men intent on capturing or killing them ran like a movie through her brain.

Josie thought back to the night she'd gone to town for the water meeting. The night the killers obviously knew she wouldn't be at home. The killer who knew she had an interest in the county water supply. As a cop with limited resources, she didn't own enough ground to be personally affected, but her neighbor Dell sure as hell did, and the killer had to have known that. The meeting was about the amount of water allowed to be pumped from an individual's well, and the use of meters to determine depleting groundwater usage. The meeting became heated on both sides, from water conservationists to ranchers trying to save fragile crops and livestock. Josie watched men and women who had been friends and neighbors for years face off against each other in a battle that would end friendships before it was over. She ran through her mind the various people she had seen at the meeting, people who had stood at the microphone to speak from handwritten notes they'd carefully prepared, to the hotheads in the back of the room catcalling. Then she wondered who wasn't at the meeting. Who was missing that should have been there? Who might have skipped the meeting in order to hunt down and kill a woman?

She felt the blood drain from her face as she mentally checked off the list of speakers that night. Who was the one person in town who lived for moments in the spotlight? Who loved controversy and the chance to stand as a voice of reason in troubled times? And he hadn't spoken that night. Josie realized she hadn't seen him at all.

She pulled her phone out of her sweatshirt pocket and checked the time. It was 10:11 p.m., too late to politely call, but she couldn't wait until morning.

She dialed Smokey Blessings, who had given the opening

address at the water meeting, and then introduced the speakers throughout the night. He answered on the second ring.

"Smokey, it's Josie. I apologize for calling you so late at night."

"It's no problem. Everything okay?"

"I'm not sure. I'm trying to piece together a timeline, and I'm hoping you can help me."

"Sure."

"Remember back to the night of the water usage meeting?"

"How could I forget?"

"I'm trying to think back to the speakers that evening and I don't remember Mayor Moss being there that night."

"Hell, no, he wasn't there. Why do you think I had to mediate that meeting? I sure as hell didn't want to. I hate public speaking."

"Why didn't he do it? It seems like he'd have wanted to be there."

"He was supposed to. We'd been planning that event for weeks. And he was going to lead it. Then he calls me at about one o'clock that afternoon and says he and Caroline have to leave for El Paso. Like, right then. Some kind of family emergency came up. He asked me to lead it—despite knowing I hate that kind of thing."

Josie was quiet for a second, taking in the information. She was certain that she'd seen Caroline's phone calls for the night of the murder, and they had been placed locally. "Thanks, Smokey. I appreciate it."

"Sure."

"And I appreciate you making things right with the media, about my suspension. It meant more to me than you can probably imagine."

"We're not done with the mayor," he said. "But I suspect this conversation may lead to further developments, so we'll hang tight."

"I think that's a wise decision."

This time, when Josie got Chester situated on his rug, and she flipped the bedside lamp off, she fell asleep within minutes of laying her head on the pillow.

———·———

Josie was in the shower at five the next morning, anxious to get to work. When she arrived she fired up her computer and went back to the same phone records she and Marta had left on the conference table the night before. Josie found Caroline's records and saw that she had placed one call from her cell phone to Mayor Moss's cell phone the night of the murder at 9:52 p.m., and received one from him at 9:59 p.m. Both calls were listed on the phone record as "voicemail" calls. If they had traveled to El Paso together for a family emergency, wouldn't they most likely have been together, instead of leaving each other voicemails? She had to find some way to confirm whether the trip to El Paso was a sham.

Josie kept a close eye on her watch, and at exactly seven a.m. she called a representative with West Texas Mobile whom she knew only as Janet. But she knew Janet well enough to know that she worked the seven-to-three-thirty shift, on a Monday-through-Friday schedule.

As the only carrier with a significant number of towers in one of the most remote parts of the country, West Texas Mobile had a monopoly on phone service in Artemis and Arroyo County. It made accessing phone records for local investigations a much easier task to accomplish. And several times in the past, Janet had provided quick access to phone records before a subpoena could be issued and granted. Josie was careful not to abuse the favor the woman provided, but an unsolved homicide was justifiable in Josie's mind.

"This is Janet. How can I help?"

"Good morning. This is Police Chief Josie Gray. How are you this morning?"

"I'm fine, Chief Gray! And how are you?"

"I'm doing well. I'm actually calling with a question for you."

"Certainly."

"I have subpoenaed phone records for three individuals with West Texas Mobile accounts. I'll be submitting a request for one more set of records today. I wouldn't ask for your help, but this is involving a murder suspect and we're closing in on the case."

"Go ahead."

"I'm wondering if I can give you a phone number, and ask you to tell me what calls were placed during a sixteen-hour period of time."

"I think I can do that." Her voice had lowered to just above a whisper.

Josie read off Mayor Moss's cell phone number and gave her the date and asked for calls between one p.m., the time that the mayor was supposed to have left for El Paso, and six a.m. the next morning.

Janet placed Josie on hold and a few minutes later read her a list of five phone calls that the mayor placed between those hours. Josie wrote down the list of numbers and immediately recognized both Caroline and Josh Mooney's cell phone numbers.

"Okay. Now for the bigger question. Can you tell me the location of the tower where each of those five calls were placed?"

"Mmmm. I can do that. I'll need to place you on hold for a bit." She paused. "And you're just looking for a verbal. Right? No printed documents?"

"Just a verbal. I need to know where the person was when those calls were placed."

"Okay. Hang tight."

Fifteen minutes later Janet came back on the phone. "I'm so sorry to keep you waiting so long. Sometimes these computers act like they don't want to wake up in the morning."

"You're doing me a huge favor. No need to apologize. Were you able to get anything?"

"I was. Nothing too complicated. All of the towers were within Arroyo County. The first four calls pinged off the tower located off of Nex Road. Are you familiar with that area?"

"Yes. I know that area of the county. I can find it. And the other call?"

"That call pinged off the tower on River Road. It's located right down near the border. You know that area?"

Josie knew exactly what tower she was referring to. It was within five miles of her home. And a four-hour drive from El Paso.

———

When Otto walked into the office at a little before eight that morning, Josie was standing at the whiteboard finishing a chart that detailed the mayor's calls, the times they were placed, and the geographical location where they were placed. When Josie turned, Otto took one look at her expression and said, "What's up?"

Josie described her conversation with Janet.

"Hot damn. So who do those numbers belong to?" he asked, pointing to her chart.

Josie pointed to the top four numbers, calls that were most likely made at or near the mayor's home. "All four of those calls, placed between three in the afternoon and just after eight that night, were to Josh Mooney."

Otto winced.

"The last call was a return call to Caroline's number. The return call was placed at 9:59 p.m. Want to guess what cell phone tower that call pinged off?" she asked.

"I'm guessing one in your vicinity?"

Josie took a moment to respond, still so shaken by the realization of what the information meant that she could barely acknowledge it. "The mayor was by my house during the time that Renata was murdered. And he made cell phone contact with Josh Mooney multiple times leading up to that."

Otto shook his head for some time before responding. "Did Josh make any calls that night that we can trace?"

"No. Nothing. Based on these calls, and what Smokey told me, I think the mayor saw the town meeting about the water tower as his chance to go to my house and take care of the problem of the two women. He knew from Caroline what a mess she was in, so he called Josh Mooney and convinced him to go with him to take care of the job."

"The question is, who pulled the trigger?" Otto said.

Tyler Holder was driving to San Antonio for a preliminary meeting with the FBI when Josie reached him and explained the latest developments.

"Son of a bitch."

"Caroline called the mayor at a little before ten the night of the murder. She left a voicemail. He called her back seven minutes later and left a return voicemail for her. That seems odd to me. If she knew a murder was about to take place, would she really have communicated by voicemail?"

"Damn, Josie. Hang on. I'm halfway to San Antonio. I'm turning around."

"I want to go visit Caroline."

"Hang on," he said. "Can you give me a minute to process this?"

"I want to know why she called him. Did she tell him to murder the girl? Did she tell the mayor to go get Josh to help take care of business? Or was she trying to call him off?"

Holder made a noise. "But you said the mayor had talked to Josh several times earlier that day."

"Maybe the mayor was trying to talk Josh out of doing something rash," Josie said.

Holder took a second to respond. "I don't think so. If you were in Josh's place, if the mayor told you even once to forget it, to let the girls go? You'd do it in a heartbeat."

"What might take some convincing, and several phone calls, was if the mayor was convincing Josh that he needed to help him catch, or murder, Renata and Isabella."

"That makes sense to me," Holder said.

"I want to talk to Caroline. I have a hunch. I saw the look on her face when I confronted her with this. She was overwhelmed with emotion. The mayor was pissed." Josie thought about the conversation she'd had with Otto and his take on the events. "Maybe she really had convinced herself she was offering a service. Maybe not quite legal, but she'd rationalized for herself that she was doing a good thing. And when things went bad, the mayor tried to fix the problem."

"And created one hell of a mess."

"Does this mean I can go grab Caroline?"

"Now hang on. You're talking about Moss's phone records. He wasn't part of the subpoena."

"That's true. This is based on a phone call with West Texas Mobile."

"All right. I'll get the judge on the phone and get those records ASAP. As soon as I get the approval from him, you get your contact and get those records. Once we have proof his phone was in the vicinity of the murder the night it took place, I'll submit a search warrant for the gun. I want that done today."

"That's great. Now hear me out on Caroline. After seeing her reaction the day I confronted her at home, I suspect she started this mess and lost control. I don't think I have anything to lose by going and talking to her."

He didn't respond and she continued. "The chance of flight for the Mosses is about zero. They're too public."

"This is sketchy," Holder said. "This investigation has been turned over to the FBI. It's a federal case."

"But the murder is local. The FBI is investigating a human trafficking case. We're looking at a murder."

Holder cursed and Josie heard him bang on something repeatedly. He finally relented. "What are you going to do if the mayor is there?"

"He should be at work. If he's at home, I'll ask to speak with her in private. I'll just take it one step at a time."

Holder was silent for a minute. "You take another officer with you. And you let me know the minute you're done with her."

Josie hung up and saw Otto staring at her intently. "I heard," he said. He walked to the back of the office and looked out the window to the spot where the mayor parked his pickup truck every day and gave Josie a thumbs-up. "He's here."

"Let's go."

Otto drove and they said little on their way to the Mosses' house. When they pulled into the driveway she said, "I think I should talk to her alone. You can stay here and watch for the mayor. If you see him headed this way, come on inside. I feel like she'd open up easier to me, so it doesn't feel like an ambush."

Otto nodded. "Agreed. I'll post outside the front door where I've got a good view of the road."

Caroline answered the door wearing an outfit similar to what she'd worn last time Josie visited, but her appearance was strikingly different. Her hair hung limp around her face, and her eyes flashed anger when she saw it was Josie.

"I have nothing to talk to you about," she said, and started to shut the door.

Josie put her hand out to stop it. "Caroline, please. Give me five minutes."

"I'm calling my attorney," she said, but she stopped short of closing the door.

"Caroline, this is important. I'd like to hear your side of things. You may be able to clear things up before this gets out of hand," Josie said, knowing that was a lie.

Caroline stared at Josie for a long moment, obviously weighing her options, and finally walked back into the house, leaving the door open for Josie to enter. Caroline didn't take her outside onto the veranda, or offer drinks; they sat in the front room in club chairs facing each other.

"I need to explain new evidence that we've found. Things have turned very serious. For both you and the mayor. We have a clear picture about how your business runs. We understand how the transportation route works, the money, the people involved, and so on. Over the past twenty-four hours we've also put together a clear picture about how the murder took place. We have phone records that link the killer to the location of the murder."

Caroline sat with her arms crossed over her chest, but when Josie mentioned the killer she squeezed her arms even closer to her body.

"The night of the water meeting in town, why did Mayor Moss tell Smokey that you and he had to leave town for El Paso?"

Caroline's eyebrows drew up in confusion. "What do you mean?"

"The mayor said he couldn't lead the meeting because you were leaving for El Paso that afternoon. For a family emergency."

She opened her mouth as if to speak and then closed it again, staring at Josie as if she didn't know what to say. "I don't know. It's been months since we've been to El Paso. Steve has a brother there, but he's fine."

"You or the mayor didn't travel to El Paso any time over the past two weeks?"

"No."

"Can you imagine why the mayor would have told Smokey that?"

"I have no idea. And I don't understand what you're saying about the meeting. He was there."

"The mayor?" Josie asked.

"Yes. He told me he'd be late, but when he wasn't home by ten o'clock I called to find out when he'd be home."

"And did you talk to him?" Josie asked.

"No. I left a voice message. He called back a few minutes later and said that he'd be late. That he was getting together with a few ranchers after the meeting to finish the discussion." She looked lost in thought, as if trying to replay the conversation. "I probably have the message on my phone still. I had left my phone on the bed and gone out to the kitchen to write myself a note, and I missed his call."

"Why wouldn't you use your home phone?"

She looked annoyed with the question. "I don't know. We don't even need it. We almost always use our cell phones. When I listened to the voice message, he said he was going back to the office after the meeting, and that I shouldn't wait up for him. So he was definitely at the meeting."

"He wasn't at the meeting, Caroline. Mayor Moss called Smokey at one o'clock that afternoon and canceled. I attended. He wasn't there."

"I don't understand what you're getting at."

"How much does the mayor know about the transportation of the women from Guatemala? Has he been involved all along, or did he just get involved when the two women disappeared and threatened to expose the trafficking ring?"

"I'm calling my lawyer," she said. "You shouldn't even be here."

"You can either discuss it now with me, or later when this blows up into a nightmare for both of you." Josie was banking on Caroline's natural desire to know what the police understood about the case.

"What are you talking about?"

"The mayor called Josh Mooney multiple times the afternoon and evening of the murder."

A dark look passed over her face but she said nothing.

"When the mayor called you back and left the voice message at just after ten o'clock? His cell phone connected with the tower located just a few miles from my house. If he had been in town, at his office, or at the water meeting like he told you, his signal would have bounced off a different tower."

Tears filled her eyes. "I don't know what you're saying."

"Two people were involved in the murder that took place in the pasture beside my home. Your husband was there, and I believe Josh Mooney was with him. One of them killed a woman that night and tried to track down another woman but lost her."

Caroline broke down and cried openly. Josie spotted a box of tissues across the room and handed them to her. She sat quietly for several minutes as Caroline cried herself out. "I'll get you a drink of water," Josie said.

She walked into the kitchen, found drinking glasses in the cabinet, and filled one from the refrigerator water dispenser. When she handed the glass to Caroline she sipped the water until she had calmed somewhat. Josie sat down and decided to remain quiet for a while to see where Caroline wanted to go with the information she'd just heard. She finally set the glass on the table beside her and leaned back into the chair.

"I've spent the last year watching my life transform from a life to be proud of to a hideous mockery. I sit here looking at you now, and I have no idea how to move forward. I would like to say that I have no idea how I got to this point, but I do. I tell you now, I wanted to help. I wanted to come up with a way to help women in terrible situations. But it's all so twisted and turned so horrible."

"But you accepted money from women, and then got them a job that's little better than modern-day slavery. How was that ever good?" Josie asked. She knew she was allowing her personal feelings to interfere, and she took a mental step back to refocus.

"I had to take money! Especially in the beginning. It was an expensive venture, helping those women move across the country, across an international border. And I did my best to connect with reputable employers."

Josie couldn't imagine how Big Ben would ever be considered reputable, but she let it slide.

"I understand," Josie said, nodding, trying to redirect the conversation. "Was the mayor involved with this from the beginning?"

She shook her head no, her expression forceful. "No. I wanted to do this on my own. It was my project."

"When did he get involved?"

"When things fell apart. The other deliveries went fine. The girls experienced a smooth trip, they had jobs waiting for them when they arrived. Then my lead driver moved to the East Coast unexpectedly, and I was stuck trying to find a new driver. And that put Josh as the lead. Obviously that was a disaster."

"When did you ask the mayor for help?" Josie asked.

"When Josh called from Piedra Labrada to tell me two of the women had escaped. I had no choice but to ask Steve for help."

Josie noted her use of the word *escaped*. How could Caroline use that word if she'd viewed what she was doing as humane?

"And how did he help?"

Caroline's expression changed. She considered Josie again, as if realizing who she was talking to. She took a moment to respond.

"I don't think I should continue this conversation," she said. Her voice had grown quiet and Josie knew her welcome had just ended.

She stood and placed her business card on the table beside her chair. "My cell phone number is on the card. If you'd like to talk, give me a call."

TWENTY-TWO

After a morning and afternoon spent coordinating with Sheriff Roy Martinez and two Texas state troopers who served the Arroyo County area, Josie finally received the phone call she'd been waiting for.

"The search warrant is approved," Holder said. "I just called the mayor's office and he's still there. You get your team out to the house. I'm going to tell the mayor in person. That'll give you a few minutes to get out there and set up with Caroline before the mayor comes in ready to blow. I'll warn him that we will arrest him for interfering with a lawful investigation if he gives us the slightest provocation. But I'd plan on him giving you grief."

Josie and Otto rode in her jeep, two sheriff's cars followed, and two state DPS cars followed them. They filled the mayor's driveway. Josie and the sheriff approached the front door together and presented Caroline with the documentation and explained that they were there to search for the weapon used in Renata Carrillo's murder. Caroline looked stunned.

"The mayor isn't here," she said, grabbing the doorframe as if she needed help standing. "I'm calling my attorney."

"Prosecutor Holder is talking with the mayor now," Josie said. "For now, we'll ask you to have a seat in the kitchen while we go about our business. You're welcome to call your attorney from the kitchen."

They wasted no time. Six officers carried out the search while a sheriff's deputy remained stationed in the kitchen to keep an eye on Caroline and to watch for the mayor.

Josie and Otto were both in the home office when the mayor arrived. They ignored the raised voices and continued the search, knowing the sheriff's deputy would take care of the mayor if need be.

Josie opened a closet door in the office and called Otto over. Two shotguns were propped in the corner of the closet.

"Let's get some photos." Josie used her digital camera to take the photos but neither officer touched the shotguns. The casing that had been found in the pasture near Renata's body had obviously not come from a shotgun. Also in the closet was a filing cabinet with nothing but paper files.

Josie dragged a desk chair over to the closet and stood on it to examine the one shelf at the top of the closet.

"Otto, check this out." Josie held up a white box with the company name Ruger imprinted in red. "It's a Ruger .380. And it was a .380-caliber bullet that killed Renata."

She shook the box and frowned. She stepped off the chair and opened the box. "No gun."

Otto sighed. "What do you want to bet the mayor's gun ends up conveniently stolen?" he said.

Josie laid the box on the desk and opened it, pulling out a lock and extra magazine in a plastic bag that had never been opened.

She picked out several pieces of paperwork that came from the gun maker and then stepped away from the box and smiled. "You won't believe this," she said, and held up a yellow sealed envelope for Otto to see. "Look what he left behind."

Otto laughed. "I bet you just solved a murder."

"I'll go test your theory on the mayor's missing gun," she said. "Can you go check with the other officers and see where they are with the search?"

"You bet."

Josie walked down the hallway and into the kitchen holding the white Ruger box. The mayor and Caroline were sitting on benches in the breakfast nook, staring at the table and not speaking.

"Mayor Moss, can you tell me where the gun is that belongs with this box?" Josie said. She kept her voice nonconfrontational and hoped her nerves wouldn't cause the same tremor in her voice that she felt in her stomach.

He stared at her and she wondered if he was going to refuse to answer. She figured what was going through his mind was, *It's none of your damned business where my gun is.* But instead, he said, "I don't know."

"You don't know where your gun is located?" she said.

"It used to be in my truck in the glove compartment. About a year ago it disappeared."

"Did you report it missing?"

"No."

"Why didn't you report the theft of a firearm from your truck?" she said.

He clenched his jaw shut before finally speaking. "Because I didn't know if I had misplaced it, or how long it had been missing. I figured it would show up and then eventually forgot about it."

Josie glanced at the trooper standing off to the side of the kitchen, who gave her a look that was as good as an eye roll.

Josie left the room and walked outside.

She found Holder standing in the driveway next to his car, talking on his cell phone. He finished his call and she asked, "How familiar are you with purchasing firearms?"

He smiled. "I have my dad's shotgun in our safe with a box of shells in the cabinet in the laundry room. I'm not even sure I could load it."

"Okay," she said, grinning. "I'll explain what we have. Several states require ballistic fingerprinting for all new firearms. Texas does not require it. Basically, in those states, every new firearm has to be fired and the casing saved and compiled in a state database. When the casing is ejected there are unique markings left by the barrel or chamber of the gun. The casing can then be used like a fingerprint in a crime using that gun."

"So why don't all states require it?" Holder asked.

"Because it's expensive and controversial," she said.

He put a hand in the air to stop her. "Okay. I have enough controversy. Let's not go there. Just tell me how this is going to help us," he said, pointing to the box.

"Though only a few states compile the casings in a database, some gun makers test-fire their new guns anyway and include the test-fired casings in a sealed envelope with the gun. That's what this is." She took the yellow envelope out of the box and held it up. "There was no gun in this box. But this is the next best thing. We have a spent casing from this gun in a sealed envelope from the factory. And we have a casing from the murder site. And we have the bullet that killed Renata."

Holder gave her a skeptical smile, as if her theory sounded too good to be true. "What makes you think the gun that was used to kill her came from this box?"

"We've already searched Josh's apartment. There were no guns." She paused when the front door of the house opened and Otto walked outside to join them. "We know that a .380-caliber handgun was used to murder Renata. That's what this gun is. And the mayor says this gun was either stolen or lost about a year ago. He never filed a report, though, because he forgot about it? Come on."

Holder nodded. "So we submit for ballistics, and take the mayor in for questioning to try for a confession."

Josie nodded. "You know that the mayor and I don't have a great relationship," she said.

He choked out a laugh. "An understatement."

"So I'm not sure about the interview. What would get the confession? Me getting him so angry that he blurts out a confession? Or Otto, who could offer sound advice. Man-to-man," she said. "Maybe Otto could coax it out of him."

"What's your opinion?" Holder said.

"I think Otto should start. If he doesn't get anywhere, then I can go in and mess with him. See if I can get him so angry he cracks."

Holder nodded and turned to Otto. "I like it. How close are we to finishing up here?"

"They're finished upstairs, and on the first floor. They haven't found anything. They're headed to the basement. We'll get back in there and should be done within the hour."

"I'm headed back to the office. Keep me posted."

———————

After the search was completed, Josie headed outside with the other officers while Otto asked the mayor to come to the jail to talk about the situation. The mayor asked if he was being charged and Otto assured him that he wasn't, but that there was important information they needed to discuss. He agreed, no doubt hoping a deal was in the works, probably hoping he could hang Josh Mooney out to dry while he skated free. That would be the mayor's mentality, thought Josie, and they would use it to their advantage.

An hour later, when the mayor arrived at the jail, Otto led him into the interrogation room. Josie was next door in the observation room, watching on a computer monitor via a camera feed.

The mayor had changed into jeans and a button-down shirt and looked relaxed and in control. Josie was certain that he figured, with no gun, the police had nothing. He was about to get the shock of his life.

Otto patiently explained the phone records, how they connected the mayor and his wife to the key players in the trafficking scheme, and the fact that his phone had pinged off a tower beside Josie's house when he had said he was going to be in El Paso. The mayor had obviously already heard the same information from his wife, and he'd formulated his explanation like a pro.

Josie watched him smile and tip his head as if he expected Otto to know him better than to assume something as sinister as Otto was implying.

"Look. You know what a mess Josh made of Caroline's attempt to help those women. She finally came to me asking for help, and I knew I had to step in and take control. She needed help, and she's my wife. Of course I stepped in. I had to cancel my speaking engagement and go talk to the kid before he did something stupid. I called and tried to talk him down several times. He said the only way out of the mess he'd made was to shoot both of those women and take their bodies to Mexico." The mayor shook his head and frowned, like, *Can you believe that?* "I said, *Josh. Get a grip, man. That's no solution. You can't kill those women because you've got yourself in a mess.*"

The mayor rambled on and on about the fatherly words he offered Josh, and the good counsel he provided, and about the fact that Josh just wouldn't listen.

"He finally convinced me to drive out there with him to see if I could convince the girls to finish the trip. That was the only way I could talk him out of doing something stupid. So Josh drove and I rode passenger. We drove slowly by the pasture. I rolled the window down and called for them but we couldn't find them. And we left. Josh drove me back to town and I got in my truck and drove home. End of story. I have no idea how that poor woman ended up dead."

"Do you think Josh went back and shot Renata after he dropped you off?" Otto asked, playing the part of the patient friend.

"I have no idea what he did."

"Did he have a gun in his car when you were with him?"

"No idea. If he did, he didn't show me."

"Did he ask you for a gun?"

"Hell, no. He knew I wouldn't give him a gun."

"Did he ever have access to your house or vehicles? Maybe you invited him over to your house and he could have borrowed a gun or taken one?"

Josie watched on the computer monitor with Sheriff Martinez, who'd stepped in the room to view with her. "Nice job," Josie whispered. "He's making sure the mayor can't later say that Josh was in his truck and stole the gun to shoot Renata."

"Come on, Otto. You make it sound like Josh and I were drinking buddies. The guy is a freak. He didn't come to my house or drive my cars. I rode with him one time because I thought I was going to save a woman's life. It obviously didn't work."

Josie noted that he said he went to save one woman's life. Hadn't he been going to save two women?

"I appreciate the information," Otto said. "Can I get you a cup of coffee, Mayor?"

Josie stood and gathered her papers. That was her signal that Otto was ready to turn it over.

Martinez slapped her on the back. "Go get him."

———

Otto grabbed the mayor a cup of coffee and led the way back into the room. Otto sat the coffee on the table and Josie entered after him, all attitude, as if she were enjoying the power trip. The mayor puffed up like a blowfish as soon as she entered the room. She slapped her paperwork down on the table and leaned on her hands toward him.

"Can we just cut all the crap?" Josie said.

"Excuse me?"

"You heard me."

Moss scooted his chair back. "I don't have to put up with this nonsense. I did you a favor by coming in here. You need to learn some respect for your superiors."

"I don't think you want to leave just yet. I learned something that I think you'll want to hear." Josie smiled, sat down at the table, and opened up the manila folder in front of her.

Moss said nothing, but he remained seated.

"So you and Josh Mooney aren't friends?" she asked.

Moss looked at Otto, who raised his eyebrows as if wondering the same question.

"You know full well I'm not friends with that moron."

"You don't offer him rides?"

"No."

"He's never borrowed your truck?"

"Hell, no. What are you getting at? I explained why I talked to him."

Josie offered a cynical smile. "Here's what we have. Not only do we have cell phone records that place you near the murder scene, as well as your own words, admitting you were there, but we've now connected your gun to the murder scene."

"What gun?"

"The Ruger .380 that we removed from your home today," she said.

"You said yourself the gun wasn't in the box. How the hell could that gun be at the scene?"

Josie smiled again. "We don't have your gun. We have the casing from the site of the murder, the bullet from Renata's body, and the test-fired casing from your gun that all match perfectly."

"What the hell are you talking about?" he asked. His forehead was drawn up into worry lines. She realized he didn't have any idea. Texas didn't require registry of the test-fired casings, so why would he know? Most people had no idea what the envelope was for and ignored it as excess paperwork in the box, having no idea there was a spent casing inside it.

"When you bought your gun, did you notice the little yellow envelope in the box?" she said.

The mayor looked at Otto. "What the hell is she talking about?"

Josie nodded at Otto, to pass the baton back to him.

"Inside that envelope is a spent casing from the manufacturer," Otto said. "That casing matches the casing we found at the murder site. Your gun was used to murder Renata Carrillo."

They were bluffing. But Moss was so flustered he'd not thought it through that they had not had time to run ballistics to confirm the match.

The mayor's face had the chiseled look of stone as he gritted his teeth, mentally recalibrating his story. After a moment he said, "Josh shot her." Typical Moss: knee-jerk reaction, deflecting the blame before thinking through the consequences. He'd already told the police he'd lost his gun, and then instantly changed his story. He'd just made it easier for the prosecution.

Josie glanced at Otto, who was recalculating his questioning strategy. This was not the way they had imagined or planned for the interview.

"Were you with him?" Josie asked.

"I watched him. I drove the car."

"Wait a minute," she said. "Earlier you said Josh was driving."

Moss began nodding his head, his expression earnest. "I know I did. I was trying to help the kid out. Trying to deflect some attention off of him, but it's done nothing but cause me trouble. I'm done with that." Moss's eyes grew wider with his story. "He did take my gun out of the glove compartment of my truck, now that I think about it. He must have had it with him when he stopped the car. He got out and ran after them, chasing them into the pasture. When he couldn't catch the first girl, he panicked and shot her. I drove the car down the road and tried to shine the headlights on the pasture to stop things from getting out of control, but it was too late."

"What did you do after you heard the gunshots?" she asked.

Moss looked at Josie, unblinking. She could imagine him spinning his tale on the fly. She noted that his order of events didn't exactly match Isabella's but let it go. "I waited for Josh to get back in the car and we left. He told me he'd shot into the air to scare them, but that they'd escaped and he couldn't catch them."

Moss paused and suddenly looked as if he was tearing up. "I didn't find out the woman had died until I heard about the death on the radio. Obviously it was too late to do anything at that point. I wanted to come forward, but that crazy bastard Josh Mooney said he'd kill me if I went to the police."

Josie stood and said, "I need to place a phone call."

She left Otto with the mayor to stall for time while Josie called Holder and explained the situation. "I don't want to let him go, but I don't know what to charge him with. We're at the jail. We'll talk to Josh Mooney next, but meantime, we have to do something with him. We can't hold him indefinitely."

"Place him under arrest for accessory to commit murder. If it falls apart we'll let him go. But I'm with you. At this point, I don't want to cut him loose."

Josie entered the interrogation room, where she found the mayor smiling at Otto as he told some story. He obviously thought he'd played his part well and was headed for home. Josie wasted no time.

"Mayor Moss, after consulting with Prosecutor Holder, I am placing you under arrest for accessory to commit murder in the death of Renata Carrillo. You have the right to remain silent."

"What the hell are you talking about? I told you, I didn't even know that woman died until days later! I didn't shoot that gun!"

Josie finished reading his Miranda rights over his protests, and then asked him to stand and follow her to the booking room.

He sat in his chair, unmoving, staring at Otto as if waiting for him to help. "Tell her! Tell her this is ridiculous!"

"I need you to stand. If you refuse to walk with us we'll have to use handcuffs, and I don't think you want that right now," Otto said.

The mayor finally stood and Josie led him down the hallway. He didn't say another word. She'd never seen anyone look so completely baffled during their booking. A female jailer who was in the booking room when they entered avoided eye contact. Josie figured the sheriff had filled the staff in on the situation, trying to control the drama.

Josie held each of his fingers and rolled them in the ink. She printed each finger on the card and then handed him off to the female jailer, who nodded and placed her hand around his upper arm to lead him toward a cell.

Josie found Otto resetting the recording equipment in the interrogation room. When he was finished they walked down the hall to collect their next suspect, and Otto said, "This is one of the most bizarre days of my career."

———•——

Josie and Otto sat across the table from Josh Mooney and Oliver Greene. Josh was still wearing his orange jumpsuit but had fortunately showered. They quickly recapped the mayor's story and got the explosion they expected.

"That frickin' scumbag! That is exactly the opposite of how it happened. And you know what? I knew that lifelong rat-faced liar would do this. So you know what I did? I outsmarted the mighty mayor!" Josh's face was bright red and his eyes were bulging with anger.

"How'd you do that?" Otto said. His tone gave the impression that he didn't believe a word of it.

"When the mayor got back in my car he shoved the gun under the passenger seat and told me to get rid of it. He told me to clean it, wrap it up, to put it in a garbage bag, and to put the garbage bag in a dumpster downtown."

"What did you do with it?" Otto asked.

Josh leaned into the table and Josie could see the veins in his neck popping. "I left it there! He shot the gun. So his fingerprints are all over it. Not mine! Go look under the passenger seat. And then let me out of this frickin' jail cell before I go out of my mind!"

———

Josh's car had been seized and impounded by Jimmy's Wrecker Service when he was arrested. The car had been the least of their worries and no one had touched it since the impounding. Josie called Holder on the way to the lot and he approved searching the car without a warrant, since it had been properly impounded.

Josie and Otto drove to the lot and had Jimmy unlock the chain-link fence to allow them access to the car.

Jimmy went into his office to make a phone call while Josie unlocked the passenger-side door. She shone her flashlight under the seat.

"What do you have?" Otto called.

"A murder weapon," Josie said. "Hopefully covered in finger-prints."

———————

On their drive back to the jail with the gun in an evidence bag on Otto's lap, Josie told Otto, "You're better at lifting prints. You take the gun and run the prints. I'll check with the intake officer and get the mayor's fingerprint card we took earlier tonight.

By the time Josie carried the card into the booking room where Otto was working, he'd already pulled several prints.

"Beautiful, full-pad print on the side of the gun, and on the butt," Otto said, grinning at his work. "I just got off the phone with Ernie Mays at the crime scene lab. You know Ernie?"

"Sure. He checked the gun and bullet for us."

"He's the one. He agreed to match the prints for us if we'll get them delivered to him in the morning."

Josie patted Otto on the back. "I believe the mayor's accessory to commit murder just turned into first-degree homicide."

TWENTY-THREE

The feds subpoenaed Steve and Caroline Moss's bank records and computer and home files, and compiled a yearlong timeline of human trafficking that would allow full prosecution under the law. The town was in shock: two pillars in the community, a husband-and-wife team, arrested for charges involving trafficking, rape, and murder. The local radio and newspaper ran little else for weeks, and the Hot Tamale was too consumed with gossip for Josie to even enter for a lunch burrito.

Selena Gomez organized a local fund-raising drive to pay transportation expenses for the four women to receive safe passage back to Guatemala. Selena was establishing herself as a local leader for grassroots mission efforts. The work she was completing had a different focus than the highbrow work of Caroline Moss, and Josie was curious to see how the change might affect the town.

Four weeks after the Mosses' arrest, Smokey Blessings came to the police department and asked to speak with Josie and Otto. They sat with mugs of coffee around the conference table and talked about the cold weather driving down from the north that was threatening a December frost that night. The change of season seemed appropriate to the conversation when Smokey finally got down to business.

"I've come with a huge favor to ask, both personally and as an elected official for the community." He looked directly at Otto. "With the trial looming ahead of us for months, and maybe even years, we won't be able to heal and move forward until we have a new mayor in place. The city council believes you are the perfect person to step in as the interim mayor. You're the former police chief, a longtime respected member of the community, and you've served on a dozen different community boards through the years. You're the right choice."

"I have a job," Otto said, looking at Josie as if she should have told him.

"I didn't know anything about this," Josie said. "I'm as surprised as you are."

"That's why we're meeting together. Obviously we'd like your blessing, Josie. With Otto taking the job as interim, you'll have to hire a temporary officer, and we all know that'll be a tough position to fill."

Josie sighed and folded her hands on the table, knowing Smokey was right. Otto still seemed too shocked to say anything, so she spoke. "Obviously I'll support whatever decision Otto makes. As much as I hate the idea of losing him, I can't imagine anyone better for the job." She looked at him. "You are the person with the integrity and experience that we need right now. You can lead us out of this mess."

"This department barely gets by on three officers," he said. "You'll be totally overwhelmed until you can find a replacement. And how many people want a temporary assignment for a job that takes months, even years, to feel competent in?"

"We'll deal with that," Josie said. "And you'll be close by to help train."

Smokey stood. "You go home and talk to Delores. Come see me at the courthouse tomorrow and we'll talk it over. Bring Delores along if you'd like."

Smokey left and Otto and Josie both sat quietly at the table, reflecting in silence on the conversation as only old friends can do.

Josie finally said, "My mom has hired a moving van."

Otto raised his eyebrows and grinned. "Moving to Texas?"

"She is. I found a small house for her to rent downtown. And she's going to work full-time as a clerk at the gas station."

"I think that's great. I really do," he said. "Families are a giant pain in the ass, but in the end, they're all we have for the long haul. I hope it works out for you."

She nodded and brought the conversation back around to the issue at hand. "What do you think Delores will say about you taking the mayor's job?"

Otto rubbed his hand across the stubble on his chin. "She'd like me to retire. She says she's tired of worrying about me being a cop after all these years, but I don't think that's it. She's used to being a cop's wife. She knows I'm careful."

"So why the push?"

"I think she's lonely. She'd like me to stay home with her and work around the farm. She'd like for us to go visit Mina and the grandkids more often." Otto lifted a shoulder and gave Josie a miserable look.

"You'd like to take the job, wouldn't you?"

"I would."

"You'd be a great mayor," she said, grinning. "Mayor Podowski. Has a good ring to it."

"So many times through the years I've thought, if I were mayor, I'd do this or that. Now's my chance. I'd regret not taking it."

Josie sipped her coffee. "I've been thinking about regret a lot lately. I want to make things right with my mom. I don't want the two of us regretting that we didn't try harder to patch things up between us. But what happens if she makes this move and it's a disaster? I'll still have regret and I'll be miserable along with it. You know what I mean?"

He narrowed his eyes at her. "You're turning philosophical."

"I'm just wondering, how do you decide? Do you chase down a dream, or do you do what makes your wife happy? Do you take a chance on something new, or do what's safe and comfortable? Life just seems like a giant game of chance."

Otto smiled. "Don't look so worried. That's the beauty of it too. You take your best guess and you make the most of it."

"What about you? Do you have regrets?" she asked.

"Well, sure. If you've lived, you're bound to have some." He took a moment to respond. "I suppose my biggest regret is losing touch with my family in Poland. But our choices were made with good intent. I miss my family, but in the end, I know we did what was best for us." He smiled then and shrugged. "So I'll go home tonight, and Delores and I will look at the pros and cons. Then we'll make a decision together."

They both stood and locked up the office for the night, turning off the coffeepot, computers, and lights. As they walked down the stairs together she said, "After forty years of marriage, I have no doubt, you and Delores will work it all out."

———•———

Josie called Nick on her way home and asked if he could make it to her house for a late dinner and whatever else that might lead to.

"I'm still in Mexico. I have a meeting with a Federales officer tonight at seven. If I make it to your place, it'll be late."

Disappointed, Josie sighed. She needed Nick's company.

"What if we meet halfway?" she asked. "I could meet you at

your cabin. I'm off tomorrow, so we could sleep in and make a fire in the morning. After a big breakfast, we can share a long walk along the river."

He laughed. "I definitely want to share. Bring Chester with you too. And can you bring a few groceries? My cabinets are pretty empty."

"I'll make you the best breakfast you ever had."

"No canned fruit cocktail?"

"Maybe canned biscuits, but I can pull off fried eggs and bacon."

"You're the best. I'll love you forever. Did you find your key yet?"

"What key?"

"I left you a key to the cabin on your hook in the pantry, just in case you need a getaway."

"You sure you want to open up your hideaway? You want to invite a woman into your space?" She paused. "No regrets later?"

"Not a chance."

Josie hung up with Nick and pulled into her driveway. She walked behind the house to catch the final rays of sun shining bright as lightning across the ragged ridge top of the Chinati Mountains. She pulled her coat around her tighter and sat down on the porch step to watch Chester gallop down the driveway from Dell's house to hers—pure joy on the dog's face. He bounded onto the steps and leaped into her, knocking her backwards, licking her face and whining with happiness. She laughed and hugged the dog, wondering why people couldn't be so uncomplicated, and she vowed to take life one day at a time with a new motto—no regrets.